Karla J.M

Blood of Angels

Tale of a Fallen One

By:

Karla J.M. Brading

Karla J.M. Brading

Karla J.M. Brading

Blood of Angels
Tale of a Fallen One

Published by:
Print Evolution

Copyright © Karla J.M. Brading
Cover Photography © LRMason Photography
Cover Model: Alexandra Kissack
Model MUA: Crake

ISBN: 978-0-9561007-0-2

This novel is entirely a work of fiction. The names, characters and incidents portrayed in it are the work of the authors imagination. Any resemblance to actual persons, living or dead, events or localities is entirely coincidental.

First Published 2008
Second Edition 2013
Third Edition 2014

Karla J.M. Brading

Also By Karla Brading

For Young Adults:

Destiny In Blood

Blood of Angels

Dark Blood Falling

Gabriel Lance and the Cursed Ones

Whispers of a Reaper

Eyes Like Death

For Younger Readers:

That Quiet Place

Zombie Jig and Jive and Other Creepy Tales

Coming Soon:

The Blood Thirsty Life of Little Drake Daley

Karla J.M. Brading

Special thanks to:

Katherine Roberts- for your letters and advice over the years. Your kindness has meant the world to me and your fantasy novels are a ray of sunshine in my life.

Karla J.M. Brading

Blood of Angels

Tale of a Fallen One

By:

Karla J.M. Brading

Karla J.M. Brading

- Prologue -

Fallen

Whenever Tarian stood in the presence of the Lord, he was always blinded by an immense and brilliant white light that masked His face from view.

No Angel was granted permission to admire His true appearance. It was an unwritten rule of His- a secret He only shared with worthy humans in the afterlife; not His winged soldiers.

Usually, Tarian would stand before the creator of heaven and earth in obedience- seeking instruction on a daily basis- it was the reason why he existed. To worship. To love. To serve Him and those He watched over with replicated fondness.

This time the circumstances of Tarian's audience with the Great One were quite out of the ordinary…

The Lord's voice was a mixture of both female and male- a strange concoction of the two that left its listener in contemplation of His true sex. Many had chosen to believe He was 'both,' whereas others believed He hid himself from view because His exterior was neither. Not human, nor animal- perhaps a compilation of stars and light?

Tarian disliked paying the Lord too much of his time in thought and wonderment since he had rebelled. He had become accustomed to ignoring the fact he was an Angel, born from the palms of God's hands and crafted to be perfect in both face and body.

The perks of being an Angel had begun to wear thin over the centuries. He had found himself neglecting his duties to find any pretty human girl he could spend the night with on earth instead… loving and leaving her swiftly and without consequence.

Until now.

Tarian could tell God was seriously annoyed with him. The bonds that had appeared on entering the Judgment Hall were cutting into his pure white wings, forcing them to remain folded and pressed agonisingly into his back. He'd never experienced pain before. Angels had deadened senses and were meant to show a lack of emotion, for they were designed purely to answer their Master's call. But once in a while, one would decide they just didn't *want* to do the right thing anymore. They would give up, or sin. And for this, they were punished.

-What do you have to say for yourself?-

The voice of the Almighty came to Tarian as a piercing whisper directly in his mind.

"Have mercy-"

The words escaped before Tarian could suck them back in and hold them there. He hadn't planned on pleading for his immortality. Not like his best friend Isaac, who had already been cast out, a few hours previous. *His* judgement had been cringe-worthy.

-You have broken a fundamental rule-

Tarian, surrounded by a mass of fellow Angels, looked down at the floor for a moment. He was on his knees, naked (which most Angels preferred to be) with his wrists lashed together as further punishment to the binding of his glorious wings. To the audiences amazement, he suddenly smiled.

"What can I say? It was worth it," he sneered, relishing the gasps that followed.

All heads turned to the white light at the end of the platform in the clear violet sky, anticipating his reaction.

-You have taken pleasure in seeking sexual gratification amongst the human race on seven *occasions-*

Tarian grinned at the crowd, beginning to enjoy himself. "Do you want me to go into detail about that? Ha-ha!

And what took you so long to realise I was down below, sleeping with some of those gorgeous bitches you've made?" he asked mischievously, winking at a female Angel to his right, who was holding the hand of a human child they had moments ago claimed in a car accident in Karanthian. The child's face was buried in the Angel's white robes, frightened to the core and having no idea how she had ended up in the court room of the Great One.

-*Silence*- the Lord cried, and a white strip of material glued itself over Tarian's slightly parted lips, keeping his words at bay. -*You disgust me*-

Tarian was quiet now, feeling his eyes stinging from the brightening light before him. A strange and increasingly unpleasant heat was kissing the skin of his forehead, nose and chest with every passing second.

-*The last girl was a virgin*-

If Tarian could have spoken, he would have said, "So what?"

-*She was nervous and unprepared*-

He rolled his eyes.

-*You told her it wouldn't hurt and that if she didn't sleep with you, she'd stay a silly little virgin for the rest of her life*-

Tarian was casting his mind back now. She had been seventeen- a couple of pounds heavier than he preferred them to be- and bearing a birth mark on her left thigh that had almost killed the mood, but he had persuaded her that having sex with him would be the best damn thing she would ever experience. No pain, no gain was how he'd put it. "You'll be the coolest kid on the block once you've told your mates you've slept with a God."

-Even when she asked you to stop, you carried through with your sick desires. She bled and when she requested a break, you told her to stop whining and get down on her knees against her will-

Tarian was giddy with pleasure. Just thinking about his evening of twisted intercourse was making him hard. The virgin girl had cried a lot he recalled, but he had never felt so truly overwhelmed with pleasure like he had when he was finishing inside her- her tears and sobs *music* to his ears.

-Stop what you are thinking- the Lord demanded, His voice like a whip lashing against Tarian's lower back.

-This human girl I speak of considered suicide three days after because she was in so much mental pain. You left her without a word. I can't believe one of my own- a creation of beauty and perfection- could maliciously treat those that

they are sworn to protect-

There were a few nods of agreement. The Angels, standing in two lines on either side of the guilty one, were clustered around, or up against, huge white pillars. White, white, white. Everything was white and spotless and Tarian was sick to death of it.

-You are no longer permitted to live within the boundaries of my Kingdom-

Tarian had known this was coming. He had been present at Isaacs's judgment and had heard the same words come from the Lord's invisible mouth then as well.

-I cast you out, to live among the people you have hurt, where you will suffer pain and sorrow and never be capable of experiencing my gift to the human race- the ability to love-

Tarian made a '*pfft*' noise of mockery beneath his gag.

-You are no longer one of mine, Tarian. You are one of the Fallen, with a life expectancy of no more than one year. After that, Lucifer- King of the Fallen and unrighteous- can have you.-

This news angered him.

A year! A year to deteriorate on earth like a filthy corpse in a cheap coffin. It was completely unfair. Isaac had not been told this and he'd been just as vicious in his actions towards impressionable young girls as Tarian had.

-Same goes for your friend-

He struggled, trying to free his wings. The Kingdom of Heaven was vast- he could hide somewhere- hide amongst the parted souls that the Lord sheltered in the afterlife. Or hide on earth- a fugitive, but an Angel still.

There was a sudden slapping sound, like two hands being clapped together, and the floor beneath Tarian's knees disappeared.

He was still bound as he fell, tumbling and rolling in the wind as the earth rushed up to meet him. When the gag was ripped painfully from his lips, he let out an inhuman wail of fear.

The impact, when it arrived, took his breath away.

He landed left side first on the rain sodden earth, after crashing through a sycamore tree, positive that every bone in his body had snapped in the process.

"Shit-" he mumbled, wheezing loudly with each breath- a new experience for a creature who had never required oxygen, until now.

Rain splashed against his burning hot cheeks as he rolled onto his back, staring up at the sky his Father had just cast him from.

Fly, he thought. *Fly away.*

Slowly, he climbed to his feet, shaken to the very core, but the wings that he had so often summoned never came.

"It'll hurt for a while-" came an unfamiliar voice.

Tarian jolted in fear and rotated on the spot, his back still hunched in anticipation of flying. His wings had gone! Taken, by *Him!*

He was in a graveyard, petite and overgrown with weeds next to a small and cheerless church. The only tolerable sight was the tree, taller than the churches crumbling steeple and sparkling with a layer of rain water. From the church door came a man, tall and gangly, with thick bristly grey hair and a dominant moustache above his thin lips. He was clothed in a black shirt and trousers.

Tarian opened his mouth to speak, but closed it abruptly when his words failed him. He was cold. So cold. The rain was coating his naked body and it was only as the man put a hand on his shoulder that he realised how completely exposed to the elements he was. It appeared the Angels above were crying at the loss of two brothers, for the downpour was becoming torrential.

"Come inside, boy. Isaac is waiting for you."

His friend's name was a flaming torch in an endless black tunnel.

"Isaac?"

The old man nodded, blinking away rain water as it clung to his eye lashes. "You're not the first Fallen Angel to land here. I help the 'Fallen' by waiting here for new arrivals. You'll get back on your feet again, don't you worry."

"How…how many?"

The man put pressure behind his palm, guiding Tarian towards the church entranceway.

"Come in. Come in. We'll talk inside."

"But there's so little time," Tarian said breathlessly, his eyes darting left and right as if Lucifer waited in the darkest corners of their surroundings.

The man smiled, "Yes, about that-"

He paused.

"The Fallen, over the years, have discovered ways around the Lord's punishment. Calm yourself now. You're in good hands, my son."

Tarian sighed. A small part of him felt as if he could relax now that he was in the old man's hands- a Priest of the church maybe?- and the larger part of him kept screaming '*Fly! Fly away!*' like a frightened bird. But without his wings, he had no choice but to use his stiff and tired legs, wandering in the direction of the soft glow of the church.

His friend Isaac stood hunched in the doorway, bruised and bleeding. In his hands, he gripped a faded red blanket, which he kindly slid over his partners quaking shoulders.

The old man laid a comforting hand on both the young men before him.

"Welcome to earth, Fallen ones."

- Chapter One -

Boys Will Be Boys

Atlanta took a tight grip on Deacon's arm, dragging him out of the busy school corridor and into an empty classroom. As she did so, she tried her hardest not to let tears spill from her perfectly painted eyes.

"This is the feistiest I've ever seen you," Deacon pointed out, smirking like the arrogant imbecile he truly was. "Perhaps I'm making the wrong choice?" He paused. "What do you think, baby? You gonna prove me wrong?"

Atlanta let go of his muscular arm immediately and tried to avoid glancing into his dark eyes. He was trying to melt her heart into cooperation with his cute little dimples and that oh-so-shiny dark hair he kept pushing back sexily.

She took a deep breath, considering silently how stupid she had been in believing Deacon could be a 'decent' human being.

They had been together for four months now, doing what couples do- walking around hand in hand, spending time at the West Meridion Mall on Saturdays, taking long drives out into the desert beyond the South Meridion Bridge, pecking each other on the lips in public, and then snogging each other's faces off when they had some privacy. Things had been great, until Deacon had slipped his big hand up her little skirt to try and tease her into submission.

But Atlanta was better than that.

She wasn't about to give up her virginity based on a short lived relationship with the handsome high-school *dream boy*. No. There were plenty who would drop their knickers for him without needing to be asked, but *she* was classier than that. She wanted to have sex only in love, like her parents had raised her to believe was the right thing to do.

And there was no love between herself and Deacon.

It had all been a phase. A silly little phase.

Nerys, her closest friend, had once mentioned overhearing Deacon's conversation about how he thought Atlanta was a 'cutey,' and from that point onwards Atlanta had succumbed to his dazzling smile whenever he'd walked by, giggling to her friend about it.

Of course she had accepted his offer when he had asked her to be his girlfriend! What lucky girl didn't want to be his?

Yes, Atlanta was pretty. Yes, she had been asked out before. But she had never really wanted to 'kiss' a guy, like she'd felt compelled to with Deacon.

And boy, did she regret it now.

"Why are you so stubborn?" Deacon leant forward, his forehead perspiring in the tension that was building. "I thought you liked me?"

Atlanta glanced over at the slither of glass mounted on the shabby wooden door and watched the other students leaving the corridors in an explosion of noise. Not one of them glanced in, which she was thankful for. She wasn't going to be able to hold the tears off for much longer.

"Are you gonna start crying on me?"

"No," she replied defiantly, giving a little sniff. "I'm angry."

"But why, Angel? Can't you see this from *my* point of view? We're leaving high school in a few months. I'm a man, and I have needs. If you don't want to part those pretty legs of yours for me then I'm gonna have to find another girl who's willing to enjoy what we were designed to lust for."

Atlanta's cheeks blazed red in colour. She still wasn't quite used to Deacon's language. She'd let out a cry of shock on the night he had first talked 'filthy' to her.

"I can't believe you don't like me anymore over such a small thing," she said, barely above a whisper. The tears came at last.

"Baby, it's no small thing, I can assure you. And it's starting to hurt because you won't grant me access to what's mine. There's only so much masturbating I can do before I get bored of waiting-"

Atlanta scowled at him.

"You're a complete *dog*"

"And you're a tease. Who do you think you are, walking around with those miniskirts and revealing tops, letting all the guys check out your rack and those damn fine legs of yours? You've got the face of an angel and the backside of a Goddess, and baby, I need to get a little something, or I'm out the door. I've wanted to have sex with you since the day I discovered what my dick was really for-"

Atlanta shuddered and stepped around the table she had been stood behind, moving to the door in a hurry. Her bag dangled loosely from the crook of her arm and her long brown hair bounced breezily on her delicate shoulders. But before she could pull the door towards her, an iron fist knocked it back onto its latch.

"Wait, baby. I didn't mean those things."

"You said it's over, Deacon, so it's OVER! Just let me go."

His eyes became soft. Gently, he cupped her face.

"I can give you another chance."

Atlanta froze. She told herself not to fall for his act repeatedly in her aching head.

"We don't *have* to have sex-"

She looked into his eyes, amazed at his words. Her heart sped up.

"-But a nice blowjob wouldn't go amiss, if you're gonna keep leaving me high and dry."

That was it.

She shoved him back and swivelled on the spot, pulling on the handle of the door once more. He didn't stop her this time.

"Fine. Leave," he yelled down the corridor, alarming a few first years who were gossiping next to their lockers. "I'm glad you're out of my life. I'm wasting my time with you. *Virgin!*"

Atlanta mustered the courage to raise her middle finger and dashed for the exit before he could verbally hurt her further.

As she ran, her left sandal flopped from her foot and

she almost tripped down the steps at the front of the school's main entrance, arousing a painful pang of embarrassment inside her chest to add to the mix of despair she was feeling.

Her breath escaped loudly as she finally reached her car, acknowledging the presence of her twin brother Phoenix. The weight on her shoulders lifted ever so slightly.

Phoenix and Atlanta Nightly shared no similarities in appearance whatsoever. Atlanta's hair was a light shade of brown, whereas Phoenix's choppy, gelled strands were jet black in colour. *His* eyes were blue and *her* eyes, grey. Being the male, Phoenix was at least six inches taller than his sister and both had a varied tone in skin colour- Atlanta a pale peach, and Phoenix, as white as paper.

"I don't want to talk about it," Atlanta announced, before her concerned looking brother could open his mouth. He pushed his glasses further up the tip of his nose instead, for they had been slipping down whilst inspecting his new trainers in the wait for his sibling.

"I warned you he was a shit-head," Phoenix reminded her, moving off the car and opening the door on the passenger's side.

"Yeah, well, how am I supposed to believe what you say?"

"Easy," he replied. "I wouldn't lie to you."

"Phoenix, you told me that kissing men could kill me unless I've had a vaccine, which isn't government issued until the age of eighteen!"

"Precisely," he smiled smugly, clicking his seat belt into place.

"And I believed you too, you big idiot, until mum told me you were fooling around!"

"Mum just doesn't want to scare you about the truths of the big wide world, and dad and I remain in quiet hope that you won't kiss a guy at least until you're thirty."

Atlanta was enjoying their argument. It helped ease the pain, especially when Deacon strode past the car in the direction of his own, patting her hood with an unfriendly force.

"So…how many girls have you killed with *your* lips?" she asked, reversing the vehicle faster than she'd ever tried before. She just couldn't wait to see the back of her bastard ex, whose oversized car stereo was blasting tunes into the quiet parking lot, making their shabby seats vibrate against their backs.

Phoenix made a whistling noise. "Ooh. I can't divulge that information."

-I'll read your mind-

He watched Atlanta closely as she drove, using their telepathy with a distinct sense of pride and ease. Both brother and sister- twin children to a magically inclined Healer woman- had developed the talent to communicate without moving their lips since the day they could cry, "Mummy!" They could speak directly into each other's minds, and even- if the other was caught off guard- read each other's thoughts.

"Stay out of my head," he warned her, his eyes narrowed sternly behind the lenses of his glasses.

"Stay out of my love-life," she retorted.

Phoenix cast his eyes upon Atlanta's knuckles, aware of how white they were becoming as she gripped the steering wheel. With a petrified expression, she noticed Deacon pulling his car up alongside hers- his window rolled down so that he could get a better view of her.

"Ignore him, 'Lanta," Phoenix advised, watching her skinny arms shudder for a moment.

Deacon was beeping his horn wildly, looking backwards and forwards from the road to his ex-girlfriend to admire the affect he was having on her.

Phoenix planted a hand on his sister's shoulder and felt the trembling of her delicate body beneath his touch.

-*It's okay*- he whispered telepathically. -*Ignore him. I'm here with you*-

Atlanta managed a meagre nod and to Phoenix's amazement, she manoeuvred the wheel suddenly and sharply, sliding into a side street that Deacon was too late to follow her into.

"Or you can drive like a maniac to lose him. Your choice-" he muttered, sounding a little angry at her rash action.

They made it home in good time, having no more encounters with Deacon along the way, and headed straight for the fridge in their kitchen, whipping out a bottle each of Meridion spring water. Together, they glugged down the sweet and satisfying liquid, bursting into laughter as it dribbled from the corners of Phoenix's lips.

It was only when they re-entered the living room- dropping their bags behind the sofa routinely- that they realised the house was devoid of their mother.

Atlanta gave her brother a worried glance.

Kiya was always home to meet her son and daughter from high school. She worked half-days at Meridion Hospital as a Healer and never changed her plans without informing the children in advance.

Meridion was far too corrupt to leave loved-ones out of the loop.

"Mum?" Atlanta called.

Phoenix put a finger to his lips and made a 'shushing' sound. He then pointed towards the ceiling.

"What?" Atlanta mouthed.

Phoenix smiled. "Dad's home early."

- Chapter Two -

All Work

Kieran's tea had gone cold. He looked at it in disappointment, feeling remorse at the idea of asking his secretary to fetch him another one so soon, and instead, took a cautious sip of the milky liquid- the skin swirling around unappetisingly on its surface. Yup. It was disgusting. So much for enjoying a nice brew in his time of need.

With a sigh, he pushed the mug further away from his laptop, fearing it might destroy the new and *very rare* gadget- a gift from the government for his participation in years of loyal service to the city. It only *occasionally* left its cupboard- when Kieran was bored and fancied browsing screen saver options.

Slaying things had become a pretty simple procedure now, unless the creature in question was a 'werewolf,' in which case interviews and 'tagging' became part of the job. Besides that, it was a kill and celebrate system. No one requested reports, because the government preferred to just sit back and assume Meridion's problems were being dealt with.

As Kieran glanced over his computer screen, a burst of static crackled in the corner of the room.

"Kieran, are you in hearing range of this transmission?"

He glanced at the radio, recognising the voice of Siren- Chinese Vampire Slayer and Godfather to his children. Siren had been around when the infamous war of Meridion had broken out many years previous; when vampires had fought to win the corroding city from the frightened human race and *lost*.

"Let me guess- you're catching some 'z's' again, are you not?"

There was more static proceeding Siren's sentence.

Kieran pushed his chair from beneath his desk, walking the short distance to the small grey filing cabinet and lifted the radio to his mouth. "I'm here."

"Good, because you'll like this," Siren said, happiness emanating from his words. "We have exterminated the bloodsucker that has been slipping past us for months."

"Spiros?"

"Yes, *him*. We found him waiting for sun-down in the old library- the one that is nothing more than a storage building for musty paperbacks down on Creeper Street.

Steevie was the one who located and dusted him."

Steevie was a new member of the team- a Slayer in training now that she'd finished high school and given up on the idea of becoming an actress. She had spoken of the 'War' in her job interview- remembering in great detail how the vampires had come up through the underground passage beneath the Stone Table- and how she had stumbled upon her mother lying bitten and bleeding on the kitchen floor. Her father had raised her to seize the day ever since that frightening period of her fragile life, and she had decided to become Siren's new trainee as soon as she had seen the advert in the newspaper.

"Congratulate her for me," Kieran replied, imagining the young woman wiping the ashes of the un-dead from her presently unscarred hands.

"We're heading back to base."

"Righty-o," he mumbled, eyeing his mug of tea and wishing it were still piping hot. He craved tea like he craved cigarettes- something his wife had demanded he give up now that there were children in their lives.

"Why don't you head on home? William said he was going to start patrolling before the sun touches ground and I've got things pretty much covered now that Steevie knows everything there is to this job. I'm going to let her do what we do best, without me being around to help."

"What about the shipment? We've got an order of silver stakes heading into the city at some point and it needs either mine or your signature on the paperwork or else they'll just send the package back to where it came from," he pointed out, trailing his eyes over his wrist at his watch. It was far too early to leave yet. The twins were still at school…

"It's covered. I assure you. I will wait for the shipment. Chances are it will arrive between five and six anyway, because when has our postal service ever been *reliable*? And you can go home and spend five minutes alone with Kiya. Doesn't that sound tempting?"

Kieran smiled, thinking of his beautiful wife and how she'd react when he turned up ready and willing to take her.

"Are you planning a mutiny or something? Since when do you offer to cover for people?"

"Since I decided you do not see your family enough."

Kieran sighed. "Siren, that's my problem. *My* choice. Someone has to put food on the table. I have two teenage children that eat like wild dogs."

"All the time you are talking, it is time you could be with Kiya," Siren interjected.

Kieran automatically inspected his watch again.

"I'm going on holiday in a few days. I can relax then."

Siren's end of the transmission was void of words for a while, until: "Have two weeks instead of one, starting now."

"Siren-"

"I insist."

He grumbled in defeat. The offer was too good to pass on after all. "Fine."

"I knew you would not be able to resist."

"Are you sure about this?"

"As sure as I know that big seat in your office provides the ultimate support and comfort for my back and behind," Siren joked.

Kieran chuckled. "Call me if anything comes up."

"I won't."

The static came louder and crisper as Siren disappeared from the other end and Kieran hooked the device back onto its latch.

"Emily!" he called suddenly. His office door always remained open a fraction, so that he could hear if anyone stumbled into the main foyer sounding distressed and in need of his assistance. "I'm leaving."

"Okay, Mr. Nightly. Enjoy the rest of the day," came

her sweet tinkling voice.

Kieran grinned wickedly at the picture of his wife smiling back at him from a photograph.

"Oh, I will," he said smoothly, exiting the building with his leather jacket in one hand and the keys to his motorbike in the other, aware that his groin was tightening already.

*

Kiya had her hands in a bowl of soapy water when she heard the door to her home opening, and without a moment's hesitation, she snatched up the butchers knife from the draining board and spun to meet her attacker.

"It's impossible to sneak up on you," implored her breathtakingly gorgeous husband, running a hand through his long brown hair- now showing vivid hints of grey at the roots.

Kiya exhaled in relief, placing the butcher's knife back with a loud clank against the clean cutlery. She then threw her arms around her man, feeling her feet lift from the ground as he squeezed her with his muscular arms, both desiring the physical touch of every inch of each other.

"This is a nice surprise!" she gushed, kissing him square on his perfect lips.

"Siren gave me the day off."

"Siren has the authority to do that now?"

Kieran shrugged. "I reckon he's gonna knock me off the top spot and become Chief Slayer someday."

Kiya pushed a strand of Kieran's hair behind his right ear. "No he won't. He loves you too much to steal your job, honey."

They shared a smile for what seemed like hours, glancing into each other's eyes with longing.

The little kitchen was glowing with sunlight, pouring in through the white netted-curtain, illuminating the pale wooden table and chairs and the bowl of apples in its centre. The pastel yellow of the walls made the room feel cool and friendly, and the curtains bore a modern pattern of silver zig-zags, which she had adored the second she'd laid eyes on them.

Kiya loved spending her time in the kitchen, especially with 'cooking' being her new found hobby. The living room was the 'family room,' which didn't give off quite the same vibe, so the kitchen was the place where she was usually happiest, when waiting for her family to arrive home. She could whip up all manner of delicious treats- proving that mothers in Meridion were capable of making something out of nothing, even though the variety of food stuffs had dwindled over the years.

Kiya managed to review the clock face above the silver bin just as Kieran lifted her off her feet and she realised with excitement that they had an hour, at the most, to do what they enjoyed best together- before the children came home from school.

Kieran, though looking a lot more 'weathered' than he had eighteen years ago, still had the strength in him to carry Kiya up the stairs into their bedroom without breaking into a sweat; tossing her onto the mattress unceremoniously before unbuttoning his jet black, silver pinstriped shirt.

Kiya bit her lip in anticipation, watching silently until she couldn't take it any longer.

"You're taking too long," she exclaimed, reaching out and pulling his belt free. His zip was down and his trousers *off* before he could decline her help.

"Eager aren't we?"

"I hate having to wait for the kids to go to sleep and I especially hate having to be quiet. I want it hard and fast and I want to be able to make as much noise as possible."

Kieran's boxer shorts slid down to the floor and he kicked them off in a random direction, keeping his eyes fixed on Kiya's cleavage as she lifted her red top over her head, revealing her round, impressive breasts, cupped comfortably in a black bra.

"Take it off," he instructed, touching himself whilst Kiya stripped before him.

She obeyed instantly, unclasping the strap and allowing her breasts to fall completely on display. Grinning mischievously, she then proceeded to loosen her own belt, shimmying her long legs out of the tight denim that had been clutching her thighs all day.

At last, her thong was shed.

"Beautiful," Kieran whispered, moving forward.

Kiya put a hand on his chest and stopped him from clambering onto the bed. His eyebrows rose in surprise, but sunk when he felt her take him into her warm mouth.

She loved the taste of him. The warmth and texture of his skin made her tingle all over.

Kieran was growling in pleasure from the moment she'd trailed her tongue over the length of him and after a mere *minute* of foreplay, he pushed her roughly onto her back and entered her with a sigh of pure enjoyment, allowing her wetness to ease him inside gradually before picking up the pace with each thrust.

Kiya cried out, dragging her nails over his back in need of something to grip onto. Kieran swooped down and met her lips, feeling a lack of coordination in her kisses as the pleasure screwed with her thoughts.

Bringing her legs up, she wrapped them around his lower back, feeling the whole of his erection touching the very back of her, ripping her apart with even greater levels of ecstasy.

When at last she came, Kieran waited no more than thirty seconds before lifting her legs up around his neck.

"Daring for a woman of my age," she commented, between ragged breaths.

"You're still young yet, Princess," Kieran replied, entering her again.

The depth Kieran was reaching made him shiver pleasantly, plunging inside until he could go no deeper, and as he watched Kiya's face screw up with the love for his performance, he felt the buildup reach breaking point- coming at last with a distinct growl from his lips.

"Feel good?" Kiya asked, her long brown hair sticking to her forehead in unnatural patterns.

"Amazing," he agreed, crashing down next to her on the comfortable scarlet bed sheets.

Kiya lowered her legs and curled up in a ball next to her husband, smiling uncontrollably at his handsome face.

Kieran had allowed his beard to grow longer than he preferred it since working all the hours the station had to offer- never getting a moment's rest- and he had also left his hair to grow past his shoulders.

"You look worn out."

"I haven't had sex like that in quite some time."

Kiya blew gently onto his face, attempting to cool his brow before saying, "You know we have to have the slow, 'romantic' style of intercourse with the kids just down the hall."

Kieran rolled his eyes. "It's not like we haven't told them about the birds and the bees yet."

"Yes, I know that, but we wouldn't want to traumatise them."

"You're the boss."

"Indeed, I am."

As silence settled, the pair felt their eyes drooping and the warmth of their touching bodies consuming one another. It wasn't long before they were both sleeping, legs entwined as they usually were at night time.

They would have slept till late evening if it wasn't for

the sound of the twins entering the house.

Kieran's eyes shot open to the sound of 'mum' echoing through the house and it was with a reluctant hand that he nudged his wife awake.

"The fledglings sound hungry," he joked, kissing her cheek tenderly.

"Hmm?" Kiya mumbled sleepily, turning away from him. She didn't move again after that.

Kieran grabbed his boxer shorts and hurriedly climbed into the legs of his trousers, leaving the shirt dangling open as he left the room as quietly as possible. It was dark in the hallway, but strips of light were cast upon the stairs as he padded down them barefoot, ready to greet the children that were not actually his flesh and blood, but had been raised to believe so.

He loved them like they were his own and had convinced himself over the years that he was truly their father.

"Hey," Phoenix said, with an expression that suggested he knew what had kept their father from them.

"Hiya, Dad," Atlanta said, with a feigned smile.

Kieran continued to fumble with the buttons of his shirt as he detected a note of misery in his daughter's voice, giving Phoenix a curious glance in hope of finding an explanation there.

He shrugged in response and passed Kieran in pursuit of his bedroom.

"Your mother's asleep," he called after him.

"Okay."

The sound of Phoenix's door closing vibrated throughout the house.

When the last button was done up, Kieran scraped his messy hair back with his rough fingertips and sunk onto the sofa next to Atlanta, who was staring at the blank television screen.

What bastard has upset my baby now? Kieran thought, examining the tear tracks down her usually flawless make-up and felt a sudden pang of sadness as he remembered Roxy- the teenage Vampire Slayer that had perished in the war when he had failed to reach her in time. But this wasn't about lost comrades. This was about his daughter, obviously upset, and Kieran had had a lot of experience with weepy women over the years.

"Do you want to talk?" he asked quietly.

And it was at that point Atlanta burst into tears.

- Chapter Three -

Teenage Issues

Kieran placed a large hand on his daughter's shoulder and marvelled at how small she seemed beneath his palm. She had grown up to be a beautiful creature, just like her mother, but seemed ten times more fragile. Her long shiny hair never had a strand out of place and her outfits were always carefully coordinated and fashionable, but Atlanta seemed to lack the confidence that a charming young lady with staggering good looks should exude.

"Why are you so unhappy, Darlin'?" he queried, moving his hand to her back and rubbing it gently in a circular motion. He wondered if physical touch was pushing it too far, but she didn't shrug his hand off, which he took to mean continue.

Her head was bowed low so that her father couldn't see the mess her mascara was causing her face. She wished she'd been able to contain her emotion, at least until her mother was around, because her father was a 'guy' at the end of the day, and she found it hard to confide in him- and sometimes Phoenix too- when the main reason for her misery was that daunting topic of sex.

"Tell me," he urged, "I can't help you unless you talk."

Atlanta found a tissue on her person and gave her lightly freckled nose a swift wipe, keeping it scrunched up in her hand for future access. She was aware that some of her foundation had rubbed off with it, and imagined how silly she must look with a patch of her real complexion peeking through.

This is so awkward, she thought dismally.

"I-" she began. "I've been seeing someone for a few months now, Daddy."

Kieran nodded. This wasn't news to him.

"Your brother *had* mentioned it," he said.

Atlanta's nose twitched.

-What have you been telling Dad about me, loser?- she thought-spoke, aiming it directly into her brother's dazed mind. He was either nodding off or absorbed in a book because the connection was hard to establish at first.

-What?- came his bleary response.

-You know what. He knows about Deacon!-

-He knows nothing 'Lanta. He asked me one night if

you were out with Nerys and I accidentally let slip you were on a date with that gorilla. He didn't even care. He just wished you'd told him you were seeing someone-

-From now on, stay out of my life, Phoenix-

-It's hard to when you're the precise same age, sharing most of the same teachers and lessons, having the same parents and also, the ability to read your sibling's mind- he muttered sarcastically, idly flicking through the pages of his novel.

"Hello?" Kieran waved a hand in front of his daughter's vacant face. "You in there?"

Atlanta blinked.

"Talking to your brother?"

"Not for much longer," she promised bitterly, folding her arms over her chest.

There was silence for a moment. Kieran was trying to decide which angle was best to go about things.

"Did you argue with him?"

"Dad, we *always* argue. He's my brother for crying out loud. I'm sure you and mum have noticed by now-"

"No-" he stopped her. "No- I'm talking about this boyfriend of yours."

"Oh." Her head sunk a little. Her eyes swam with

images of the break-up she had undergone no more than two hours ago.

"Yes. We argued. It's my fault really-"

"How so?"

"Well. He's...he's grown *impatient.* And I don't blame him! But I thought he'd at least have a bit more respect for my feelings, you know?"

Kieran frowned at his daughter's words. She was twiddling her fingers around and around in her lap, showing signs of discomfort.

He was pretty sure there was only one 'thing' this guy could be impatient about, and it had nothing to do with marriage or sharing a house together.

"You've told him no I take it?"

Atlanta chanced a look at her father's face. He had turned so that he was facing her, and his hair hung across one side of his handsome face, partially shielding eyes that were fixed on hers.

"Dad- this is too weird. I'll talk to mum about it later-"

He raised his hands to cut her off.

"Wait a minute. What does your mother know about sex that I don't?"

I knew this would get weirder! Atlanta thought to

herself and she made a move to leave.

"You *are* a virgin still, *right*?" Kieran was standing now, holding onto Atlanta's shoulders.

"Yes, Dad," she assured him. "And that's what seems to be an issue with the boys at my school-"

She tugged her body free from his grip and rushed to the stairs, taking them two at a time.

"There's nothing wrong with staying a virgin, Atlanta!" he yelled after her. "In fact, I'd prefer it if it *stayed* that way! Don't let any boy pressure you into doing something you don't want to do! If this boyfriend of yours upsets you again, I swear I'll ride down to his house and smash his genitals in with a sledgehammer!"

"Oh- that's really mature Dad! Just be quiet about it, okay? I don't want to talk anymore!" she shouted back, slamming her bedroom door.

-He's right you know- Phoenix said, sensing his sister was crying. *-There's nothing wrong with waiting for the right guy-*

-It didn't sound like Dad was suggesting I should wait for the right guy. It sounded like he wanted me to remain a virgin for all eternity-

-He just wants you to be safe. We all do-

-Just back off out of my breathing space would you? I know you're my twin brother, but that doesn't mean you can pester me with your opinions all the time. Quite frankly, I've had enough of it-

Phoenix felt a stab of pain in his chest. It hurt him to hear his sister reject his help when she had sought it out so often in the past.

Rarely had the twins been separated. They had grown up doing *everything* together. They had learnt how to swim and ride bikes at the same time, ran at the same speed on sports days and had even bathed together before they were old enough to notice they were of different genders.

Now they were teenagers- gradually moving further apart it seemed- Phoenix didn't like the idea of Atlanta exploring the ever popular world of love. But he knew, deep down inside, he had no right to stop her.

He dreaded the time she would fall for someone. Someone who would take her from him.

-You know where to find me if you want to talk- he said, with hope laced through each word.

But Atlanta's end of the telepathic connection was unsurprisingly dead.

- Chapter Four -

Arguments

Kiya was staring out the window when Kieran cautiously entered the bedroom, checking if she was still asleep. It appeared she had been roused by the sound of the slamming bedroom door, but didn't look too disgruntled by it.

"Dare I ask…," she said, after a loud yawn, "Are the kids okay?"

Kieran slipped onto the bed behind her and began working his thumbs into her soft skin, gently grinding them into her muscles to help ease some tension. He hadn't given her a massage in weeks, and he knew how much she loved his fingers probing her body in all the right places.

"I think our daughter is in a bad place right now."

Kieran moved his hands further down her back, knowing by the way she growled and moaned that his skills were being appreciated.

"I think her boyfriend has been pressuring her into having sex."

Suddenly, Kiya shot up off the bed. "She didn't did

she? She didn't actually let him… Oh God!"

"Lower your voice-" Kieran advised snappishly, waving his hands now that her body was out of his reach.

"If that guy laid a finger on my little girl-"

Kieran stood up and put his hands on either side of her face. Most of the make-up was missing after the heated sexual activity, but she still looked beautiful to him. So beautiful he wanted to kiss every inch of her.

"She didn't. I'm sure of it. But Kiya, you need to wake up and smell the hormones. She's a teenage girl. And Phoenix is practically a man now! The pair of them are gonna start wanting to experience 'things.' We know, as well as most, what it's like to want someone bad enough. It won't be long and they'll be getting up to all kinds of…stuff."

Kiya shook her head forcefully.

"Not my little girl," she vowed. "Atlanta wouldn't. Not yet anyway."

"And what about Phoenix? He's kind of a dark horse. I'm his father and not even *I* know what goes on in that boy's head. For all we know, he could have done it already!"

Kiya turned away from Kieran's touch and put her hands on top of her head, trying to push a headache back with all her might.

"This is the last thing I want to think about before we go away together."

"I know. I know-" Kieran said soothingly. "But I think they're both good kids and that we'll have nothing to worry about. Sex and parties and all the other *stuff* that teenagers do is far from either of their thoughts. I mean, Phoenix is a book worm and Atlanta is- well- Atlanta."

Kiya let out a breath she didn't realise she'd been holding in.

"Are you sure?"

"Yes," he lied, hoping his perspiring brow didn't give him away.

She stood on her tiptoes and kissed him.

"I better make some dinner."

As she turned, Kieran gave her behind a firm slap. "You just wait until we reach that mountain resort. You won't be able to walk after I'm done with you."

She smiled at her husband.

"Is that a threat?"

He winked. "It's a promise."

*

"I want to have sex," Atlanta announced, getting goose bumps as she listened to the silence at the end of the phone. "Am I insane for thinking that?"

Her friend was rustling something, so she knew she was still there.

"No, honey. You're not insane for thinking that."

She sighed audibly. "I just wish I could bring myself to do it."

Her friend made a 'hmm' noise.

"Did you find it hard? You know, the first time you and Malcolm-"

"No way!" she cried, and Atlanta had to move the earpiece away before her eardrum exploded. "We'd been ready for a *long* time and as soon as my parents were out of town for the weekend, we jumped at the chance."

Atlanta thought about this.

"I want to, but just not with Deacon."

"Understandable," her friend agreed, chewing on something that made a loud crunching noise between her words. "That guy doesn't deserve you."

Atlanta smiled. "You think?"

"I *know*."

"So why did you encourage me to go out with him in

the first place?"

"Because you needed some action in the kissing department! Some lip to lip experience! Deacon's hot- we all know that- so it was perfect timing that Mr. Handsome wanted to take you out for a test drive."

"Nerys- I hate it when you say things like that! I just feel even more *used* and kind of *cheap*."

"Awww, I'm sorry, sweetheart. I didn't mean it like that. What you need to remember is that it's *his* loss. You'll find someone new and will fall in love with him and then you can tell everyone- including Deacon- how amazing the sex is when the pair of you get frisky in the bedroom. Deacon will find himself masturbating on cold winter nights with thoughts only for you and what he's missing out on."

"Atlanta!"

The sound of her mother yelling up the stairs came loud and clear as the smell of home-grown potatoes and melted cheese wafted through the crack at the bottom of her door.

"I have to go. Dinner awaits!"

"Sure thing. I'll see you tomorrow in school."

"Yup."

"Oh…and Atlanta."

"Hmm?"

"Wear one of the sexiest outfits you've got because I want all the guys looking at you when that idiot *Deacon* is around to see."

She laughed. "Maybe-"

"No *maybe's*."

"*Bye*, Nerys."

Atlanta hung up and turned to face the long mirror attached to her lilac coloured bedroom wall. Her reflection was most unattractive. The mascara was still dark and smudged beneath her moist, red eyes and her skin matched her pearly white teeth. The only thing she thought looked decent was her hair, held back with a pink headband she had found at the bottom of her desk drawer.

Atlanta had anticipated awkward silences at the dinner table, but to her amazement, conversation was never sparse. It seemed her parents were still planning to go away to the mountains, though her mother's rigid, pale face betrayed her calm tone of voice.

"I'll make sure the cupboards are full, I promise and I'll leave some money for the pair of you-" *Why do I have such a bad feeling about this?* she thought.

"Money? Great, because there's this new series of

books I wanted and they are so-o not cheap-" Phoenix said through a mouthful of spud drenched in mature cheddar. He received a stern look from both parents. "Kidding-" he added, with a grin.

"I want you to be prepared. If anything should happen, just give Siren a ring."

"I know how to fight," Phoenix pointed out coolly.

The twins had been placed in martial arts classes from the age of seven, but only Phoenix had stuck it out. Atlanta had shown very little passion for the art of defending oneself. She just assumed her father would always be there to save her.

"I'd prefer it if you didn't have to," Kieran replied, cutting his potato up to allow the heat to escape from its piping hot centre. "But just in case the situation arrives, I'm leaving you the keys to the basement."

Phoenix's eyes lit up. "Really?!"

His father nodded.

The basement had become a place for weapon's training and general storage. Every Sunday, Kieran would go down and either practise with, or clean, his fine collection of sharp and dangerous objects that had aided him in the slaying of demons over the years. And once again, only *Phoenix* had ever shown an interest in any of it- learning techniques from his father, usually in the early hours of the morning, whilst the women of the household slumbered soundly.

"You can use anything you need- except my shotgun."

"Excellent!" Phoenix twisted the melted cheese around his fork, thinking about the swords and knives he would soon have access to. His father obviously didn't want to leave them unarmed.

"Why are you telling us this now?" Atlanta spoke up, earning looks from everyone at the dinner table. "You're not going until next week."

Kieran looked at Kiya suddenly.

"*Actually*," Kieran said, "We think we're going to head out in about two days' time, just to get a head start on travelling."

Kiya nodded. "Serendith is a fair distance away and we want to make the most of your father's time off work."

-*This is brilliant*- Phoenix projected into Atlanta's mind. -*Think of the freedom we'll have!*-

-*For you to do what exactly? Read until your eyes fall out of your skull?*-

Phoenix glowered at his sister, not seeing any humour in her retort.

"Hey- would you two knock it off?" Kieran snapped, clicking his fingers in front of his son's eyes. "I'd rather hear what you have to say to each other if that's okay with you?"

Kiya smiled warmly at Kieran. She loved the way he handled the twins. From day one, when the twins had first arrived into the world accompanied by a lot of pain and blood, Kieran had been there- showing no fear towards the new and challenging prospect of parenting. He loved Kiya dearly and had raised the children with an equal amount of devotion in his heart for both her and her babies.

Not a day went by that she didn't feel content in her relationship, and even on visiting the Stone Table, where the twins true father had perished, she knew she was doing everything right by them. The stones had whispered their approval, or so she imagined.

"He's right. It's not fair that the pair of you can hide things from us, especially when we're at the dinner table."

"You just *hate* the fact you're not always in *control*," Atlanta said, and regretted it as soon as the words had left her mouth.

Kiya looked flustered for a moment, thrown from her pleasant thoughts into a state of speechlessness.

"Atlanta-" Kieran scolded.

-Simmer down sis-

-Piss off, Phoenix-

-Hey! You're just ratty because your stupid boyfriend tried sleeping with you when you weren't ready. Now he doesn't want you because of it-

"Stop talking about him!" she screamed, forgetting to use telepathy in her rage.

Kieran and Kiya shared confused looks, remaining silent for the time being.

"Sex isn't everything, you know."

"Will you shut up?! You don't know *anything*!"

"I think you both need to take a deep breath and think about where this is heading... *Nowhere*." Kieran intervened, since Kiya was in a state of non-cooperation.

Atlanta slammed her knife and fork down. Hard.

"He thinks he knows everything about me, and he doesn't."

Phoenix's expression was wooden. He was trying not to display any of his true emotions, chewing his food slowly and determinedly.

"Why are you two always jumping down each other's throats so much lately?" Kieran asked, looking from one twin to the other.

"Because I need space, Dad. Just because he doesn't have any friends of his own he has to get involved with *my* life to make himself feel wanted."

That stung.

It stung a *lot*.

Silence settled at the table.

Phoenix slid his chair back, calmly, and left without a word, leaving the last half of his meal untouched.

Atlanta was breathing heavily from her outburst, and she knew she should apologise, but felt too damn frustrated with her brother to make him feel better.

"That was very unfair of you, young lady." Kieran shot her a disappointed frown, refraining from jabbing a finger her way.

Atlanta shrunk in her chair.

"You two need to sit down and talk this through, if you feel strongly about needing time away. Perhaps, when high school is over, you might want to think about studying in separate universities?"

"Mum-" Atlanta whispered, feeling guilt eating her insides.

The last thing Kiya wanted was to force her children apart. They'd been so close from the day they were born, but the pair of them obviously had issues.

"We can't cancel the holiday now because we'll lose our deposit, but I have to say, you've ruined this for us."

Kieran rested a hand over Kiya's. He knew how much she hated telling the twins off- especially as it was a rarity in their lives.

"I didn't mean it."

"So go tell Phoenix that."

Atlanta bit her bottom lip.

"Don't worry about us," she said, diverting her mother's request. "Enjoy yourselves. We'll be fine."

"I hope so," Kiya said simply, and decided to busy herself with the washing up now that it appeared dinner was well and truly over.

- Chapter Five -

More

Phoenix didn't leave his bedroom for anything that night, other than to relieve himself in the bathroom close to twelve p.m.

He had immersed himself in an English essay that still had a good two weeks left before its due date, finding it a helpful distraction from his sister's cruel words at the dinner table.

He hated being angry with her, but as much as he loved her, she could be a real bitch at times.

Then again, he wondered if he had deserved it.

Midnight came and went.

The first draft of the essay was complete- the ink dry on the paper and a staple neatly clamped in the corner to hold everything together- and Phoenix was beginning to feel the need to rest dominating his sight.

The following morning, he woke up feeling cranky.

There was never a day he didn't sit with his sister to eat a bowl of cereal before taking off, but this time, he skipped breakfast entirely.

Atlanta, dressed in a denim mini-skirt with a rainbow design on one of the pockets and wearing a bright pink top that had a ribbon to tie around her neck, was sat waiting in the car, bearing a meek yet hopeful smile.

She waited patiently for her brother to leave the house, taking deep breaths, and sighed in misery as he strolled away from the car in the direction of the bus station.

"Phoenix!" she called through the crack in the window, but he ignored her completely.

-*Come back here. Don't do this. I'm sorry, okay?*-

Still, he chose not to reply and it felt as if she were suddenly carrying a weight on her shoulders that she really could have done without.

As she had expected, Atlanta arrived at school before Phoenix did.

"Hey!"

Nerys; petite, slim and dark skinned, bounded over to the car as her friend climbed out of the driver's seat. She was clothed in a white t-shirt and dungarees that covered large breasts and most of her flawless legs. On her feet she wore little white sandals that made a slapping noise every time she took a step. Regardless of how bad the weather was, Nerys *always* wore as little as possible and it had started to rub off on her best friend.

"Hi, Ner'," Atlanta said, trying to muster some enthusiasm.

"I *love* your outfit," her friend sang, putting a hand out and pushing Atlanta's hair behind her back so that it didn't obstruct the full-frontal effect of what she was wearing. "Deacon's gonna eat his own heart out."

Her heart fluttered- in a negative way. As well as dealing with her brother ignoring her, she still had to get through the day without being bullied by her ex.

"I always wear clothes like this," she muttered. "It's nothing new."

Nerys didn't know how to respond to this, and instead mentioned Phoenix's absence.

"So, is your brother ill? Where has he disappeared to?"

Atlanta moved to the boot of the car and retrieved the pink folder and denim shoulder bag that was hiding within.

"No, he's not ill. He just took the bus for a change."

Nerys sensed the tension immediately.

"You guys are fighting, aren't you?"

She nodded.

"I think it's best if we avoid the 'P' word for a bit. I'm not proud of myself and I have a feeling he hates me."

Nerys shook her head. "You pair always make up in the end. Don't worry about it."

"I'm trying not to," she whispered, just as Phoenix came into view. He was walking with his head down and his faded navy blue rucksack sagging over his right shoulder. Just as he looked up in her direction, she looked away.

"Let's go."

Atlanta moved to depart from the car park, and as she did so, felt her side smash into something pretty solid.

"Oh...I'm sorry! I wasn't looking where I was going."

She glanced apologetically into the purple irises of a female she had noticed on the school premises occasionally. Her hair was the colour of blood, short and spiked out at the tips and her eyelashes strangely had the same scarlet colouring. The shape of her lips was exquisite- plump and contoured in the centre, swathed in bright red lipstick, and her nose glistened with a small silver ring. Her outfit was of a gothic nature- black lace t-shirt that revealed a red bra beneath and a belt designed to look as if there were bullets attached to it. Her jeans were tight and black and on her hands she wore red lace gloves that allowed her fingertips to poke through at the ends.

"Are they real?" Nerys asked.

The girl glanced down at the bullets, but ignored the question.

"Sorry about that," Atlanta repeated.

She received a slight curling of the lip that could have been considered a smile of recognition from the girl, and watched her march off, bag bouncing on her hip as she moved.

"Weirdo," Nerys said, none too discreetly.

"I quite like her style. It's got *edge*."

Nerys rolled her eyes. "Don't go all devil worshipper on me, *please*! I'm already in shock about your statement last night."

"What statement?" She sounded confused.

Nerys leant forward as if it were a secret.

"The fact that you want to have *sex*."

Atlanta blushed. "Did I mention it's got to be with someone I *love*? It could take years before I find Mr. Right, so don't act all surprised. We're almost eighteen after all. Who doesn't want sex at that age?"

"*You're* almost eighteen," she corrected. "I'm already there honey!"

The girls entered the school with the usual feeling of dread. Days always dragged at Meridion High and the staff count was absolutely phenomenal. They had Maths teachers covering Geography and Physics; Games teachers attempting to tutor Religious Studies students and I.C.T, and English teachers that had a bash at bringing the actors and actresses out in people, in very uncoordinated Drama lessons.

The school itself was made of red brick and greatly lacked in colour. The grass outside was patchy and dull to say the least and the concrete paths were all cracked and vandalised. Students were very rarely involved in artistic studies, so the walls of the corridors were vacant of anything interesting, besides the odd 'bin your litter' flyer. Phoenix had once tried to put in a request for some decent paints and a sturdy surface to design something grand for the main foyer, but it was sadly declined, and he was left with nothing but corner shop quality watercolours in tiny pallets- quite useless in his vision of grand design.

"I hate Wednesday's," Atlanta grumbled.

"I hate all days."

"All days?"

"Okay, *school* days. Weekends aren't *too* bad."

As routine foretold, the girls' extracted books from

lockers and slammed them shut again with a strong sense of foreboding. In an unhurried pace, they eventually made their way to registration, until Atlanta froze in fear at what was coming her way.

"It's okay," Nerys encouraged. "I'm here."

Deacon, tall and dominating in the thin corridor barged his way through with his pack of imbecilic comrades, having eyes only for her.

Atlanta tugged on Nerys' wrist automatically and pulled her to the side, hoping the boys would just pass on by.

But it was too much to ask.

"Hey, Angel,"

Be strong, she told herself. *Show no fear.*

"What do *you* want?"

Deacon was leaning against the scratched metal lockers as smoothly as he could, smiling his big dumb smile and admiring her outfit with a critical gaze.

"Daddy like," he whispered. "Very nice."

"If you have something to say, *save it*." Atlanta told him firmly, and made to push through.

Deacon stopped her with the palm of his hand, sneaking in a squeeze of her left breast.

"Hey, hey!" he said, ignoring her apparent outrage.

"Slow down. We were together for a couple of months, so the least you can do is give me five minutes of your time."

Atlanta sighed audibly, rolling her eyes in Nerys' direction. Her friend was biting her lip, showing all the signs of awkwardness.

"I'm going to leave you pair to it," she offered, sliding amongst Deacon's group of gawking buddies- all of which shared good looks and up-to-date haircuts. One of the lads had the audacity to put a hand against Nerys' backside, barking like a dog as she squirmed away out of his reach.

"Will you guys clear off. I need to talk to my girl."

Atlanta scowled. "So I'm your girl again am I?"

Deacon shrugged. "Maybe." He ran a hand through her hair, and before she could protest, kissed her exposed neck, sending shivers coursing through her already quaking body.

"Stop it!" she objected, edging away.

Deacon cared little for her display of discontent.

"Have you thought about what we talked about yesterday?"

She glanced around the corridor for help. No one, not even a late first year was present now.

"It's over," she said. "And I'm glad."

"Oh come on, babe. You act like I meant nothing to you."

She didn't know what to say to this.

He grinned, trailing a hand gently down her arm.

"I think you do want to have sex with me, but you're scared," he whispered in her ear and with a yelp of surprise, she felt his hand slide under her skirt, touching her underwear, which was providing a *very* thin barrier for the goal Deacon was trying to reach.

She squirmed away, but Deacon progressed expertly, sliding the underwear aside and stroking her teasingly, his fingers warm.

"Deacon!"

She wanted to scream, but at the same time, she was enjoying the sensation. After all, she *had* had feelings for him, even if they weren't very strong anymore. Perhaps a part of her could forgive him?

"See," he cooed in her ear, warming her earlobe with his breath. "You do want me. I can tell. Girl's don't get wet like this for no reason."

It was at this point that reality hit, just as the tips of his two fingers tried forcing their way inside her.

She was in a school corridor for crying out loud.

Expulsion was just a heartbeat away at the rate they were going.

"*Deacon!*"

He ignored her cry, but she rammed him with all her might, causing him to lose connection at last.

"Aww...Angel! I was so close. Why'd you have to go ruining my fun?"

"*It's over*," she reiterated. "What part of that doesn't make sense to you?"

"But I'm hard for you. Look what you're doing to me."

"I couldn't care less what your dick does around me."

He grinned. "Well in that case-"

Deacon made to loop his arms around her waist, but she twirled away.

"Stay away from me!"

She retrieved her bag from the floor where it had fallen, tucked her folder under her arm, re-arranged her underwear into a more comfortable position and ran away.

"Virgin!" Deacon spat after her- left to his own thoughts as he remained the only student out of class.

- Chapter Six -

Serenity

Dhampir's were a rarity, and in Serenity's eighteen years of living- what some might consider a 'cursed' life- she had never met another like her.

Born of a human mother, and having a *vampire* for a father, Serenity had all the abilities of the despised 'blood sucking' race, but was blessedly capable of walking in sunlight without turning extra crispy. She craved blood like any other demon, but was able to keep her thirst under control with ample amounts of animal blood from the butchers.

And as a rule she had set herself from the moment she could speak, she vowed *never* to use her abilities for evil.

She preferred to call herself a Slayer; able to detect the pungent scent of evil and spending countless nights fighting those with a desire to kill and maim the innocent- winning every battle she ever participated in.

Her night hunts were the reason why Kieran and Siren had fought very few enemies in recent years, since the great war. She was the first to know when a bad guy strolled into town, and was the *first* to put a silver bullet or a blade between its eyes.

With hair a natural shade of blood red and eyelashes to match, she had always known herself to be different from the rest. It had taken a long time to come to terms with her lust for blood and even longer to control the rage that brewed inside her at random times- an inheritance from her now *vaporised* vampire father- but her mother was always just a phone call away if she needed to talk to someone, even if she *was* locked up in a psychiatric hospital at Lake Molly, half way across the big wide world.

The split from her mother- Mrs Danielle Heller- was Serenity's decision. She had never liked the feeling of hopelessness when trying to care for her. After the wound in her mother's neck had left her drained and practically immobile, coupled with the rape, she had lost her mind gradually until it became entirely necessary for Serenity to hand her to professional care staff.

Mrs Heller had feared everything that breathed and would not step a foot outside, even if the building she resided in was burning down around her. And at times, she had even feared her own daughter- the result of her horrific rape when she was coming home from a trip to the movies with a female friend. The friend had been killed on sight. Mrs Heller, it seemed, was the lucky one.

Meridion had always been Serenity's first choice for re-location. Something about the hopeless city gave her a warm feeling in her gut, and she had taken it upon herself to keep the demons at bay.

She was truly a Slayer- a pretty good one she thought, none too modestly- even though her thirst for blood was a constant reminder of the dark secret she bore.

The secret that part of her was an intolerable night creature.

If people truly knew her, she was sure they would question why she bothered going to high school at all. Her future was pretty bleak in the sense that she probably wouldn't be able to work comfortably among humans' nine till five, once her education was at its end.

She thought about why she attended school almost every day and always came to the same conclusion: teenagers were the future, and they needed her protection. By stationing herself at a high school, she could observe the activity among potential victims and ensure they didn't get caught up in anything life threatening.

And as much as she hated to admit it, Serenity liked

the company. Yes- she didn't talk to people- but she liked the hive of activity around her; the bustling of students; the gossip; the changes in fashion; the boys.

Dhampir's could have crushes too, so it seemed.

*

Serenity shook the strange feeling from her head as her contact with Atlanta replayed in her mind and she almost stopped moving altogether when she came inches from Phoenix.

Her heart beat faster.

She stole a look his way and noticed he looked unnaturally solemn.

The smell of grief cloaked him like a strong cologne.

Registration urged her to pick up the pace when she feared she had stared at Phoenix for too long, and she disappeared around the back of the building, entering through the vacant sports hall.

She didn't like going through the main entrance. Too many people congregated there in the mornings, so she preferred the quiet route, taking the cracked-slab pathway that was sheltered by trees. The only people she was likely to meet there were nicotine junkies, puffing on their first cigarette of the day.

Registration was swift.

The students behaved as normal- ignoring the teacher who was struggling to yell names out over the din and scratching black marks in the appropriate places on her clip board. When this was complete, the students shimmied back into the corridors and on to their first lesson.

Serenity was always last to leave the room.

No one had ever tried to get to know her at Meridion High, and it suited her just fine. It meant she didn't have to cook up excuses when female friends questioned her absence at the local pub on Friday nights, or why she didn't show up for the ten o'clock showing of the latest flick. It also meant she didn't have to pretend she was normal.

Normal girls didn't realise how easy life was for them.

When the first break period blessedly came, Serenity headed straight for the library. She spent all her free time there- enjoying the sight of books and the single, ancient computer that made funny whirring noises when a member of staff attempted to use it. But as well as all that, it was a place that Phoenix Nightly haunted.

Serenity had noticed Phoenix the very first day she'd

joined the colourless high school and she was aware- over careful weeks of observation- that he read a lot. But it was the *power* she sensed in him- the power to do great things- that became a drug she just couldn't give up.

There was fire in Phoenix's soul. A distinct warrior's spirit blossoming in his heart and she liked the impression he gave- silent, but potentially dangerous. Also, Phoenix was *gorgeous*. Beneath the thick frames of his glasses was the unthinkably handsome face of a God. His black hair beckoned her to touch it and his eyes put her under a spell every time she found herself looking at them.

Phoenix was the one person she desired more than anyone else.

If she had to, she'd die for him, a thousand times over.

Even if he never knew her name…

Serenity, the keeper of peace.

Slayer of evil.

Both selfless heroine and blood drinking *demon*…

- Chapter Seven -

The Library

Phoenix swiped the glasses from his nose and rubbed his eyes, trying to coax them into focus. He was feeling unbearably tired, no thanks to his decision to write an essay from start to finish the night before, and was also feeling an overwhelming sadness at how pathetic he allowed himself to be.

Wearing glasses when he could wear contacts? His family had always been baffled by his decision to obscure the true beauty of his face. But Phoenix liked doing the opposite to what was expected of him.

If he started flaunting himself, he would become the type of person he despised. So until he could truly discover who he was, he preferred to remain in the shadows.

Deacon and his crew of bullies had wanted Phoenix to sign his soul over to them the day they had started high school. But he was smarter than that. Being an insufferable bully wouldn't get you anywhere, especially when high school was over. And for Phoenix, the end of high school was only a few more months away.

The boy's bathroom was filling up now. He had been alone when he had first entered to re-establish some life in himself, but the silence was now disturbed with the sound of urine hitting toilet water and chains flushing.

It was time to go to his refuge.

Atlanta was nowhere to be seen as he dodged his way to the second floor of the school at a casual pace. He was hoping to catch a glimpse of her, just to see how she was holding up- even if he felt she didn't deserve his concern for her well-being. But alas, she was not amongst the crowd and he pushed her to the back of his thoughts as soon as the door handle to the library was in his clammy hand.

The library was his little sanctuary. Every break period, he went there, unless he was involved in extracurricular activities or helping a student to catch up on class notes. (He was the reliable one). It was a peaceful haven- a place to relax and read something imaginative. To forget about exams and surviving the school year.

He got the impression his family thought he read a little *too* much. Perhaps they were right too. He did chose reading over a lot of things. It was because of the library that he didn't have mates to hang out with on weekends and in the holidays. But Meridion High boys were- the majority of them-

assholes and not worth his precious time.

Taking up his usual chair at the long desk that ran the whole length of the room, surrounded by shelves of books on both sides, he nodded to the regulars and proceeded to extract a novel from his rucksack.

The temperature was high. As he settled, he shed his jacket and rolled the sleeves of his shirt up until at last, he was comfortable.

"Sorry about the heat," the librarian said, peering over her spectacles. She had noticed the student's discomfort and felt the need to explain. "Radiators are on full power for a change and the knob had broken off. We can't lower the temperature until someone comes to fix it."

"It's no wonder," a boy piped up, his hair bright orange in colour. "Everything in this place is a piece of crap."

The librarian scowled and returned to her paperback, patting the back of her brown bun absentmindedly to double check her hair wasn't coming loose. All was satisfactory it seemed.

Phoenix blew air upwards to cool his forehead, but stopped thinking about how hot his skin felt when something caught his eye.

The girl, with hair the colour of blood, was reading the

same novel as him and it appeared she was further into the story than he. As he pondered this, she looked his way.

Her white cheeks went scarlet.

And Phoenix, though it was not in his nature, found himself burning with embarrassment too- for being caught looking at a girl with an expression of pure intrigue.

He looked at his book and tried reading, but the lines didn't make sense to him. He kept reading the same sentence over and even in doing so, he didn't understand what the author was trying to say. So he gave up trying and stole another look at the girl.

He thought it was odd that he hadn't really *looked* at her before. She was in the library just as much as he was- he was sure of this- and it wasn't as if a person could miss that unusual shade of red, spiked out hair. Her lips were the reddest he'd ever seen and her body was a perfect womanly shape that could make a guy go insane for one touch of her skin. The nose piercing was pretty cool too.

When he was caught staring a second time, he felt he had to react. With his cheeks aflame, he threw a dazzling smile her way, then opened his mouth to mention their matching taste in the fantasy genre…until his sister walked through the doors, looking slightly peaky.

"Atlanta-!"

"Oh, so you're speaking to me now?"

Phoenix dropped his book onto the table and stumbled over his words. The red-headed girl had allowed his thoughts to get all scattered and he had forgotten to remind himself that he was no longer on speaking terms with his sister.

-If you're gonna talk, use your mind, would you? This is a library. People come here for peace and quiet-

Atlanta nodded furtively and slid into a chair beside her brother, trying to pull her skirt a little further towards her knees as it rode up unexpectedly. Phoenix caught her doing so, and rolled his eyes.

-Don't you have an appointment with the girl's lavatory? Your hair could do with a good brush and your lip gloss has become practically non-existent since the ten layers you put on first thing this morning-

-I didn't come to argue-

-What did you come for?-

-To be friends again-

Phoenix picked up his book, pretending to read it so that the pair of them didn't look too suspicious just staring into space like zombies as they used their telepathy.

-I have no friends, as you pointed out less than twenty

four hours ago-

-You know I didn't mean it-

-Well it's true isn't it? I guess we can't all be as popular as you are-

-Just stop it, okay? What else do you want from me? I'm sorry-

-Why did you really come here, sis?-

-For you of course-

Phoenix watched her face closely. *-This has nothing to do with avoiding Deacon does it?-*

She shook her head. *-No-*

-Because I heard you this morning-

Her eyes twinkled in bafflement.

-I heard you screaming- he continued. *-You were crying out in your mind for a while. It wasn't a major yell for help or anything, but I got the impression something was making you seriously uncomfortable-*

Atlanta blushed. She hadn't realised Phoenix was so in tune with her thoughts.

-Deacon wanted to talk-

-And?-

-And what?-

-Are you okay?-

-Don't I look it?-

Phoenix sighed aloud. He knew he wouldn't be able to get much else from her. Atlanta was always rather private when it came to her relationship with that buffoon.

-Why does that girl keep looking at you?- she asked, changing the subject. She wanted to draw the conversation away from the experience she'd had that morning, involving Deacon's hand reaching up her mini skirt. *-Does she know you?-*

-No- he told her simply.

-She can hardly keep her eyes off you-

-What of it?-

Atlanta gave her brother's shoulder a little push of encouragement. *-I think she fancies you, bro'-*

Phoenix suppressed a smile.

-This could be interesting- she laughed.

-What could be interesting?- he queried, with a note of worry in his voice.

-The fact that you have a girl eyeing you up-

-It's not like I haven't caught a lady's eye before, Atlanta-

-I reckon there's definitely something there. A little fire in her eyes. Perhaps she wants you to be her man?- she

giggled telepathically, and Phoenix gave her a stern look.

-I think you've overstayed your welcome-

-I think someone has a crush-

-I didn't say I liked her! Jeez!-

Atlanta sent kissing noises into his thoughts as she gathered her bag and folder.

-Would you shut up?-

-I could, but I don't want to-

She left, giving him a little wave and a sly wink just before she disappeared out of view, and Phoenix sat in silence once more, finding it a struggle to keep the grin off his lips and his eyes on his book.

When break was over, he was eager to leave. The sooner he got through his classes, the sooner lunch would arrive- as well as his second session at the library.

- Chapter Eight -

Heaven Sent

As much as Atlanta desired the rare rays of Meridion sunshine, she was fully aware that Deacon would be outside, lolling on the benches or cruising through the crowds to high five friends and irritate blatantly insecure students. Because of this, she stayed *well* away from his regular haunts, leaving her with very little ground to roam. It didn't help her mood either. She was uncomfortable and glum, though her visit to the library had cheered her a little. Teasing her brother always picked up her spirits.

  She was alone now. Nerys was taking a walk with Malcolm somewhere off the premises (final year students were permitted to leave the grounds during free lessons or break periods) and so, Atlanta realised quite sulkily that she had nothing better to do than to head in the direction of her next class.

  The brief burst of sunshine meant the corridors were empty, besides a teacher or two coming out of classrooms to grab a hot beverage from their staffroom. She took her time reaching her destination; carefully placing one leather booted foot before the other and working her hips into a tantalising rhythm, pretending to observe notice boards on passing. It was just a shame there was no one to see her walk... One thing Atlanta knew was how to work her body. She wasn't overly confident in her looks, but she knew there was something about her that guys liked. And it wasn't that she craved attention like the popular girls- she just liked the uplifting feeling she gained from being noticed.

On entering the English room, she assumed it would be vacant. Her teacher, Miss Hathaway, usually spent break periods flirting with male members of the games department, but instead, she was perched on the edge of a table- flashing more leg beneath her skirt than a teacher realistically should.

After getting over the initial shock of finding the tall, slim and blonde member of staff present- still pretty enough and *young* enough for clubs and bars- Atlanta found herself paralysed by the sight of *another* person.

An *interesting* person.

A down right *gorgeous* mass of flesh standing at six foot five, with long blonde hair touching his broad shoulders- slightly layered at the sides of his face. *Perfect* from the top of his head to the tips of his toes, born with the bluest eyes she had ever had the privilege to feel gazing at her body, and the most *fantastically* fit toned and sculpted body she had ever come across. He was one of those legendary 'pin up model' look-alikes - the type of guy a girl could only *dream* of bumping into.

Her radar for stunningly handsome individuals was blaring in her head and it *wasn't* about to shut up anytime soon.

She had found a prince among men.

A God among rodents.

The young gentleman before her made a simple white shirt look like it was worth a million pounds and a pair of light blue denim jeans fit snug around his magnificent backside.

If Atlanta didn't stop gawking soon, she was sure Miss Hathaway would call the hospital and have her taken away, suggesting to the paramedics that they wipe the drool from her lips.

My gosh, she thought as the young man flashed her a smile of recognition and performed a curt nod. His dimples were the cutest thing *ever*!

Miss Hathaway didn't hide the fact she was unimpressed with Atlanta's interruption. She wrapped her arms around herself, perking her breasts up to make them appear more ample and she bit a glossy lip in annoyance.

"Hi," the boy said, with a voice like an angel. It wasn't like the other boys. It sounded seductive, yet, had a kind of rough 'edge' to it. It was a voice layered with an intriguing hint of innocence, as well as *power* and a great big dollop of 'don't you just want to come over here and taste my lips with yours?' *magic*. He *knew* how to make a girl shiver with every word that left his mouth.

Atlanta, dumbstruck, accidentally flitted her gaze over his crotch. It appeared the boy had caught her doing so, and he couldn't help but crack another breathtaking smile.

She blushed ridiculously red.

"Is there something you *want*?" Miss Hathaway asked, fearing the start of some chemistry in her English domain. She didn't mask her tone of bitterness. Science belonged in the labs.

"Excuse me?" Atlanta managed to mumble, not even attempting to look the teacher's way.

"Why are you *here*?" Miss Hathaway asked, firmly.

"Eager to start I guess-"

She rolled her eyes and stood up straight, dropping her arms from beneath her breasts. She straightened the plum coloured, long sleeved top and patted her black skirt hurriedly. "Well I was just leaving."

Ten guesses where to, Atlanta thought.

When the teacher departed, giving the boy a wistful 'once over' before closing the door, Atlanta felt as if a bright spotlight had just been cast upon her in a darkened room full of eyes she couldn't quite make out. Her hands became clammy and her mind reeled for things to say.

The boy looked relaxed and she wished she could borrow some of his breeziness. Some of his calm.

How did he get such amazing biceps?

She realised how stupid she was being, standing there like a little girl who had just witnessed Santa Claus coming into the building with a plastic white beard, patchy red clothes and a musty smelling bag full of cheap toys.

"Julian," he said, brandishing an open palm her way,

Atlanta stared at it for a second before gripping it in her own.

He waited expectantly.

"This is the part where you tell me *your* name," he urged.

Atlanta smiled goofily and she tried taking a deep breath without making it appear obvious she was doing so.

"Lanta," was all she managed to get out.

"Lanta?" he repeated.

"No…I meant, *At*lanta."

He nodded.

She looked earnestly at the clear desk next to Julian and made to sit in a chair, changing her mind at the last second and favouring the table top instead. Her skirt rose around her thighs, and she giggled nervously, placing her balled up fists on top to obstruct any view of her underwear.

"I haven't seen you around here before- where are you from?" she questioned him bravely. *Brownie points for not messing up your sentence,* she thought.

"The north," he told her, without giving any specific name of a city or mountain village.

"I see," she replied. "And you came to Meridion because…?"

"Change of scenery."

Atlanta wondered why anyone would want *Meridion* to be their next choice of place to stay. You could count the amount of trees it had with your fingers! And the only places that offered a bit of colour was either the West Meridion Mall, with all its fairy holograms and fake plantation, or the Stone Table, which had become vastly overgrown with big white lilies that never seemed to die.

"Any brothers and sisters?"

He shook his head. Atlanta's heart skipped a beat as he took up the space beside her unexpectedly. For a brief moment their sides touched, until he skimmed over a bit.

"So... you're studying at Meridion High I take it?"

"Well, Meridion High is the only school in the entire city for kids our age. It's not like I have much choice."

"No, of course not," Atlanta said. She was looking at her boots now, trying to stop her eyes from obsessively scanning over the new and extremely handsome stranger. If she were the confident type, she would have stroked a hand over his thigh and maybe tried to make a move for a kiss on those irresistible lips-

"You okay?"

His voice was a knife to her throat.

"What!?"

"You seem to be absorbed in something."

She physically shook her head, trying to clear the cobwebs. Did she really just let her mind concoct a crazy fantasy involving Julian? By the Lord Himself, she didn't know where such ideas were coming from! It was *most* unlike her.

Julian looked at his gold coloured watch, with its shiny black face.

Atlanta assumed he had somewhere else to be. Other people to meet. Friends to make.

"Well... I need to make a move."

Elegantly, he swung his legs and sprung from the tabletop, landing lightly on the cracked tile floor. Atlanta's disappointment showed, and it was clear she wanted him to stay and keep her company.

"Sorry it's been such a short introduction. I have to consult the games department to see if I can join them. With the school year so close to completion, some teachers will probably reject my request, so I just need to persuade them I'm a fast learner and can catch up easily enough. I've done most of the work at previous schools."

"Why did you move here when you were so close to finishing school? Wouldn't it have made sense to finish first, then find a change of scenery?"

"There were complications. I had no choice." His head sunk.

"Oh... I didn't mean to pry for information or anything. I just wondered why you might have-"

"My mother is very ill," he cut across her, looking

darker- haunted with bad memories perhaps? "We couldn't find help where we were staying previous to this, so I moved us here in hope of seeking medical help from the hospital."

"My mum works at the hospital! Perhaps you might have seen her-?"

"Perhaps." He paused. "I really should go."

Atlanta jumped off the table, feeling the heel of her right boot wobble disconcertingly. Luckily, she kept her balance.

"It was nice meeting you. We should hang out sometime."

Atlanta scrunched her face up in painful thought. *We should hang out sometime? What am I, twelve? Jeez*! She wished she'd just said her goodbyes and left things with the *possibility* of re-meeting.

I bet he thinks I'm some desperate loner in search of a friend- a handsome friend to perhaps raise myself on the social totem.

Well, no matter what he thought of her, she hoped to God he would seek her out again.

- Chapter Nine -

Old Age

Kiya was distracted. It was hard washing up breakfast dishes when her partner was nipping at her neck, but she refused to give in to his little game.

With a smile she couldn't keep contained; she swilled the dish cloth around a breakfast bowl and almost cried out as Kieran tickled her two inches below her right armpit.

"Stop it!"

"Make me."

He persisted, changing tactics and swapping to her left side so that she wriggled back into his path.

Kiya almost dropped the bowl that was in her dripping wet hand.

"Kieran!" she laughed, uncontrollably. "Kieran you're making this more difficult than it should be! *Ah!* Stop it!"

He chased her around the room for a while, and when he managed to get a grip on her clothing, he tugged her roughly to his chest.

"Look," Kiya groaned. "You've ripped my new

blouse!"

"That's because I *despise* it," he explained matter-of-factly. "You may be a woman in her forties, but you're still gorgeous. Don't wear 'mum clothes.' You can still dress like you used to." He sighed loudly. "Hmm, to see you in those leather trousers once more… and for me to take them off at my leisure. Would you put them back on for me, baby? Just this once?"

Kiya pushed him away, but he clung onto her for dear life.

"This isn't funny," she scolded him, though she didn't sound truly angry. "We can't afford to be ruining clothes for the sake of flirting and the leathers are all boxed up in the attic for Atlanta to pick and choose from if she wishes-"

"Oh, just shut up with the mum stuff for two minutes and kiss me."

"Kiss yourself!" she grinned, grabbing his arm, spiralling free and twisting it behind his back. When his bones clicked loudly, she let him go, biting her lip in apology. But Kieran kept any signs of discomfort hidden. He wasn't about to let his wife make him appear so easily conquerable.

"Sorry honey!" She reached a hand up and touched his cheek. His muscles were on fire from the simple exercise he had undergone- running around the dining room table. Though he would never admit to it, Kiya was sure Kieran was succumbing to old age.

She worried about him. Every day he spent at the Slayer Headquarters, she dreaded the thought of receiving a phone call that he was injured, or worse. Kieran had been a warrior his whole life. It was all he knew. But she feared it would put him in an early grave.

"Why are you looking at me like that?" he asked, slipping onto a stool near the counter, directly opposite the sink.

Kiya jostled her head in exaggeration, shaking the thoughts away, and placed the wet bowl on the draining board. As she turned back towards the sink, she was aware of Kieran's eyes roving up and down her body.

"I wasn't," she assured him.

He leant forward, putting his head in his hands.

"You feeling okay Kier'?"

"Yup," was his sudden reply. "Just thinking about leaving this place behind for a few days."

Kiya made a sound of agreement. "It's going to be great, isn't it? Our first week away from the kids."

Kieran smiled, but it faded.

"What's wrong now?"

He made an expression as if she were accusing him of something he wasn't doing, glanced at the bread bin pointlessly, then turned back to face her.

"Do you think they know?"

Kiya wrung the dishcloth out and draped it over the tap before turning to face her husband. "Know what?"

He looked down at the floor. "That I'm not their father."

Kiya sucked in a deep breath. She'd had a feeling Kieran would bring this up again. The last time they had discussed it, the twins were just starting high school.

"I wouldn't think Atlanta could figure it out," she said, keeping her voice from wavering to the best of her ability. "But Phoenix is a smart kid. He may have his suspicions…What does it matter anyway?"

He sighed again. "It *doesn't* matter. I just often wonder, you know? Do they think I'm some sort of impostor in their lives? Do they think we're keeping something from them?"

Kiya approached him and placed her hands on his thighs.

"They love you, Kieran. Isn't that enough?"

He feigned a smile, but Kiya could sense he wasn't completely satisfied.

"I wish I *had* been, you know? Their true father, I mean."

Kiya didn't regret the fact that the children were the last gift she'd had from Rycan, but Kieran's discomfort was effecting her too.

"We should have had another."

Kiya stood stiffly.

"You never said-"

"I know-" He reached out and grabbed both her hands.

"I'm not saying I regret any part of the time we've had together. It's been perfect. Every minute of it. But I was thinking, it would have been nice to have had a child…you know…made by *me*." He chuckled half-heartedly.

Kiya put a hand to her heart.

Minutes that felt like hours lolled by.

"We could still try," she said slowly.

He stared deep into her eyes, stirring her soul into life.

"Do you want to?"

Kiya didn't need to think about it.

"Yes."

A broad smile stretched across Kieran's face.

"Another baby," he smiled, as if it were already in his arms.

She kissed him gently.

"And just think of all the fun we'll have making it," he joked.

Kiya went to slap him on the chest playfully, but as she moved her arm, he caught her by the wrist, proving his reflexes weren't *entirely* dead.

"Now get upstairs and put those leather trousers on because I'm gonna do things to you that'll make you insane from the pleasure of it."

Kiya looked at him mischievously. "I hope you keep to your word. It's going to take ages for me to find that box in the attic-"

Kieran rolled his eyes and with a quick flick of his fingertips over her jeans, the button came free and the zip slid down.

He winked. "Fine, forget it. But just as long as the leather's end up in our suitcase-"

She laughed.

"You read my mind."

- Chapter Ten -

The Note

Nerys put her pen down on the table top. She'd given up trying to write anything with Atlanta talking so animatedly beside her- something about a guy being the hottest thing she'd ever seen- and considered pulling some nail varnish from her bag to add to an already dazzling layer.

At first, it had been a relief, seeing her friend regaining her quirky, cheerful nature, but the daunting task of starting an English essay with a voice constantly singing in her ear wasn't going to help Nerys get a decent coursework grade. Her usually mellow attitude was becoming clouded with anxiety. If she didn't finish school with good results, she had a feeling she would end up in the cheese. And Nerys *hated* cheese.

Miss Hathaway had stepped out of class for a moment, after having received an urgent message from Mr Benson- the head of the sports department- which the students were about ninety five percent sure involved 'copping a feel.' With her slim frame vacant at the front of the class, they had the perfect opportunity to put their feet up on the tables, lean back in their chairs precariously and gossip like their lives depended on it.

"Do you think they let him join the class?"

"Hmm?" Nerys replied distractedly. Her concentration was slipping into the abyss and she decided to give up trying to write any sentences that made sense. As a means to keep herself from fidgeting, the nail varnish came out at last.

"Julian. He wants to study Physical Education-"

"Atlanta-"

Atlanta's eyes were wide and sparkling with imaginative thoughts of where Julian might be at this point.

"Yes?"

"I honestly couldn't give a shit."

The harsh tone of her voice bit into Atlanta like a rabid dog, leaving a wicked sting behind. "I'm sorry. I…I was babbling again, wasn't I?"

"Just a little, honey."

Atlanta sighed, tapping her pen on the desk. The level of noise in the classroom was growing in magnitude. Any louder, and the Headmaster would come bounding in to shut them all up with threats of detention.

"He was just so dreamy."

"I'm sure he was," Nerys replied, with no commitment

to the conversation in her voice.

When English ended at the sound of the bell, Atlanta couldn't wait to leave for lunch. She tossed her pencil-case in her bag, half opened- to which the results involved stationary swimming around with her make-up, purse and deodorant- and almost left her pink folder on the desk as she made to leave.

"What's the rush?"

"Hungry," was her one word answer.

Nerys was sure this wasn't the *real* reason as she blew on her nails- double checking they were bone dry.

"I'm sure he hasn't forgotten about you," she muttered sarcastically.

"And I'm sure you're right," Atlanta responded, ignoring the true meaning behind her friend's remark. "But I really want you to see him. Believe me, you will *not* be disappointed."

"No one is better looking than my Malcolm."

As Atlanta rounded the corner- with Nerys in tow- she thought she saw Julian in the distance and almost dropped her folder in excitement.

Her thoughts were so focused on the new-guy now that she completely forgot to avoid Deacon as he passed her in the corridor.

He stood in front of her- all muscle and strategically gelled hair falling over the right side of his face- and raising two of his fingers, he sniffed them loudly.

Deacon's friends, standing like a pack of handsome fools behind him, burst into raucous laughter, patting their leader on the back.

Atlanta's face burned hotter than ever before.

He said nothing as she stepped around him, but continued to hold his two fingers beneath his nose, sniffing the feminine scent she had left behind there.

"What on earth was all that about?" Nerys queried, twiddling the dial on her locker without even looking at the numbers. The pair of them were keeping their heads down, in hope of convincing people they were not involved in Deacon's taunting.

When the locker clicked open, Nerys planted her English textbook safely inside- blank sheets of lined paper tucked between the pages in wait. The essay was going to kill her over the weekend.

"He's a big idiot. He's just trying to piss me off."

As Atlanta's own locker swung open, a note slid out and floated to her feet.

Her heart beat wildly in her chest, shaking her very ribcage.

Could it be from Julian? No…wait…he didn't know where her locker was situated in the hallway.

The note was folded, and with trembling fingers, she revealed the message within.

It was Deacon's handwriting.

In big black letters, the word 'VIRGIN' sprung out at her.

Nerys shook her head in disgust. "Asshole," she breathed through gritted teeth.

Atlanta sucked in a deep breath.

I'm not going to let this get to me, she thought determinedly. *I'm not. He can't hurt me.*

"You okay?"

"Yes!" she exclaimed. "I'm fine! Just shut up asking me that!"

Nerys looked hurt as her best friend brushed passed her, still clutching the note in her hand.

Atlanta didn't feel like eating anymore. All her enthusiasm for the rest of the day had been man handled into a box and locked up tight. She wanted nothing more than to go home and lie on her bed watching something that had nothing to do with sex, love or *men*.

"Catch you later then," Nerys called after her.

Atlanta grunted, but the sound was lost amongst the cries of hungry students, young and old, heading for the exits to seek food. The school couldn't provide lunch like most educational buildings. It couldn't afford to employ lunch ladies, so the children had to leave the grounds to find a shop. The younger students, who were unable to leave the grounds, were forced to bring pack lunches.

Atlanta's nerves were now masking her desire to eat.

God, I hate this place, she thought.

A part of her regretted leaving Nerys behind. It wasn't a wise move, because she had made herself an easy target if she were to bump into Deacon again.

The corridors were clearing and the sunlight beckoned to her, but she was too afraid to make a move. Torn between hiding and holding her head high outside, she went to walk one way, then turned at the last minute, walking face first into the chest of Julian.

If her nose didn't hurt so much, she would have smiled.

"Sorry!" she cried sheepishly. "I've been doing that a lot lately."

Julian showed no sign of understanding what she meant.

"Your nose…it's bleeding," he said.

Standing all red in the face, she felt the warm trickle of blood and tried to hide it behind the palms of her hands. In doing so, the note from Deacon slipped from between her fingertips.

"I'll get it," Julian offered, as she made to dive for it.

"No really-" she pleaded, but his hand reached the paper first.

The word virgin was clear as he handed the paper over, but he pretended he hadn't read what it said.

"Let's get you cleaned up," he said stoically.

"It's quite alright. This happens all the time," she lied.

"I can escort you to the girl's bathroom if you like?"

She scowled at him. "Why would you want to do that?"

He shrugged. "Because from what I've gathered, you're looking for a way around bumping into the guy who sent you that note, and I don't think anyone should be made to feel afraid like that."

Atlanta's mouth was hanging open and she could feel the blood from her nose sliding towards her lips. There was far too much of it to contain in her hands now.

Defeated, she allowed Julian to walk at her side in the direction of the girl's toilets. The fact she was in pain, made her uncomfortable.

"How did you know?" she asked him as they went.

"Know what?"

"That I was…afraid?"

"There were a bunch of guys in the changing rooms throwing your name around and one in particular was being a bit of a dick, so I gathered you've been having a rough time lately. It would explain why Miss Hathaway was so surprised to see you attend her class when we first met."

Atlanta was in shock. Her world was crashing at her feet. She hated the thought of being talked about behind her back. Deacon was laughing at her in the changing rooms! He was probably telling them about how close he'd been to…to…*urgh*! She was furious and felt so helpless!

When the toilets came into view, she rushed ahead, leaving Julian standing there- tall, handsome and alone. Like her bodyguard or something.

She was surprised to find he was still standing there ten minutes later, after she had wiped and reapplied some foundation around the nose area, followed by a quick spritz of perfume to the neck and a rapid brushing of her long brown hair.

The sight of him was staggeringly good.

Perhaps God *had* sent him?

"You didn't have to wait," she smiled appreciatively.

"Well, I feel somewhat responsible for causing you pain."

"It's okay, really."

She stood still, wondering where to go. She hadn't thought about any particular direction to take and now that she had found Julian, her hunger was returning tenfold.

"Do you want to grab some food? I know a great Chinese that sells their stuff at discount prices to the students- and they have *excellent* egg fried rice there-"

"I'm trying to lay off the greasy stuff." He said coolly.

Atlanta was crushed. She took this as his way of saying he'd had enough of her company.

"Okay. Sure."

Losing her confidence a little, she walked in his general direction and made to go around him.

Suddenly, he put an arm out to stop her from advancing further.

She opened her mouth in surprise, about to protest-

"I didn't say I didn't want to hang out with you though," he told her silkily.

Where his hand touched her, she tingled. It rippled through her body and gave her soul a zap of electricity.

"Shall we?" he said, crooking his arm for her to link with his.

She smiled uncontrollably, aware of how red her cheeks must look. But she didn't care.

Julian is such a gentleman, her mind gushed. *He's fresh meat in this school, and there's nothing I wouldn't give to have the first bite!*

- Chapter Eleven -

Liquid Lunch

The sound of humans talking was louder than ever as Serenity made her way into the food district of the city, with the rest of the students all in groups up ahead. No thanks to her vampiric abilities, all conversations and domineering screams ripped through her mind like a heavy metal band at a live concert. Her ribcage rattled with the vibrations of their screeching and her head ached intolerably, so she decided to hang back- letting the mixture of young adults scatter as the shops came into view.

When she knelt to tie a shoelace on one of her shiny black boots, a strong smell of *dog* wafted up her nose, making her gag unexpectedly.

Velkon- the youngest werewolf she had ever encountered- was coming up behind her, having been kept back to explain to his teacher why his homework appeared incomplete and bearing teeth marks.

On passing, Serenity gave the fifteen year old boy a nod, to which he mirrored back in confusion before hurrying on.

Velkon was a good lad who had suffered the misfortune of being scratched by his father in 'wolf form.' Now, he had to chain himself up in the basement every full moon, with a little assistance from his mother, who kept her son's disability a secret from the government. Serenity had observed Velkon the second she had smelt the dog inside him- following him back to his house every full moon for six months to ensure he was capable of preventing any incidents involving dead people with missing hearts. He'd proved to be reliable... so far.

Velkon had made Serenity realise just how many secrets were being kept at their school, and if it wasn't for her unnatural strengths and powers, there might well have been a serious disaster by now.

One year previous, she had been the person to put a stop to dark magic being performed in the Science labs. A student- with anxiety issues- had planned on summoning a demon to consume all the students that had bullied him. If Serenity hadn't arrived on time to behead the beast that had torn a blazing hole in the school floor during its manifestation, the boy would probably have succeeded and a lot of teenage miscreants would have lost their limbs.

The only reason why the anxious student hadn't revealed Serenity's identity was because she had threatened to tell his parents what he practised in his spare time.

Her secret was safe- her mother being the only one who knew her true nature. The boy in question had committed suicide just after Brad Sutton had stolen his clothes in the boys' changing rooms and left him there to be discovered by a female cleaner at the end of the day.

When she had first burst into the labs, her eyes had flashed silver- a tell-tale sign of a hungry, or very pissed off vampire- and her teeth had elongated during the battle to 'gonna bite your neck' style.

But all was well now.

The bullying had become too much for him, and Serenity had been too late to persuade him not to put a knife to his throat.

Poor kid.

But she couldn't save them all.

Velkon, on the other hand, didn't know Serenity had taken an interest in him- going to his house to witness the process of him 'turning' into a werewolf. He didn't know she had been the one to slay his father on the eve of Serenity's seventeenth birthday either, when she was trying to enjoy a midnight stroll- alone, as usual. The werewolf had come at her in an alley, teeth glistening in an outstandingly huge mouth, and she had barely reached for her blade in time to drive it into one of his big yellow eyes. From her jacket, she'd pulled out a handgun- loaded with silver bullets- and planted three of them in his heart.

Summer was on its way now. Although she could walk in daylight, the sun's rays always pained her during the hottest time of year. Her pale skin burnt viciously if she was out between one and five, and no amount of lotion to protect against harmful rays helped. She had dealt with this hindrance by sticking to the shadows- just one more reason why she couldn't have any kind of social life.

Uh! She thought, as she watched Velkon's back disappearing into a greasy old shop, *I always know how to depress myself! If there was one person I'd rather not have to be around, it would be* myself!

As was to be expected, the shops were riddled with customers, and Serenity ended up sitting on a brick wall outside a derelict church in wait for a break in the thick crowds. Students came and went, as well as a mass of crows that landed amongst the many feet of pedestrians to snap up any crumbs that might have fallen. She watched the black birds squawking, until finally, when the boredom and hunger became overwhelming, she slid in the direction of the butcher's shop.

"Ah, Serenity!" came a loud and enthusiastic bellow from the back room.

Shirley, the owner of the shop, must have noticed her crossing the road in her direction. She was rosy cheeked, oily faced, *extremely* overweight, and the *only* person in Meridion that didn't question Serenity's repetitive order for bags of pigs blood.

"One enough?"

Serenity cast a wary eye to the door. The students outside were too busy to care about anyone standing in a butcher's store.

"Yeah, that would be great."

She handed over the correct amount of money- having the prices memorised- and gave the female butcher a smile of appreciation.

"See you next time, Darlin'" she said cheerfully, wiping a chubby hand in her bloody overalls.

Leaving the butcher's shop, Serenity scrunched the brown bag up into a more convenient bundle and left the food district behind for a back alley. It was in this alley, upon a giant green dumpster, that she ripped the plastic corner with her jagged teeth and glugged down as much of the blood as she could manage before coming up for air.

Hmm, still warm.

The blood was kissing her muscles into life and clearing her head of all fatigue. If she could see her own skeleton, she'd find it glowing as a result.

Finishing the last few tasty drops, she almost choked on the final gulp as two figures appeared from the shadows.

She looked left- then right- for some place to scarper, but realised with horror that the only way she could go was in the direction of the strangers.

"Hey!" one of the shadows yelled with a distinct Chinese accent.

Serenity's vampiric nature was fighting to unleash itself. The fact she had just drained a bag of blood was making it harder to resist hissing like a feline at the oncoming humans.

"Come out from there," someone instructed- this being a woman from the sounds of it- "We're armed, so put your hands up."

Unsure of what to do in her current situation, Serenity obeyed- sliding off the lid of the green dumpster and landing neatly on the floor.

A fraction of sunlight lit the face of a Chinese man, whose black hair was greying. In his hands, he held a deep blue Samurai sword aloft.

"It's just a school kid," the female implored, as if the Chinese guy didn't have a set of working eyes.

He lowered the sword.

Serenity felt this was an optimistic move for him. If she had decided to use her abilities for bad instead of good, this guy would have been dead by now, as well as the younger specimen an inch or two from his hip.

"What are you doing down here?" He demanded an explanation from her.

Serenity shrugged. She had a feeling she was going to have to play the quiet school girl act- looking for a place to hide from all the bullies. *Yeah right*!

"I like it here," she told them, putting on a meek and pathetic tone of voice.

"It's not safe for little girls to go wandering down alleys, even in the day."

Was this guy for real? *Little girl*? He really *was* blind!

If you knew who I was, you'd realise it wasn't safe for you to be walking down this alley with me here, I can tell you!

she thought coldly.

"Go back to the food district, or return to your school."

"Yes, Officer," she said innocently. "I'm sorry to have caused you any trouble."

The Chinese man looked at his partner as if to say '*aww!*'.

"It's no trouble. We're just keeping people safe, that's all."

Safe from what? She argued in her mind. *I'm the one that kills most of the bad guys before you even know they're here! It should be* me *wearing that flashy uniform and getting paid a ton for the amount of demons I slay.*

"Have a nice day." The woman smiled warmly at Serenity as if she could make her feel safer with her pleasant and promising attitude- face all aglow.

What can you *do?* Serenity thought. *You can't even hold a gun like you mean it.*

She couldn't wait to put distance between herself and the patrolling Vampire Slayers. If they had arrived ten seconds earlier, they would have seen what she'd been drinking, and she would have been arrested- or worse!

It shook her up to say the least, and all she could think

about was getting to the library and sitting down with her book.

No one would think of her as a potential threat to mankind at the library.

- Chapter Twelve -

Look My Way

Walking with Julian was a dream.

Atlanta couldn't believe the turn of events in her life and had convinced herself that the break up with Deacon was just another act of God.

God had *wanted* her to be single for Julian's coming- it was so obvious!

She walked with new-found confidence, keeping a tight grip on Julian's arm, though not enough to hurt the guy, and as they walked towards the food district, she was aware of all the people stopping and gawking at them both.

That's right, Atlanta thought pompously. *Get a load of this! Atlanta Nightly, linking arms with the hottest thing to hit Meridion since her father was a young rebel.* The conversation wasn't too heavy- just simple questions about studies and things to avoid whilst living in Meridion. The war between humans and vampires was mentioned and Atlanta gushed on about how her father and mother had fought together and that it was during this dark period of their lives that they had fallen in love with each other.

"Sounds just like the movies," Julian commented. "Two strangers meeting and falling in love whilst undergoing frightening situations. A hero and a heroine- that kind of thing. It would make an interesting novel, don't you think?"

Atlanta beamed at him. She'd never thought of her parents as being cool, but she was certainly addressing the idea now. They *had* been warriors. You couldn't get much cooler than that!

"It *would* be pretty awesome."

Atlanta continued to glide along the sidewalk as if she had wings on her back. She was so content with how things were progressing that the sudden interruption of her brother's thoughts were *most* unwelcome.

-*Who is* that *guy*?-

Atlanta swung her head around, trying to locate Phoenix.

-*Don't make me talk to you like this. It's embarrassing for me! I might miss something Julian has to say*!- she snapped, somewhat aggressively.

-*Julian? Where'd he come from and why are you leaning so close into him? Have some dignity and stop throwing yourself at the guy. People will start calling you a slut-*

-Better a slut than a virgin-

-Don't be so bloody ridiculous. Are you insane?-

Atlanta pushed Phoenix out of her head, trying to mentally sever the telepathic connection they had, but his voice continued to invade her thoughts loud and clear.

-So, is he your new boyfriend? This morning you came to the library looking like a lost sheep and now you're hanging out with a complete stranger. Don't you realise how dangerous that can be?-

-He's okay. Leave us alone-

"Are you okay?" Julian asked her, looking bemused.

"Huh?"

"You keep looking at that boy and haven't said anything in a while."

Atlanta tried to laugh the accusation off as they drew nearer to Phoenix, who was sitting on the pavement curb in a pool of sunlight, enjoying a ham roll.

"He's my brother. My twin brother actually."

"Twins?" Julian looked impressed. "Can't say I've ever met twins before. They're quite rare in this day and age."

Atlanta nodded. "So I've heard. Strange that-"

As they walked by, Julian smiled warmly at Phoenix

and muttered an "Alright?" to which he received a frown.

"Nice guy," he said, slightly offended.

"Just ignore him. He's been moody for days now."

-I heard that- Phoenix complained.

-Bye Phoenix- she waved a hand, the one with silver bangles around her thin wrist that jangled musically like bells.

-Bye yourself-

Food consisted of a chicken and mayonnaise baguette for Julian and a tuna and sweet corn roll for Atlanta, which she immediately regretted as the smell of fish hit her in the face. She hated the thought of smelling like tuna all day long, and only took nibbles at areas relatively devoid of fish- as if it would have less of an effect on her breath.

"This has been nice," she said, as they headed back the way they'd come.

Julian was still eating his food, so he had refrained from offering his arm to her, but Atlanta didn't mind. It meant she could walk more freely, without bashing into his hip- although; the physical contact between them was nothing to complain about.

As they walked at a leisurely pace Atlanta was soon aware of the milky white girl with the blood red hair, walking on the opposite side of the road. She seemed to be in a hurry, but stopped abruptly as they drew nearer and turned to face them.

"What's *her* problem?" Atlanta asked, without expecting an answer.

The girl's lilac eyes were pinned on them both, giving Atlanta shivers.

"Seriously, what's wrong with her?"

Eventually, the red-headed teen came out of her trance and took off once more, her pace a lot faster.

"That *was* odd," Julian mumbled out of the corner of his mouth.

"Tell me about it."

"She in on the bullying?"

Atlanta blushed and gave a nervous laugh. "Oh…no! She…uh…well, I think she fancies Phoenix."

"Your twin?"

"Hmm."

"What gave you that impression?"

She shrugged. "Caught her staring at him a lot. I know Phoenix insists on wearing those stupid glasses, but underneath, he's not a bad looking guy. I think it's his brooding nature that girls probably find attractive. They think he's just *too* cool to be as openly arrogant as most of the boys around here."

"Deacon being one of those arrogant boys you're referring to?"

"Exactly."

The end of the road came too soon for Atlanta. Gingerly, she slipped her half eaten tuna roll into a bin and brushed the crumbs from her hands.

"What do you want to do for the last twenty minutes of lunch?"

Julian smiled, his blonde hair rippling deliciously in the breeze.

"As long as I'm with you, I don't care."

Good answer, she thought.

- Chapter Thirteen -

Tongue Tied

Serenity pondered the possibilities as she headed back to the school.

Walking down the street, she could have sworn she'd caught the scent of something unpleasant, and she didn't mean dog's mess or decaying food. It was the stench of evil, but an evil stench like nothing she'd ever come across before. A strong perfume tainted with an even more dominating smell of sweat? Yes- that's how she'd put it.

It was foul.

But with there being so many houses in the street, she couldn't just pin the blame on the two people around at the time- one of them being Phoenix's twin sister.

She'd have to come back another time and scope the place out. See what the people of Meridion had to hide behind closed doors these days.

She couldn't shake the thought of that horrid aroma for the entire lunch break. Just when she would start feel content in her surroundings, a reminder of how powerful the smell had been clawed its way to the front of her thoughts.

"Hi-"

Serenity let out a yelp of surprise, bringing a hand to her chest as a shadow fell over her. She'd been thinking so much- trying to match that smell to a breed of demon- that the sound of Phoenix's voice almost had her in a fighting stance, ready to kick some ass.

"You scared the living daylights out of me!"

Phoenix looked genuinely apologetic at her perturbed expression.

"I didn't mean to," he lightly put a hand on her shoulder, but moved it away hurriedly as he caught sight of her reddening cheeks.

"It's okay. I'm just not usually one for letting my guard down like that."

He nodded in understanding. "Mind if I take this seat?"

Serenity looked at the chair in awe, wondering distantly what might be the problem with Phoenix's usual spot at the table. There was no one there, so why did he want to sit so close to her?

"Um… if…if you want to-"

Her heart was pounding as if she'd just run the entire

perimeter of Meridion. With her heightened sense of smell, she could detect the natural scent of Phoenix's body and could even smell the blood that coursed through his veins.

Now, she was confused. Did he want to sit next to her so they could chat? Or was it that he just wanted a change of seating? Did she continue to read or was she supposed to open the conversation with talk of the weather?

Waiting, she smiled at no one in particular and lifted her paperback novel into her line of vision. Her brow began to prickle with sweat. She was struggling to keep her cool with Phoenix's arm being just an inch from her elbow.

Was he playing a game with her?

Did he know she adored him?

No- how could he?

Phoenix cleared his throat behind a balled up fist and turned to face the Dhampir.

"What...um...," he looked away suddenly, struggling with his words. "What do you think of the...er...the story so far?"

Serenity grinned stupidly. She hadn't expected him to seem so nervous, and she drew confidence from it somehow.

"Interesting. Although we have enough demons to worry about in our lives, I still find myself enjoying novels about them. Of all the novels by this author so far, I prefer her stuff about werewolves than the stuff about vampires. Somehow, she paints too nice a picture of blood suckers and I find that absurd."

"Well, it *is* fantasy…"

"It was once. These novels have been around for centuries. They're more a fact of life now than they are 'make believe.'"

Phoenix nodded. She was right. Books about vampires, magic and werewolves were still labelled 'fantasy' when in reality, they were a part of their everyday lives in Meridion. People weren't surprised by such phenomenon anymore. Evil existed. *Fact*. The ability to manipulate nature and wounds was becoming more common. Magic was growing in the veins of the next generation and the amount of witches in the area was on the rise.

"My dad's a Vampire Slayer,"

"Oh really?" Serenity pretended she hadn't known this, when really, she had done her research on the Vampire Slaying business years ago and discovered that Kieran Nightly was Phoenix's father.

"Yeah, and my mum was a Slayer once too, but she's a Healer now."

This information was new. "Your mother was a Slayer?"

"Yup. For a brief period in her life she was."

Serenity thought about this. "Is it something you'd like to do when you leave school?"

He shrugged. "I'm not sure. I kind of want...," he paused, "...to be a writer."

She smiled at him. "I'll buy your books."

He blushed. "Thanks."

Silence lay thickly over the table at this point.

Serenity moved her foot slightly and felt it nudge Phoenix's shoe. Her cheeks burned instantaneously.

"Sorry," she mumbled pathetically.

"It's quite all right,"

He smiled warmly.

"By the way... you haven't told me your name."

"Oh...," she touched her burning face nervously. "It's Serenity."

There was another pause.

"Don't you want to know what my name is?"

Her eyes widened. "Yes. I mean. *No-*"

His brow was furrowing at her.

"I mean, I know your name already."

Her heart was about to escape. She was sure of it.

"Let me hear you say it, so I know you haven't got me labelled as a Brian or Jacob."

She laughed softly, feeling a little silly because of his request. "Phoenix," she said, barely above a whisper.

He nodded and suddenly, the closeness of his body became too much. She looked at his arm as it brushed against her on the table, feeling compelled to lay her hand over his, but shook the thought aside- grabbing her jacket and bag from the floor.

"I...I have to go," she told him pensively.

"Why?"

She tried forcing her book into her bag- her mouth hanging open without any words slipping free.

"Did I offend you? Tell me... what's wrong? Please...don't run out on me."

"Why?" she asked ineffectually, ignoring his many questions.

"I just wanted to get to know you."

Took you long enough, Serenity thought grimly.

"I'm a very private person," she said, before thinking her words through. "I like being alone."

And with that, she left the library, using all her

strength not to look back at the boy she loved.

- Chapter Fourteen -

Isaac and the Watcher

The cobwebs lay thick over the furniture in the old church building, bearing crusty, dead flies and fat black spiders that never particularly bothered Isaac, hence the reason why he left them to dangle from the ceiling and crawl all over the table. They were a mild form of entertainment to him. Friends almost, when he was alone.

The old man was sat in his usual chair on this particularly dry afternoon, puffing on a wooden pipe and rocking back and forth- his eyes vacant.

He was the Watcher. The man who provided guidance for the Fallen. He whispered wise words to those that were cast out from Heaven- informing them that Lucifer wouldn't leave a friend- a *brother*- to die, just because their wings couldn't carry them to God's holy dwelling any longer.

Isaac feared the Watcher. Although he had been around since the day he had crash landed, he had been suspicious of the old man.

Almost two years had passed since they had known

each other, and yet he never offered his real name. Isaac had never verbally expressed his need to know why however, and instead, argued with his Fallen friend- insisting they just get the hell out of there and make a new life in another city.

There was very little trust between the mysterious Watcher and the young Angel, who had been living under his roof for quite some time now.

"Stop your tapping," the old man demanded croakily.

Isaac had been looking at the calendar propped against a broken mirror on a dusty set of drawers. His fingers were moving up and down as he sat in thought, making a slight 'thudding' sound on the table top as they landed amongst the grime.

The old church had lost its stained glass windows to vandals many years previous, and the spaces where they had once been were all boarded up to keep the homeless outside its walls. Because of this, light was very limited in the building. The old man's face was a shadow, surrounded by smoke from his pipe.

Isaac looked at the calendar once more. It wasn't long now. Not long at all when the ritual to prolong his life on Earth had to be performed in the very same place he had fallen from Heaven.

"Why don't you go and find yourself a nice bar and get drunk, until you can hardly move your body where you will it, huh? I know how you kids like to mistreat your God-given bodies after all-"

Isaac snorted. "Not when the ritual is so close. I'd rather be here. Ready."

"There's little that could go wrong. The ritual is a few days away."

Isaac disagreed. "I could end up beaten up, or worse. I want to be in perfectly good health when the time comes. And what's to say my drunken state doesn't take me outside the city? It's not like it hasn't happened before."

The old man grunted. "Are you nervous, boy?"

Isaac shook his head. "I've done it before..."

"It gets harder though. Each time you stretch your life for another year- when technically, God wants you to be a dead man- it gets harder to complete the ritual."

"But it's only my second time-"

The old man removed the pipe from his cracked lips and rested it inside a decorative wooden ash-tray.

"I know. I know. But I'm just warning you, is all. It might feel different this time round."

Silence fell. The ticking of the clock nailed to a

wooden beam above seemed louder than ever as Isaac watched the red second hand rotate, and he almost jumped from his chair as a strangled cry came from the corner of the dark, gloomy room.

The old man sighed.

Natalie was awake.

Isaac slid the chair back and slowly approached the shadow from which the noise had come.

He stood there for a moment, drinking in what he saw.

Another loud sob burst from the darkness.

"Shh," Isaac whispered. "Hush now, beautiful."

"Why'd you have to pick a girl so soon? Her family are probably tearing the city down to find her and if they come here I'll take you to Hell's gates myself!"

Isaac ignored the old man's ranting. He had found the girl sooner rather than later because he didn't want to be in a panic at the last second. Natalie had been the perfect catch- a lonely waitress at a grubby little café, working all the hours under the sun. She had no time to fall in love, because she had bills to pay, and no time to go out with friends. Her only companion was a cat and Isaac had heard her talking to her mother on her mobile phone in a parking lot, discovering that the pair of them were *not* on very good terms. She was one of those pretty little things that worked hard in life, only to get trampled over. And now, she was going to be sacrificed to assist in maintaining Isaac's fair complexion- staving off rapid decaying, like the good Lord had promised would happen.

Natalie was a skinny girl- all bone and no muscle. Her hands and feet were tied with rope- red raw and bleeding- and her mouth was taped shut. Once in a while, Isaac would rip the tape free to feed her something left over from his dinner and would persist with a few rough kisses- forcing her to accept his tongue whilst he rubbed a hand in places she'd much rather he wouldn't. She would squeal in protest, begging to be freed, and when she did this, Isaac would kick her as if she was a stray dog with fleas, so that in time, she'd learn to keep her mouth shut.

"The little miss is hungry. Why don't you go out and buy her something to eat?"

Isaac threw a look of suspicion at the old man.

"She ate yesterday."

"I know, but how many times do I have to tell you? Human's eat three times a day- not like you Fallen Angels, with your meagre snack once in a blue moon."

Isaac thought about it, and decided it was best not to

leave the church. At least not until he truly had to. He didn't like going anywhere without his partner.

"No. Not now. She can wait."

Natalie burst into tears that left tracks through the dust that caked her cheeks and Isaac 'tutted' loudly at her.

"Stop it, would you? I can't think when you're whining."

She cried harder, trying to grab at Isaac's leg with her bound hands.

"Get off me, you whore!" Sharply, he kicked her in the face and the pain in her eyes caused him to question whether he had broken her jaw. Strangely, remorse plagued his head.

"You certainly need to learn how to treat a lady," the old man piped up from his chair, chuckling to himself. He was reading a newspaper now- one that was twenty three years out of date.

"Natalie…*Natalie*," he whispered. "I'm sorry, baby. I just can't risk going out. I have to keep my eyes on the prize. I promise to order you a pizza tonight…or maybe tomorrow. Okay? Tarian hid most of the cash we had left from the heist we pulled a few months back."

Natalie's eyes were closed as he spoke. They were

stinging from so many tears escaping and her head felt as if it were splitting into jagged pieces.

Isaac put a hand to her face and drew her head towards his chest, patting her back in what he believed was a consoling gesture.

"That friend of yours better start thinking about bagging himself a sacrifice soon, if he wants to live another year."

Isaac continued patting Natalie, who surprisingly wept less.

"He'll be okay. He's better at this than I am. Somehow, it's like he's always been a human being. He's a natural. He spent too much of his free time studying them from Heaven I guess-"

"And yet *you* act like a baby, taking its first steps in the world- never taking any risks without mummy to hold your hand."

"Fuck you, old man!"

"Fuck yourself," the man laughed.

It appeared, the conversation was over.

- Chapter Fifteen -

First Kiss

It was at times like these that Atlanta hated Meridion for its lack of beauty. She wanted to take Julian somewhere nice to sit and chat, but the crumbling city was devoid of pleasant parks, vast forestry or riverside walks. The only thing that offered a mere *crumb* of beauty was the white lilies within the Stone Circle.

It had been reported in the local newspaper that even if a lily were crushed underfoot, it replenished its broken state before your very eyes! *Extraordinary*.

But the Stone Circle was too great a distance from the school grounds and Atlanta had no choice but to lead Julian in the general direction of the playing field- a field made purely of dry mud and little holes from the studs of football boots.

Together, the pair circled the field at a leisurely pace.

Atlanta squinted up at the sky. It was cloudless and pleasant- a friendly pale blue that contrasted with the rooftops of dark, miserable houses. It made her smile, knowing that no matter how derelict and old Meridion looked, the sky was untouchable, and would always be there. A place of peace. Heaven's home.

"I have to admit," Julian spoke up suddenly. He breathed in the air, enjoying the sensation as it filled his entire lung capacity, "I was dreading coming here." He paused and looked at Atlanta, keeping the pace of their walk to a mild stroll. "But you've made it perfect."

Atlanta smiled back at him. "You've certainly made *my* day a whole lot more interesting, if you don't mind my saying so."

"Oh, I can tell. You have colour in your cheeks and I sense any previous grievances have left you, for now."

She thought about this. It seemed odd. Was Julian suggesting he could see into her very soul? They'd been together for a very little length of time and yet, he spoke as if they shared a strong bond already.

Oh, I'm just being silly!

"I do feel better," she admitted brightly.

"I'm glad. No one deserves to be bullied."

His words silenced her.

When their trek was over, Atlanta unnecessarily explained the appropriateness of attending registration, no matter how pleasant the afternoon was outside, and led Julian back to the main building.

"It's a shame we're not in the same class," she said conversationally, becoming lost in Julian's eyes. She would have liked to swim in them, if such a thing were possible.

"Lucky for me, I get to be in a room where even the *teacher* avoids Deacon's general line of vision."

Atlanta scowled. "He's such a slime ball. I wish I hadn't been so bloody foolish, letting him sweet talk me."

Julian shrugged. "You live and learn, right?"

"Right," she agreed in a small voice.

Atlanta was standing with her back to her registration room now, feeling the eyes of the students fixated on her as she stood before the staggeringly handsome new guy that had got a lot of blood racing in the halls, by the look of it. She twiddled her thumbs and shifted her weight back and forth from one leg to the other as he leant nearer to touch her shoulder.

And although she appreciated the sensation of his touch, it couldn't have been more ill-timed.

"Well, well, *well*," came an exaggeratedly aghast exclamation from Deacon. He was alone, which was a small blessing, but it didn't make him any less melodramatic. "Do my eyes *deceive* me?"

Atlanta glanced at Julian for help and noticed how his jaw was clenched. She'd never seen a guy look so angry in the presence of the bully- as if he was physically struggling to keep his fist from connecting with Deacon's face. Not even her own *brother* had participated in confrontation with the school's pain in the arse.

"Are you sniffing around my girl?"

Deacon's question was a bullet to Atlanta's heart and she prayed to the good Lord that He might intervene soon. *Oh, strike him down if you can*! she thought in desperation.

"From what I've heard, she certainly isn't *your* girl." Julian stood his ground as Deacon sharply rammed his shoulder into his opponent, making his footing falter.

"Atlanta- tell this guy he's barking up the wrong tree."

"Don't you dare speak to her," Julian demanded.

Deacon looked at them both with an expression of disbelief.

"I don't think you understand me. She's an ex-girlfriend of mine and if I want to talk to her, I sure as hell *will*. So keep your interfering mouth shut."

Atlanta's breath caught in her throat as Julian reached out and grasped her hand.

Deacon made a noise of pure distaste at what he was

seeing.

"Are you serious?" he cried belligerently. "We've been apart…what…a day now? And you're already making a move on this guy?"

Atlanta made to open her mouth, but Julian got there first.

"I believe it is *I* that is putting the moves on *her*, and you're the fool that has to witness it." With these words, he blocked Deacon from his thoughts and planted a soft kiss on Atlanta's lips, receiving loud 'ooh's!' from the by standing crowd. As he parted, he grinned at Deacon. "Hmm. *Delicious.*"

Deacon opened and closed his mouth, looking for some support from the people around him, but his friends were all in registration, waiting for their great leader to return from his visit to the toilet.

He moved forward, noticing how the breath caught in the witnessing crowds throats and jabbed a finger in Julian's direction.

"You may as well quit while you're ahead," he suggested vehemently. "She may look like a fine piece of ass, but she won't give you any satisfaction. She's gonna leave you high and dry, buddy," he tore his eyes from Julian and glared frostily at Atlanta, finishing with, "Pathetic *virgin.*"

Julian didn't look at all perturbed.

"Did you ever stop and think Atlanta had higher standards when she was with you? That maybe you weren't worthy?"

Deacon's nose crinkled up in preparation for the verbal attack. Julian's words were stingers.

"Perhaps she allowed herself to fall for you, but realised you weren't worth her time and affection?"

He made a 'pfft' noise. "You've known her for five minutes and you're acting like you've seen into her fucking heart, *Romeo.*"

Julian persisted.

"She has every right to turn down your offer of sex. Why would she want to waste her first time with a heartless, pig-shit like you? Because that's the reason you're going to be lonely for the rest of your life Deacon. Lack of compassion and lack of respect for women. And let me tell you, *no* amount of hookers will fill that void in your heart. So I suggest you change your ways, or else you'll *always* be the guy that goes around telling people how women leave *you* high and dry."

Deacon's face turned a distinct shade of white. The

fact that Julian had turned his carefully crafted accusation of Atlanta being the 'pathetic' one into a description of himself made his blood boil.

"Keep smiling," was all he managed to say. "But it won't stay that way, I promise you."

Atlanta watched in awe as Deacon stormed off, pushing students from his path and kicking a bin over before disappearing from view. At last, she felt the air leaving her lungs.

"Oh…my…*God*."

Julian flinched at her words for some reason, but then burst into a smile.

"Thank you," she whispered.

"My pleasure," he replied, and with a bow, he left her standing outside the classroom- two fingers touching her lips as they tingled with the memory of his kiss.

I hope it wasn't just part of the show, she thought as she entered the room at last.

As she did so, Nerys ran over- arms flailing all over the place in her excitement.

"I want to know *everything*," she babbled. "What's his star sign? What school did he go to? How many girlfriends has he had? Which gym does he work out at? Does he want kids in the future-?"

Atlanta lifted her hands up to halt the flow of words bombarding her.

"Be quiet for a second!" she laughed. "How am I supposed to know all that stuff?"

Her best friend pouted her glossy lips.

"You didn't grill the guy for info?"

"No. Don't be insane."

Nerys gripped Atlanta's arm and directed her to their usual table and chairs. "Sit there," she instructed, forcing her into the seat, "and tell me what you can."

Atlanta smiled dreamily.

"I think he's the guy I've been waiting for."

Her friend let out a squeal, turning the heads of a neighbouring group. "Good! Because Malcolm and I agreed to do the double-date thingy, if you were ever interested."

Atlanta couldn't help but grin. "I might just take you up on that sometime."

"So he's definitely interested in...you know...*you*?"

"I think I caught a vibe."

"A strong vibe?"

"I hope so."

"Well in that case, I have to come by and go through

your wardrobe. We need to plan *every* outfit for the upcoming days because they're crucial if you want to make a good impression. I don't mean to scare you, but this guy is *seriously* handsome and I think it's safe to say he's probably used to sleeping with *really* hot chicks."

"Uch!" Atlanta made a face. "You sound like Deacon, using words like that."

Nerys clicked her fingers. "I don't want to hear that guy's name in any part of our conversations from now on. If it is totally necessary to refer to him, we can replace Deacon with the words 'Dip-Shit' or 'The Dog.' The only male name I give you permission to use freely is Julian." She stopped. "And Phoenix once in a while, since he *is* your twin."

"Fair enough."

"So...Julian."

"Yes."

"You're certainly going to be the envy of every girl who's ever dreamed of God sending them an Angel."

Atlanta settled into the chair as her friend gushed on about how handsome Julian was and how cool it would be to persuade him to join them on a night out at 'The Sword and Stone' nightclub- their regular haunt for cheap alcohol and no question of age, for legal purposes.

But after a while, Atlanta's mind drifted off.

All she could think about was her next encounter with Julian and how much she wanted to sample another of his kisses before the week was through.

- Chapter Sixteen -

Speaking Out

Atlanta considered whether she was 'over doing it' as she stood outside the main entrance at the end of the school day, waiting impatiently to catch Julian on his way out of the building. It had been a choice she had made after coming to the conclusion that he was probably looking for *her* too.

She found it increasingly hard not to keep standing up on tip-toes, watching the bobbing heads of students closely in hope of catching a glimpse of that fine, shiny blonde hair. But so far, all she had seen was the unimpressive locks and styles of nobody that interested her.

"What's *your* problem? Heading back in to use the toilet or something?" Phoenix asked, shifting his rucksack more comfortably onto his shoulder as he approached his sister. Her face told how completely oblivious she had been to his presence, which then melted into an expression of pure disappointment as he showed no sign of leaving her.

Clouds had rolled in ten minutes before the school bell had tolled much to everyone's disappointment and it looked as if the evening promised light showers. Already, the air carried a drop or two of rain- and Phoenix didn't feel like hanging around outside with his love-sick sibling for too long.

"I'm sure he'll still be alive tomorrow," he pointed out.

Atlanta glowered at him, stomping a foot melodramatically.

"I just wanted to say goodbye," she said.

"I don't think he came out this way, sis."

"Are you positive?"

"He joined my Science class after lunch and left the room before I did. Unless he's hiding in the school somewhere, I think you've probably missed him."

Disappointment was etched into the creases of her pale brow and without a word, she obtained her car keys from the bottom of her bag- a sign that she was ready to leave.

"Come on then," she sighed.

On the ride home, Phoenix entertained her by retelling some of the stories he had heard from students in the labs.

"I heard Lucas Mayhew say something about a kiss. Did you...?" he made a sound of scepticism. "I mean...I would *hope* you'd have waited to get to know the guy first, but... did you kiss? In front of everyone?"

Atlanta was gripping the steering wheel as tight as she could without even realising it. She hated the thought of Phoenix disapproving of her actions. It was horrible- especially when she believed the kiss was far from a mistake.

"It wasn't a *proper* kiss. He did it to wind up Deacon." She hoped Phoenix would cut Julian some slack if he knew he was protecting her from that slime-ball.

His eyebrows rose.

"So he *used* you?"

"What? No! It wasn't to help himself! He did it because Deacon was trying to make me feel like the world's most pathetic human being- as he's suddenly grown accustomed to doing- and Julian just put the guy in his place."

"I wonder what dad's gonna say about this?"

"He's not going to say *anything*," she said firmly. "Because he's not going to find out."

"If you say so," Phoenix muttered, casting his gaze out of the window to his left.

The dark, dirty streets were cluttered with broken furniture and old newspapers and the only cars on the road were the really battered old ones.

Dustbins outside the run-down houses were piled high with rubbish and around them were heaps of bulging black bags, sitting in wait for the pick-up that occurred once every two- sometimes three- weeks. It was because of the rare pick-ups that the air always smelt so foul in Meridion.

The stench of decaying food wafted through Atlanta's car window, making Phoenix gag as they drove through the poorest region of Meridion. Here, children sat on sidewalks with grubby little faces, throwing stones at each other, or into drains along the gutters and listening to the rats squealing in protest.

Atlanta and Phoenix hated seeing them all- looking forlornly at the passing vehicle. One time, they had made the mistake of offering an apple to a little girl from the safety of their car, and caught a glimpse in the rear view mirror of her brothers hitting her viciously in an unfair fight for the prize.

Never again did they even *suggest* helping the needy by handing out food.

The image of that little girl being smacked in the head by her older siblings would haunt Atlanta until the day she died.

Why on earth would Julian want to come to a city like this? she asked herself. She breathed a sigh of relief when the worst of the starving, decaying neighbourhood was behind her.

When they finally reached their own driveway, the twins were met with the warm and loving glow of their parent's smiles- both of them sitting hand in hand on the little wooden bench beneath the front window.

"Hey," they said in unison as they slammed the car doors behind them.

"How was school?" Kieran asked predictably.

"Atlanta has a new boyfriend," Phoenix announced, before his sister could even open her mouth to reply.

Kieran's face fell to the floor instantly. Kiya squeezed his hand.

"Already?" he asked in bewilderment. "Weren't you upset about Daniel yesterday?"

She rolled her eyes. "His name is Deacon… and my love life is none of your business."

"So it's true. You have another boyfriend?"

Atlanta threw her brother the worst 'I'm going to kill you' look he'd ever seen.

-He had to know- he said, leaving them to interrogate her as he headed in the direction of the fridge.

Atlanta sighed in exasperation.

"We'll talk later. I want to get out of these boots. My feet are killing me-" her voice trailed off as she left her father to sit in contemplation of what he had just discovered. Kiya was gripping his thigh, keeping her lips sealed for the time being.

"I can definitely see myself cancelling this holiday."

It was Kiya's turn to roll her eyes.

"Give her the chance to get her thoughts in order. We'll talk about this tonight."

Kieran stood up, stretching his arms and feeling the rain beginning to pick at his exposed flesh.

"Can't wait," he groaned, urging his wife to join him in the comfort of their home.

*

The butterflies in Atlanta's stomach were enough to convince her she didn't want dinner with the family as her mother yelled for her to come and eat. Instead she politely declined, and returned to preening herself in the mirror.

Nerys had called her mobile literally the second she had got home and had begged Atlanta to let her come over to her house. It took some persuading, but she managed to steer her friend away from the idea- assuring her she could dress herself and that she was a 'big girl' now.

"Fine. But don't be afraid to dress up a bit. So what if it's high school? These are the best years of your life, so you bloody well better look your best! Guys will always remember what you looked like, you know- especially if you looked *good*."

Now, Atlanta was alone in her room, holding up a selection of tops, skirts and dresses to her slender frame and parading around in her many pairs of flat shoes, high heels and boots.

After the clothes were decided, she experimented with hairstyles- whipping out curling tongs and accessories to dress her hair up.

It was as she was coughing on the fumes of her hairspray that the door to her bedroom creaked open.

Kiya peeked through the crack cautiously, waiting for admittance. When Atlanta refused to speak, she walked in regardless of her daughter's wishes, taking a seat on the ruffled sheets of the bed.

"You can't avoid us forever."

Atlanta squeezed the silver and red butterfly shaped clip free from her hair, allowing it to cascade down her back in a dark brown waterfall of shimmering strands and then began her next attempt at styling it. This time, she would weave the strands into small, tight plaits.

Kiya saw this and moved to her daughter's side, taking three strands of hair in her hand and weaved them together.

"It's been a long time since I did your hair," she said.

Atlanta didn't mind her mother helping, but the atmosphere was tenser than she preferred it to be. She kept a wooden expression, holding her tongue for as long as the awkward silence would allow.

"Your father doesn't mean to be so nosy when it comes to boyfriends. He just... doesn't want to see his little girl get hurt."

Silence.

"And as much as you hate talking about it, you can't blame the people in your life for wanting to make sure you're okay."

She bit her lip anxiously.

"Did this Deacon boy break your heart? Is that why you're trying to start a new relationship so soon? To help ease the pain?"

Atlanta stopped playing with her hair, but her mother continued- getting into the flow of it.

"I didn't love him," she explained stiffly. "I was... overwhelmed by the concept that someone found me to be 'girlfriend' material." She looked up at her mother with watery eyes. "I know you must think I'm pathetic."

Kiya shook her head slowly. "It's not wrong to want love."

"I think love was far from Deacon's mind. And I'm glad it ended sooner rather than later." She sighed loudly. "I think I might have done something I'd regret if I'd carried on listening to his demands."

Kiya squeezed her daughter's shoulder affectionately. *Good girl*, she thought.

"And now… you're seeing someone else?"

"No. Phoenix doesn't know what he's talking about."

"Then what made him think such a thing?"

She glared into the mirror at her face, but only saw Julian's image staring back at her in her mind's eye.

"There's a new guy at school. I think he likes me. I'm just showing him around- helping him get to know the school and then probably the city too, come the weekend. He says his mother is at the hospital, so he's really lonely."

"That's a shame," she replied. "So what's this guys name?"

"Julian."

"And he's nice?"

"I wouldn't be around him if he wasn't. I've had enough of *jerks* to last a lifetime."

Kiya felt the weight leaving her shoulders.

"I trust your judgement, so I'm going to leave you to it."

"Thanks."

Kiya could see a change in Atlanta's face. She looked completely relieved, as well as happy.

"I'll tell the boys to stay out of this."

Kiya finished styling Atlanta's hair in silence, and the result was perfect- just what Atlanta had wanted. As long as she didn't sleep too fitfully, she would be able to roll out of bed tomorrow and do nothing but run a comb through the under layer, just to tidy it up.

"Thanks mum," she smiled appreciatively.

"Anytime, sweetheart."

- Chapter Seventeen -

When the Hunter Becomes the Hunted

Her acute senses told Serenity that somewhere in the 'poor' district of wretched Meridion there hid a vampire and his living-dead lover.

It was the smell of blood hanging in the air like an angry cloud that provided her with a means to find the sick bastards.

Being a Dhampir, she was drawn to evil like a police dog to drugs, but smelling them out was just a small part of her accurate 'locating' abilities. It was as if invisible hands pulled at her, leading her in the direction of her prey. This ability worked at its best mainly when locating vampires- perhaps because she was half vampire herself?- but if she concentrated hard enough, other hell spawn, such as werewolves, could be pin-pointed for extermination with little strain on her part.

The rain was easing off as she stealthily made her way down the street now, avoiding lamp light and automatic porch lights (although she assumed no one in the poor district could afford them). In her hands, she held a twelve inch blade, with a crimson handle that bore gold tentacles curling fashionably around it. The gold never warmed to her touch, which she had never really understood or questioned. Her favourite blade- hands down- was always like an icicle in her hand, but she bore the discomfort. It reminded her that killing wasn't supposed to be fun.

"I smell you," she mouthed as the invisible hands released their grip on her. She was standing outside a house with a hole in its roof where the chimney should have been standing tall. It lacked in many things- glass panes in its windows being one of them- and in the muddy front garden, a dead Doberman lay, its throat missing and its eyes rolled back in its head.

Serenity put a hand on the dogs belly and felt a dwindling warmth on its skin.

It hasn't been long since they started, she realised, gripping the blade tighter in her hand.

The wooden panels keeping the wind from howling through the gaping holes in the windows were flickering with light in the upstairs level of the building. People were moving around up there, casting shadows, and Serenity was about to crash their party.

Here goes nothing.

The front door was already open. It swung on a broken latch pitifully and allowed her access, revealing a set of stairs that she took three at a time.

On the landing, she met the first vampire.

"Well look-ey what we have here then," the creature drawled. It was a man, six foot five in height, with long brown hair tied back in a ponytail and big silver eyes. In his hands he held a little boy, dressed in blue and white pyjamas- his head lolling about lifelessly.

Serenity didn't hesitate. Kicking the big brute in the stomach, but avoiding the injured child, she knocked him into the wall and watched him stumble to the floor. The little boy fell from his hands, and to Serenity's relief, jerked awake. Cries erupted from his mouth immediately as he witnessed the fight.

The vampire threw a punch that landed against one of the thin walls, knocking plaster and dust into Serenity's eyes as she ducked and came up behind him. Before he could even blink, she plunged her blade into his spine- once, twice- and forced it so hard into the guys neck that it burst out of his throat on the other side.

The vampire fell- not quite defeated, but as good as-

and he hit the floor face first.

It was at this point that the door behind Serenity opened, and from it, a female vampire shrieked in despair at the sight of her partner lying awkwardly on the narrow landing. From her lips, globules of blood and flesh dripped onto her white, short sleeved dress and in a rage, she rushed at the Dhampir.

Serenity caught the dead woman's wrists in her hands and drove her back into the room she had just exited, entering into a bloody mess of torn bodies. On the bottom bunk of a child's bed, two little boys lay mutilated, and in the corner of the room, against a wardrobe, two adults rested with their heads against one another.

"You killed Blaine!" the vampire screeched through her fangs.

Serenity kept her head clear of emotion and her expression blank, trying not to show how much of a struggle it was to keep the vampire from tearing free. As she steered her around the children's bedroom, she forced her towards a corner and pushed her into it.

The vampire hissed menacingly, raising her arms to shield her face. Blonde curls danced around her pale head, which Serenity took pleasure in cutting off in one fluid motion.

Swiftly, Serenity returned to the landing.

Blaine was dragging his barely responsive body towards the little boy that was cowering against the wall.

"I don't think so," she scolded him.

Blaine lost his ugly head also.

Calmness fell over the house- only for a brief moment- and then the little boy reached out a hand to her and started crying loudly.

"Keep your hand on your neck," she instructed, lifting his palm to the place where blood flowed from teeth marks in his tender flesh.

Her purple eyes flashed silver for a moment, but the boy didn't notice.

"My mummy-"

Serenity put a hand up to silence him and entered the bedroom once more. The children on the bed had lost too much blood to regain consciousness, but it appeared the parents were unscathed.

With a shake, she brought them around.

The screaming began.

"Listen to me!" Serenity barked over the sound of the mother's hoarse voice.

"My boys!-" she wailed.

"You need to phone an ambulance right away."

She shook her head and gripped her husband's dirty, blood drenched t-shirt. "They're dead! They're dead!"

As if on cue, the surviving child wandered into the bedroom on wobbly legs and peeked out from behind Serenity's leg.

"She saved me," he told his parents.

The father reached out for the child and dragged him onto his lap.

"They made us...watch," he whispered, barely able to uphold his sanity. "Watch our son's being...*eaten*."

"You need to phone an *ambulance*." Serenity repeated sternly.

"We have no phone," the father explained, placing a hand on his sobbing wife as she buried her head into his chest. The child kept one hand on his bleeding throat and placed the other amongst his mother's curly black hair.

Serenity bit back tears.

This family had been destroyed because for the first time in her life, she had allowed vampires to slip past her and kill before she could do her job.

"I'll use my mobile," she promised, slipping her blade

into its sheath on her right hip. "I'm…I'm sorry for your losses."

"Thank you for helping Benjamin," the father said graciously, kissing his son's head. "Please…tell me your name."

She turned her back on them suddenly.

"No. You can't know me. No one can. I work in secret. You were never really meant to see me…" She held her tongue as she realised she was talking more than she should be. "I must leave."

Outside, the putrid air consumed her and just as she went to click the call button on her mobile, a gush of vomit erupted from her throat, landing on the muddy ground at her feet. The retching lasted a minute or so, and once it was over, she felt a whole lot better.

Finding those children dead had been the worst thing she had ever seen in her days as a Slayer. It had been absolutely *horrific*.

How could a person do that? She thought in outrage. *But of course- a vampire isn't a person, which is why it's so easy for them to do the things they do…*

When the ambulance men clarified the address, she gave the house one last look and disappeared into the cool blessed darkness of night.

*

Her feet took her to Phoenix's street and as much as she hated to admit it, she had planned on heading that way all along.

The Nightly's place was situated in a far more preserved area, even though Meridion had nothing that could really be deemed 'nice'- besides the Mall.

There was no one around, not even a stray cat, and Serenity sat on the icy cool pavement outside Phoenix's home, weeping into her hands.

Don't be so bloody stupid Serenity, she snapped at herself.

She didn't know why it was hurting so badly. All she knew was that killing had never had this effect on her before.

For the first time in years, she wished she had her mother to hold onto and tell her everything would be alright.

What was even more upsetting to her was the fact she was thirsty for blood.

When the tears stopped coming, she wiped her nose with a tissue from her jeans pocket and dragged herself to her feet.

She had a bed to get to before the sun came up, marking a new school day...

*

Phoenix turned in his bed to face his alarm clock.

3:50.

Damn.

He couldn't sleep from thinking about his conversation with Serenity in the library and kept suffering unbearable waves of embarrassment.

Why are you worrying? he thought heatedly. *You got rejected by* one *girl. So what? She's one of those crazy chicks every high school has anyway.*

Embarrassment was replaced with guilt.

With a sigh, he rolled out of his bed and went to open the window. The room had become stiflingly hot. As the cool rush of air came through the gap, the sound of crying came with it.

What the...?

He squinted through the darkness.

Is that?

He couldn't be sure, but his gut told him that *Serenity*

was outside.

Could it be?

Hurriedly, he slipped a pair of trainers onto his bare feet and made for the front door. It was locked, which slowed him down, but it didn't take long to get passed all obstacles to reach his goal...

And when he got there, he discovered that the street was in fact *empty*.

You're seeing things, he thought, puzzling over what had just happened. The sound of crying played its tune in his head. *And hearing things apparently*.

-Phoenix, what are you doing?-

The sound of his sister's voice filled his mind in a blast of unexpected noise.

-*Saw something. Go back to sleep*-

Atlanta didn't need telling twice. Her eyes were already closed and her dreams already in motion.

Weird. Phoenix concluded, closing the front door behind him.

- Chapter Eighteen -

To the Mountains

Kieran lay in the light of dawn, watching Kiya as he so often did, battling with his thoughts.

Kiya had told him, before they had settled down for the night, that she trusted Atlanta to make the right choices with her new male 'friend' and that she was confident the children could be left without parental guidance for the next week or so. Their bags were packed and waiting beneath the window and Kiya's heart was set on leaving as soon as she stirred from her sleep.

He sighed and put a hand on his wife's bare back, causing a sleepy mumbling in response. The touch had roused her ever so slightly, but she still appeared to be consumed by dreams.

When he couldn't take the silence anymore, he coughed *intentionally* loud.

Kiya bolted upright.

"What's the matter?" she asked in confusion, her hair sticking out at odd angles. She noted that Kieran was sat upright with his back propped against the cushioned headboard. "You woke me on purpose didn't you?"

Kiya waited for an answer but Kieran said nothing. Instead he moved away from the headboard and began to massage her back.

She growled low in her throat.

"You woke me for this?" she queried sceptically.

He had decided that if they didn't leave soon, they would never leave at all.

"I woke you because I want us to get shot of this mad house as soon as possible."

Kiya yawned. "So you've decided it's okay for us to go today?"

There was a nod from her partner.

"I didn't save all that money for a trip just to throw it all away now. So, go make yourself look beautiful," he said, "And let's leave. *Soon.*"

Kiya rolled over, revealing more of her naked body. "But the kids... I wanted to make them breakfast before we run out on them."

Kieran ignored her, putting one hand on her face and the other on her right breast. He moved his head until his lips touched her neck and kissed her softly. Kiya closed her eyes, savouring his touch. She could feel his hand beginning to trail over her thigh, slipping down further between her legs and to his surprise, she pushed it away.

"Not now."

He assumed an outraged expression at the prospect of ending his fun, giving his hard-on a despondent look.

"When we're at the mountains you can sleep with me all you want."

He pulled on her arm as she tried leaving the bed. "I want you now," he whined, forgetting about the holiday for a moment. His penis had other ideas...

But Kiya stayed strong, wriggling free from his grip and slipped into a white dressing gown.

"I'm going in the shower."

"Can I join you?"

She didn't need to think about it long.

"Grab your towel."

*

Phoenix examined the bulging bags on the kitchen side as he poured himself a glass of orange juice and felt a smile pulling at the corners of his lips. His parents were leaving them- *at last*! He would have full access to the weapons in the basement and the television remote on the arm of the sofa, for a whole *week*!

"We're gonna be late for school," he intoned as his father entered the kitchen.

"Atlanta still getting ready?"

He nodded.

"Where's mum?" he asked.

"She decided to change her outfit at the last second because she thinks she'll be uncomfortable on the journey in skinny-fit jeans."

"Women," Phoenix muttered.

Kieran switched the button down on the kettle, listening vaguely to the sound of the simmering, bubbling water within.

"So," he said casually. "Are you thinking about girls yet, son?"

Phoenix almost choked on the last mouthful of his drink. "Had enough of interrogating Atlanta have we?" he said, avoiding the question.

Kieran pushed his hair out of his eyes, feeling a pang of misery at the knowledge that its shine and fullness was lacking now that he was getting old. No amount of conditioner gave it that healthy glow he once boasted about to the slayers on his team.

"You're almost eighteen. Most boys your age are at least *looking* for someone. So what about you? Got your eye on anyone special?"

Phoenix peered over the frames of his glasses into the questioning gaze of his father. "Maybe," he replied evasively.

Now that they were on the subject, Kieran felt the need to offer some friendly advice. "Why don't you try taking your glasses off once in a while? You've got a handsome face under all that hair and those damn spectacles-"

"Handsome you say? Must be good genes, eh Dad?" Phoenix smiled. "But I don't particularly care about my appearance. If some girl takes a fancy to me, it'll be for my personality. Not for my face. At least I hope that's the case."

Kieran was trying to keep a rising 'blush' at bay at the mention of good genes as his son- *Rycan's* son- spoke.

"Of course," he smiled back, trying not to think about it anymore. "You're absolutely right."

"My glasses give me an edge anyway. They work for me. Ever since 'J K' wrote about that wizard-dude, glasses and scruffy black hair have become attractive in the eyes of some women. Well... that's the impression I get."

"If you say so," Kieran said, as he poured the water from the kettle into a mug. To Phoenix's relief, his mother and sister finally joined them in the kitchen, stealing the spotlight that had been cast upon him.

Atlanta was dressed in a loosely fitting red dress with three quarter sleeves, and had her uncomfortable black leather boots on once more. Kiya was wearing a white t-shirt and loose fitting denim dungarees.

"Honey," Kieran said, with a wrinkled nose. "Seriously... Did your fashion sense die when you woke up this morning?"

She shrugged. "I'll change into something more attractive when we reach the mountains, but for now, I want to wear these."

Kieran swapped a disgusted look with his son, and received a smack from Kiya on the firm muscles of his stomach.

"I'll dump the bags in the boot shall I?" he offered, pretending to wheeze breathlessly from the blow.

"Damn straight," his wife replied, turning her back on him to grab an apple from the fruit bowl. "Start loading up and we'll head off as the kids leave."

Atlanta rattled the car keys in her hand and gave her mother a small smile as they caught each other's eyes.

"I know I don't have to tell you both to be careful, but as a concerned parent, I'm going to say it anyway," Kiya told them. "Be good. Be safe. And look out for each other while your father and I are away. There's bad reception in the mountains so if you need something, call Siren."

-We know all this crap- Atlanta grumbled to her brother telepathically.

-Just smile and nod as she speaks. It's only to make her feel better-

"Don't worry about us mum."

"I'll try not to."

In turn, Kiya planted a kiss on the forehead of each of her beautiful children, receiving grimaces as a result.

"If there's lipstick on my face, so help me God-" Atlanta complained, but Kiya wiped the red smear clean before her daughter could grab a mirror from her handbag.

Kieran entered the kitchen once more and picked Kiya up, throwing her over his shoulder- causing the apple to slip free from her hand.

"Kieran! Stop it! Put me down," she screamed playfully. "You're making me waste good food!"

Phoenix swapped a smile with his sister as they followed their parents to their car, locking the house behind them.

"We don't have all day," Kieran announced as he dropped Kiya to the floor. "Get in."

Kiya feigned a look of seething anger, but burst into laughter as Kieran pointed at the car suggestively.

"I love you both," she said, with a warm, motherly smile.

"Bye mum," the twins said in unison.

Now it was Kieran's turn to say his farewells.

"Atlanta- I've got invisible camera's all over the house, so I'll know if you bring someone home and I swear, I *will* come straight back to kick his ass."

"Shut up, Dad," she mumbled, looking at the floor.

Kieran turned to Phoenix.

"No parties. Check the doors are locked every night and then check them *again*. Keep your eyes open guys."

"Yeah, yeah," Phoenix groaned.

"I love you." He patted his son firmly on the shoulder and gave Atlanta a big bear hug- almost crushing her small frame beneath his bulky arms.

When the car finally sped away, Atlanta moved to her

own car and unlocked it.

"Oh shit!" Phoenix exclaimed suddenly. "SHIT!"

"What? What?!" Atlanta yelled in fear. She looked at the floor and at the car but could see nothing that would be a cause for concern.

Phoenix exhaled loudly. "Dad forgot to give me the keys to the basement."

Atlanta sighed. "You scared the crap out of me, you idiot! Don't do that! I thought something was seriously wrong."

"I just know today's gonna be a bad one," he grumbled and together, they left their unnaturally empty home behind for another day at Meridion High.

- Chapter Nineteen -

Obsession?

Atlanta turned the heads of many gormless students as she clomped down the corridors in her leather boots, keeping her eyes as unfocused as possible on the faces that swam before her. She regretted drawing attention to herself, and knew she would only feel better when either Nerys or Julian were at her side. It sucked- having no one to help shake off her anxiety issues with a little conversation. But she knew she shouldn't complain- she'd brought this upon herself.

Deacon was standing in the presence of a fresh-faced young girl, on this particularly dreary school morning. She had long ash-blonde hair and a figure that resembled a runner bean, standing just a few paces ahead of her, and with a quick glance Atlanta's way, Deacon started feeding the girl his tongue in wet, slobbery, *forced* kisses.

Atlanta scowled at him and plucked up the courage to say, "What you're doing *really* doesn't bother me," on passing the busy couple- feeling his eyes on her back as she strutted away.

When she was safely in her registration class, she found Nery's table empty, and sunk into her seat feeling downright miserable. Nervously, the heels of her boots clapped against the dirty old linoleum floors and her eyes flitted backwards and forwards to the clock above the white board.

"I'm in!" came a breathless bellow from the door as her friend tumbled into the room, her cheeks all rosy and her hair a little messy at the back. One side of her coat collar poked up whilst the other side remained folded down.

"Where have you been?" Atlanta queried as Nerys plonked her belongings onto the desktop.

"Malcolm's. I went to his house yesterday evening and the kissing lead to other things, so he let me stay the night."

"You guys are *really* getting serious aren't you?"

"As serious as it can get for a girl still in high school and living with her nagging mother."

"I can't wait to start visiting Julian in the evenings," Atlanta whispered, before she had even thought about what she'd said. Immediately, a vibrant blush stung her face. Nerys was grinning from ear to ear.

"It won't be long. I'm sure you'll be holding hands around school before you know it."

Atlanta returned the smile her friend was beaming at her.

"Hey!" Nerys exclaimed jovially. "Malcolm is playing at The Sword and Stone tonight and he asked if we wanted to go and support him. His band has a few new songs they want to try out and they're hoping we can encourage some excitement from the audience. You could totally ask Julian to join us!"

"*Hmmm*. I don't know. What if I just bring Phoenix instead? He could do with getting out of the-"

"Don't be so lame!" Nerys cut in swiftly. "Phoenix likes his books. Let him read himself a bed time story whilst you and I dance and let off some steam. The Sword and Stone is the perfect place for you to snuggle up to Mr God-Features and re-enact that kiss you guys have the whole school buzzing about."

"What if he says no?"

"What if he says *yes*?" Nerys replied archly.

Atlanta's eyes twinkled with the possibilities.

"Okay. This could be fun," she agreed, to the excited squealing of her friend.

"It most certainly will be."

The girls spent the rest of registration flicking through

a magazine that had been left at the back of the classroom, and discussed some of the stories that were featured inside. The magazines in Meridion were not your typical high street fashion, celebrity photo shoot and style guides they used to be. They were more... a colourful newspaper, spreading news of wars and misery in other parts of the decaying planet. This month's hot gossip- tigers were officially extinct, along with ladybirds and Dalmatians.

"This sucks," Nerys remarked, feeling grateful for the school bell as it reverberated through the school. "Onward march," she muttered, filing out of the room with the rest of the people around her.

Atlanta was last to leave. She was captivated by the moving clouds outside as they spread across a pale blue sky. And for some reason, its beauty reminded her of Julian.

*

Where is he? she fretted, taking the long way to the labs and then doubling back to check any corridors she had missed. It appeared he was nowhere on the premises, but she refused to give up looking for him.

"Lost something?"

Atlanta spun around, only to find Phoenix standing next to the drinking fountain nestled in an alcove in the wall. His hair covered most of the left side of his face, like a black waterfall spilling from his scalp. He looked dark and mysterious. *Like a creature of shadows,* she thought.

"Do you know if Julian's in today?"

"Obsessed much?"

"Just tell me," she sighed.

Phoenix shook his head. "I haven't seen Lover Boy."

Atlanta saw an opportunity to poke fun and took it. "I'm not talking about *your* boyfriend Bro,' I'm referring to *mine.*"

"Har de har har."

He departed at this point, mumbling something as he went.

Julian?! Where are you?! Atlanta cried inwardly, as she stood alone.

A soft breeze tickled her neck as she began moving down the corridor, and she paused as two hands slid around her, pressing warmly against her eyes to shield her vision.

"Oh!" she said, fearing the touch of flesh as her mind conjured images of Deacon's face. The kiss that followed was even more alarming. Lips touched her neck and she could feel the brush of a nose against her ear.

"Relax, it's only me," Julian whispered as Atlanta slipped free.

Her rapidly rising chest heaved, but became regular once more as she allowed a smile to light up her face.

"I thought you were... oh, never mind," she shook her head automatically. Her skin still tingled where his lips had touched her. "Where are you heading?"

"Free period," he said, flashing pearl white teeth.

"Me too," Atlanta lied. Her mouth was on autopilot. Words were escaping without her brain giving them any kind of approval.

"Do you want to go somewhere?"

Fireworks exploded in her stomach.

"Without a doubt."

Julian smiled. "I'm glad you said that."

- Chapter Twenty -

Rose-Red Lips

Break time.

Phoenix had been waiting for this.

He positioned himself in the library, hidden from Serenity's view and waited like some sort of predator between the book shelves.

Serenity entered on cue, looking timidly around, and for some strange reason she visibly sniffed. Before she could take her usual seat, Phoenix put a hand on her shoulder and whispered something in her ear.

"We need to talk."

She paled instantly, but said nothing.

Inwardly, Phoenix scolded himself for sounding so dark, but he wasn't sure how he would get her to follow him if he didn't seem assertive- like he wouldn't take 'no' for an answer.

"In here," he instructed, opening the door to an empty religious studies classroom, a few doors down from the school's library.

She obeyed without question.

The room was eerie within. The now cloudy sky outside cast very little light through the murky windows and only one of the four lights in the room appeared to be working. On the white board, the words "Jesus Died For Our Sins," were scrawled in red pen and at the teacher's vacant desk, a blue doodle of Satan reaching towards the sky triumphantly, surrounded by flames, had been cruelly left by a student- and signed 'Lucifer.'

Serenity glanced at a chair, waiting for Phoenix's approval, which he indicated was fine with him. She sat and listened.

Man, I feel like an idiot. Phoenix thought, scratching the back of his head anxiously. *But I've got her where I want her. There's no going back now.*

"I wanted to talk."

She nodded meekly when it became apparent he needed permission.

"Were you out late last night?"

Her face turned even whiter. The initial thoughts in her pounding head were that Phoenix had discovered she had visited the needy family- on the verge of a bloody death- and knew she had saved their lives. That was until her rational thoughts kicked in and reminded her of her visit to Phoenix's house.

"You saw me?" she asked, in a small voice.

"Outside my house. Yes. I came outside, but by the time I got there-"

"I was passing by and needed a rest," she explained. "I wasn't aware it was *your* house."

Lies. She hated lying to him.

Phoenix took his glasses off and rubbed the bridge of his nose.

All of a sudden, Serenity forgot that she had been coaxed into the room to be questioned and felt her heart do a somersault at the sight of Phoenix without his spectacles, shivering physically as he looked her way.

Her pulse sped up and she felt hotter.

"I'm sorry if I woke you last night," she spluttered, feeling embarrassed for distinctly gawking at him.

His cheeks went scarlet in colour.

"I didn't mean to-"

"It's okay," he interrupted, putting a hand up.

The room felt stiflingly hot to him- and it had nothing to do with radiators.

"I heard you crying. I just wanted to know if you were

okay. You can speak to me if you need to. I won't bite-"

Serenity would have loved to speak to Phoenix about everything that laid heavy on her heart, but she knew he wouldn't be capable of handling her dark truths.

"I'm fine. Really."

"You're sure about that?"

Her heart beat faster at the sound of his concern.

"I wouldn't want to trouble you with my life, Phoenix. Things are best left unsaid."

Silence dripped thickly between them.

Serenity could hear Phoenix's heart beating with her advanced hearing.

Is he afraid of me? Afraid of what I might be perhaps? Out late, stalking the streets... what if he'll convince his father to investigate further...?

"I'd better go."

He moved forward to stop her.

"You don't have to run off again."

She came to a stand-still.

"Why are you doing this to me?"

She noticed as she spoke that he was looking at her lips- rose red in colour.

"I just-"

"Yes?"

The heat was unbearable now.

"I-"

She tilted her head to one side, and he copied the movement with a building ache.

Their lips touched.

Serenity's eyes grew wider with surprise as the kiss she had dreamed of became a reality, but slowly, the rhythm of his tongue against hers made her lids heavy with a new-found weakness.

Phoenix lifted a hand to her face and fed his fingers through her blood red hair, caressing her scalp and bringing her body closer to his.

For the first time in Serenity's life, she truly felt human.

She had hated denying herself a person's touch and felt her body reacting instinctively as Phoenix kissed her with even more passion. His hands came to rest on her hips and her hands moved up around his neck.

"Sinners!" came a sudden unexpected yell. From the classroom door came a dumpy woman with a long black cardigan and grey flecked auburn hair.

Serenity broke free from Phoenix's hold.

"Sinning in my classroom! I can't believe my eyes! Get out of here!" she spat, in a frenzy, waving her arms like a mad-woman. "Suspension. No! Expulsion. I'll throw you out of school if I catch you in here again!"

Phoenix grabbed his glasses and the rucksack that had fallen from his shoulder and made a dash for the door, realising with despair that Serenity had already left him.

He hadn't even seen her move.

*

Serenity ran as fast as her feet would allow her, passing the gang of nicotine junkies and cutting across the concrete tennis courts in an uncoordinated manner. She wasn't sure where she was heading, but her lungs needed oxygen and the crowded school just wasn't providing any. On the verge of hyperventilating, she put her hands against the fencing surrounding the far side of the tennis courts and forced her body to breathe properly before she ending up blacking out.

Oh, what a fool I've been! she thought. *I let Phoenix lead me into an empty room and sat there like a sucker while he offered me... friendship? I'm stronger than this! Much stronger! And to think I let him kiss me, before even having a proper conversation with him. Gosh! I'm insane!*

She kicked the fence in agitation, making it ripple and rattle. Looking back the way she had come, she was sure he hadn't followed her, and felt her knees weaken to the point of falling cross legged on the dirty floor.

Boys certainly know how to mess your head up, she reflected, picking up a small twig and tapping it on the ground. *He won't be able to accept the fact I drink blood to survive, so it'll never work between us. It has to end before it even begins.*

She glanced in the direction of Meridion High and made up her mind.

I'm done with school...for today at least.

- Chapter Twenty One -

Invitation

Julian took Atlanta's hand, noting the slight tremble, and together they walked the corridor in search of an empty classroom they could duck into.

He liked the way she looked at him nervously- unsure if the dream that was 'him' might fade at any moment- and he could sense her emotions were running high; heart beating wildly in his presence. It made him feel warm inside knowing she was so captivated by his gaze, whenever he caught a glimpse of her pretty eyes.

"You have lovely soft skin," he commented, his breath a warm and welcoming breeze against her ear.

"Thanks," she replied, barely above a whisper. "Is this okay?" They had come to stand still outside a darkened room used for meetings between student groups and teachers on training days. It wasn't meant to be accessible to students during the school day, which was perfect for Atlanta's intentions.

"After you," Julian smiled broadly, pushing the handle down and holding the door ajar for her to slip inside.

The room was almost pitch black within, due to dust encrusted blinds that masked the sunlight. In the centre of the room was a cluster of tables, all pushed together to form a neat, giant square surrounded by chairs and along the walls were shelves of untouched books listing what few colleges and universities were left all over the world.

"It's spooky, isn't it?" Atlanta whispered.

"Not with me standing here, surely?"

Atlanta scooted onto the tabletop, keeping her legs clamped together and her dress flat over her thighs. She was anxious, imagining all the things she would like to do to Julian, but having no intention of doing them until he made it clear he really wanted her.

"Meridion seems so quiet, don't you think?"

"Pfft," she snorted. "Are you sure you aren't partially deaf and perhaps slightly blind?"

He shook his head, which Atlanta felt wasn't necessary. She didn't *really* think he was hard of hearing- the cutie!

"When I'm with you, it's as if the world around me doesn't exist and all I can hear is the sound of your breathing, and the sweet melody of your voice."

"Julian," she chuckled timidly, feeling the heat in the room increasing.

He was sitting beside her now, breathing gently on her neck as he whispered into her ear.

"I can't stop thinking about you."

She turned to face him.

This was too good to be true.

"I feel like I've been waiting for you my whole, miserable life."

She sighed deeply. His words were melting her soul.

Julian lightly touched her face.

"Do you...," he blushed. "Do you... feel the same way?"

Atlanta didn't feel words were necessary and pounced on his lips, kissing him with a wild intensity. He reacted in the same way, holding her tightly and prolonging the kiss with masterful touches that kept her wanting more and more.

"There's a gig tonight... at The Sword and Stone...," Atlanta said between ragged breaths and caresses. "Will you come with me?"

Julian kissed her lips gently. The pace was slowing.

"Will you dance with me?" he asked, eyes burning

with a new light that almost frightened her.

"If you like…"

He practically purred under his breath.

"I'll be there. Wear this dress- it looks incredible on you."

She went red in the cheeks.

"But I have other-"

"No," he interrupted abruptly. "Please wear this," he touched the material that coated her left thigh, pushing it up to reveal more skin. "Red is my favourite colour and you, my beautiful angel, look good enough to eat in it."

She nodded, weak with lust for him.

"Okay."

He smiled and planted a kiss on her forehead.

For a long time, they just glared into each other's eyes, grinning stupidly and stroking parts of each other's exposed flesh- arms, neck, face and hands- whilst talking about random upcoming events, such as exams and school proms. When the bell sounded for the end of period, Atlanta was surprised at herself for even considering what had been going through her mind- something along the lines of two people stripping and making love in an extremely risky environment.

"This is where I leave you," Julian stated, passing

Atlanta's school bag over to her.

"Not for good, I hope," she joked, but feared his answer none the less.

"I won't have lunch with you today,"

She frowned, her gaze questioning.

"I'm going to allow my longing for our next kiss to overwhelm me and then find you tonight, if that makes any sense?"

His lips were so close to hers now, she could taste them.

"I understand." She didn't, but she wasn't going to tell him that. Damn him for being so mysterious!

"See you around." He made to kiss her goodbye, but stopped a mere millimeter from her parted lips, lingering for a heartbeat, and disappeared from the room before she could open her eyes and wonder why he hadn't touched her.

If he doesn't show tonight, she thought, *I think I'll cry.*

*

Phoenix was agitated.

He had kissed Serenity and now he was left with a sense of longing that was driving him to the brink of insanity.

She wasn't anywhere to be found.

He had checked all the places he'd ever noticed her haunting with no result and eventually came to the conclusion that she had fled the building.

I've blown it, he thought miserably. *She won't talk to me again.*

As he moved through the hordes of students, he noticed the new guy- Julian- strolling by with a particularly cheerful grin on his handsome face that spelled out satisfaction. At least, Phoenix *thought* that was the case.

-*Have you been kissing that guy again?*- He sent out a mental question to his sister, welcoming the distraction from his search for Serenity.

-*I don't know what you're talking about*- Atlanta replied, but her voice sounded bright and laced with joy throughout their telepathic connection.

-*He looks happier than a pig in a puddle of mud*-

-*I should think so!*- she laughed.

Phoenix rolled his eyes and moved on, dragging his feet slightly- taking his time to move through the school.

Face it, he thought, *Serenity's gone. She ditched you.*

What hurt the most was the fact it had been his first kiss.

He never imagined that the girl on the receiving end of his lips would make a run for it afterwards.

"This sucks," he whispered, defeated.

- Chapter Twenty Two -

The Sword and Stone

"Dad would *kill* you if he knew where you were going," Phoenix said unhelpfully from the sofa as Atlanta unzipped her boots and swapped them for her mother's gold, sparkly high heels. She would probably cut Atlanta's fingers off if she knew she was stealing them, but while the cat was away…

"Dad would kill *you too* if he knew some of the things you got up to."

"*Like?*" Phoenix queried, ignoring the adverts that were flickering brightly on the television screen and watching his sister prepare for her evening.

"I don't know," she kept her eyes on her shoes. "I could make something up-"

"That's downright bitchy!"

"Call it what you want." She shrugged. "Just don't tell Dad and you won't have to suffer the consequences."

Phoenix exhaled loudly and turned the volume down on the television. He was feeling antsy. His kiss with Serenity was lingering on his mind and he couldn't concentrate on anything. He'd tried picking up a book when he had first got home from school, but the female character in the novel reminded him of her, which then led to a replay of what had occurred in the Religious Studies classroom that very day. So now, he was sat in front of the television, secretly hoping his sister would extend an invite to him and take away the misery he was feeling.

"I think I should go with you," he said, when he couldn't bear it any longer. He peered hopefully over the frames of his spectacles.

Atlanta blew her perfectly straightened hair out of her face and scowled at her brother.

"Why so eager? You usually hate bars and ridiculously loud music."

"I fancy a drink with my sis'."

Atlanta glared at her brother for a long time, trying to read his thoughts. She calculated slowly the tone of his voice, the look in his eyes, his posture on the sofa and mentally went over a few of the things he had said to her that evening. Interestingly uncharacteristic things, one could say.

"My God-" she gasped, her mouth forming a large 'O.'

"What?" he cried in alarm.

"I know why you're acting so weird! It has to be-" she clicked her fingers. "The red-head, am I right?"

Phoenix couldn't hide the shade of red that rose to his cheeks.

"Something happened, didn't it?"

She left the armchair and bounced onto the sofa next to her twin, slapping his thigh eagerly in a new lust for gossip.

"Talk, or I spend the night guessing until your ears bleed."

Phoenix sighed loudly. He loved his sister- he really did- but sometimes she could be a real pain in his backside. Occasionally, though he hated to admit it, he wished his twin had been born male. That way, they would have grown up with more in common. At least he assumed they would.

"We spoke. It's no big deal."

-And I kissed her- he thought, but forgot to mask the words from his sister's telepathic mind.

"You *kissed* her?" she bellowed, louder than she had intended. "We *are* talking about the girl with the blood red hair, *right?*"

There was no use in hiding the truth any longer, so he nodded meekly in response.

"What happened?"

"She ran out on me when a teacher caught us. I haven't seen her since."

Atlanta's expression reflected sympathy immediately and she squeezed his leg with affection. She hadn't thought her brother would have even attempted to make a move on a girl- not until high school was over and forgotten.

"Oh, bro'… I'm sure she'll find you again."

Phoenix looked blankly at the wall opposite. "Something tells me she didn't want me as much as I wanted her."

Atlanta's stomach did a somersault. She'd never heard her brother talk about a girl in such a way before. It was almost… creepy.

"So," he said suddenly. "Can I join you tonight?"

Atlanta bit her lip, followed by the creation of a hissing noise.

"Sorry Phoenix, but it's kind of a double date tonight. Me, Nerys, Malcolm and-"

"Goldilocks. Right, I get it," Phoenix cut in.

"If you wanna bring…what's her name?"

"*Serenity.*"

"If you wanna show up later with Serenity, by all means, come with us, but I can't baby-sit you all evening. I love you, but I hate it when you get all moody and broody on me. It's not fun, for either of us."

It pissed him off to hear it, but he had to admit, Atlanta had a point. Maybe if he had a few friends of his own, he could have called them up to take his mind off crazy females, but as it was-

"Well, enjoy yourself," he mumbled, receiving a kiss on his left cheek.

Atlanta snatched her little gold bag from the coffee table and sprang to her feet.

"Don't wait up!" she sang.

Phoenix glanced at the clock.

He would of course. He'd wait until he heard her key turn in the door and only rest his eyes when he heard her bedroom door close behind her. Only *then* could he relax entirely...

*

Nerys was precisely where she had promised to wait- around the back of The Sword and Stone with her boyfriend and the rest of the band.

Two large doors were open, allowing access to the stage of the old, run down bar, so that the musicians could lug their instruments inside and set up.

Nerys was sat inside Malcolm's black van, shivering uncontrollably in a little black dress and trying to keep warm by rubbing her arms continually. But the hairs on her arms refused to go down and the shake in her knees remained consistent.

"Trust you to be the sensible one," she muttered, teeth chattering as Atlanta slipped into the seat. She was referring to Atlanta's cosy black jacket, zipped all the way up to the girl's neck. "How'd you get here?"

"I booked a taxi."

"Didn't Julian offer to pick you up?"

She shook her head. "We agreed to meet here. If he had a car, he wouldn't be able to drink-"

Nerys rolled her eyes. "That wouldn't stop Malcolm. He'll end up getting killed one day."

Atlanta glanced at her watch. "Shall we go inside?"

Nerys nodded. "Yes! Oh God yes! I'm freezing my arse off in this outfit and the heater doesn't work in this piece of shit van!"

The two girls slammed the vehicle doors hurriedly- Atlanta leaving her jacket on the car seat- and linked arms, passing the band members with excited grins on their faces. It wasn't often Atlanta got to go to bars with her friend, thanks to her father, and she felt all the more happy that her parents were completely out of range- unable to come and sweep her away anytime soon.

"Nice legs," one of the band members commented, flicking a cigarette butt onto the cracked concrete parking lot. He eyed up Atlanta's slim frame with a lopsided smile.

"She's taken," Nerys called over her shoulder, saving Atlanta the embarrassment.

The Sword and Stone was relatively packed inside. The dance floor was clear of bodies, but every seat surrounding it appeared to be taken. Girls wearing next to nothing pressed their warm bodies against guys that were in their best shirts, standing at the bar or leaning against walls as sexily as space would allow. The lights were dim, casting shadows over faces, unless they were directly beneath the colourful fairy lights hung around the room. The bar was so packed with people that you couldn't even tell it was there.

"Malcolm had nothing to worry about if he thought people wouldn't show!" Atlanta pointed out, gripping onto Nery's hand like a vice.

"What?!" Nerys yelled.

Someone had delved into their pockets for some coins

for the jukebox and a loud dance song with beats that shook the walls kicked in.

Atlanta saved her breath. There was no use in repeating herself.

"Let's get a drink and head to the balcony," Nerys suggested. Her voice was far more powerful than Atlanta's, so she was able to hear her without too much deciphering.

At the bar, three men in their early twenties passed pints to each other and were more than happy to part for the two beauties that approached. One of the men, in a black shirt and with hair as dark as night, tried offering his pint to Atlanta with a wickedly delectable smile.

"That's quite alright," she said, putting her hand up.

"Please?" he mouthed.

She shook her head. He got the point and moved away.

"What'll it be?!" came a bellow. A boy at the bar rubbed his hands together and raised his eyebrows in anticipation of the girl's order. He was a teenager, barely of age to drink, with hair spiked up at jagged angles and a lip ring that sparkled brightly.

"Four shots and two of your cheapest alcopops," Nerys called over the dripping wet surface of the marble black bar-top.

Atlanta put a hand on Nerys' arm. Her flesh was freezing. "Ner'- I don't want to drink *that* much. We've only just arrived!"

Nerys made puppy eyes at her friend, pouting professionally.

"For me?"

"One shot."

"One shot *and* an alcopop."

"No shot. Just an alcopop."

"If you don't drink, I'll be drinking for the both of us and I'll end up waking in a hospital bed."

The bar-boy placed four shots of green liquid before them and two bottles of murky, frosty alcohol, extending his hand for the note Nerys held precariously in his direction.

Atlanta rolled her eyes and silently took one of the shot glasses into her hand. She raised it in time with her best mate.

"To finding 'the one!'" Nerys declared.

They drank. Their faces screwed up simultaneously until the burn in their throats dissipated. Nerys then took her change and drank another shot, offering the spare to the bar-boy, who glanced at the other members of staff worriedly and downed it before anyone could give him a stern look.

"Let's go!"

With the alcopops in hand, the girls pushed through the crowd in the direction of the stairs.

Atlanta felt the hairs on the back of her neck lift as she brushed against exposed flesh and cotton shirts. Men of all ages were keeping a wary eye on her, observing the movement of her body and noting her destination. It made her incredibly fearful of what she had gotten herself into.

"Won't be long now and Malcolm will get this place bouncing."

"It's already pretty packed in here," Atlanta complained, receiving an angry glare from a female who was tonguing a boy at the top of the stairs- refusing to part for them as they squeezed by onto the balcony.

Atlanta sighed. She looked at her watch and sighed again.

"He's here," Nerys whispered suddenly, prodding her friend in the ribs.

Her drink almost slipped from her hand as her eyes settled on the beautiful visage that was Julian.

He was standing coolly amongst the heaving masses, staring up at the balcony in wonderment as Atlanta waved a petite hand in his direction. Before she could take in a breath, he was at her side.

"I'm going to mingle!" Nerys called, leaving them to it.

"You came," Atlanta said, her lips curling in a sheepish smile.

"Did you think I would stand you up? Such a beautiful specimen as yourself doesn't deserve mistreatment, and I promise you, I would be the last person to deal it to you."

Atlanta shivered as he stroked the length of her arm.

She reached up and touched his face, feeling the rough texture of his stubble and warmth of his flesh.

"You are so amazing, Julian."

He dipped his head and kissed her.

"As are you," he whispered back.

It didn't take Malcolm and the band long to get their equipment set up and their sound-check completed, and when the first explosion of sound came from the drums, the room silenced instantly. People at the bar turned their heads in the direction of the small stage and the bodies leaning against the walls became upright in posture, shuffling forwards onto the dance floor.

Atlanta spotted Nerys at the front of the crowd, staring

up in adoration at her scruffy partner holding the microphone in his hand. She was bobbing up and down, capturing his gaze with her excitement and received a seductive wink as he introduced the band to the room.

"If you have anything important to say, I recommend you do so now," Atlanta told Julian, whose hand was tightly gripping her own.

"Why's that?" he queried.

A guitarist played a few deafening notes between Malcolm's longwinded introduction.

"Because it's going to be too loud to hear each other over the music," she pointed out, just as the first song came into play.

Malcolm sang a long, high pitched note that had people standing in awe of his voice and as the music kicked in, the room shook with the volume of the speakers and the thumping of feet on the dance floor.

Atlanta nodded along, keeping her eyes on her friend and sipping at her alcopop every now and again. Julian seemed mesmerised by the band, leaning as far over the balcony as he possibly could and squinting at the movement of the guitarists fingers as they plucked at strings.

"Fascinating," he mused.

Four ear-exploding songs later, Julian appeared to have had his fill of rock and roll.

"Outside?" he suggested.

Atlanta raised a hand to her ear, by way of saying, 'I can't hear you.'

He led her away from the balcony regardless, pulling her down the steps and gave the bouncers a curt nod as they moved beyond the doors of the Sword and Stone into the freezing cold kiss of night.

"That's better," he said, revealing a mouthful of perfect white teeth. His breath came out in misty clouds.

"What's wrong?" Atlanta asked.

He shrugged. "I want to speak to you."

She moved her weight from one leg to the other. Her alcopop bottle was empty and she discarded of it before giving Julian her full attention.

"Go on," she urged.

He kissed her on the lips, soft and with a hint of desiring more.

"Come home with me."

A weak burst of laughter escaped her parted lips. "Excuse me?"

"I'm sorry," he apologised. "That sounded wrong.

Think about it…the night is young. We could head to my house and watch a movie. I'll make sure you get home okay, I swear to you. It's just, my mother is still in the hospital and the atmosphere here is amazing but… I just feel it's a bit restricting."

"Restricting?"

He nodded. "I can't hear you. I can't relax because the world is so alive with hormones in that one small space. So many bodies, so many emotions! I want us to be alone. I want to have you all to myself."

Atlanta shivered. The night breeze was biting at her skin with needle-sharp teeth that wouldn't allow her to remain still for more than three seconds.

If her parents knew what she was doing, they would come straight back home and lock her in her room until her hair went grey and her skin wrinkled. As much as she trusted Julian, she knew there was usually only one thing on a man's mind when they suggested going back to their place.

But she didn't want to put too much thought into it. If she did, she would end up living her life in regret, wondering what might have happened.

She took a hold of Julian's hand.

"Lead the way."

- Chapter Twenty Three -

Running Out of Time

The mobile phone nestled in his trouser pocket began to vibrate just as he was leaving his domain, veins pumping with adrenaline.

"Yes?" he snapped, after pushing the green button to accept the call.

"Don't you think you're cutting things a bit fine? I thought you would have had someone by now."

He sighed, kicking a mouldy apple core across the dirty, dead street in frustration.

"I'm bringing her in tonight."

"So you say-" came the caller's dismissive response.

"I've studied her. She'll be easy to get a hold of I'm sure."

"Where are you?"

"On my way to a bar."

"Oh great! So I'm stuck here putting spoonfulls of rice into *my* girl's mouth to stop her from dying of starvation whilst *you're* out drinking."

He grit his teeth.

"Why do you have a tendency to make stupid assumptions?" he asked, with no desire for an answer. "You know me, my brother. Would I be the type of Fallen One to risk losing my life here on earth for an alcoholic beverage?"

"No-"

"Then stop calling me and let me do my job. I'll have her by this evening. Just be ready to meet me half way."

"Of course."

"Until then."

He hung up and shoved the rectangular device- that was becoming the bane of his life- into its resting place once more.

Tonight he would have his virgin for the coming sacrifice on the eve that marked the day he was cast from Heaven.

She would perish. And he would live on.

A small, but troublesome price to pay.

- Chapter Twenty Four -

Sweat and Perfume

Night came earlier than she'd expected as Serenity drank a large helping of warm blood from a glass, feeling her skin tingle and her bones strengthen with every gulp. When the glass was empty, she swilled it under the tap and placed it on the draining board, along with all the other glasses that were piled there.

Serenity didn't own plates. She had no need for them. Never in her life had she felt compelled to sample a cheese and ham sandwich or a warm jacket potato drenched in butter. Blood was the only thing on the menu. Blood and the occasional cup of tea- the only human drink she could stomach.

Leaving the kitchen for the lounge, she caught a glimpse of her face in the big round mirror above her mother's favourite cabinet. The reflection was almost sinister. Her eyes glowed silvery white and on her chin, vivid against the milky white skin of her flesh, trailed a thick line of blood that had managed to miss her mouth.

She waited until her eyes faded back to their natural

shade of purple, but kept her gaze on the blood. The frightening trickle of truth- her lust for blood would never die.

In a sudden spurt of anger, she smashed her fist into the glass, sending silver shards to the floor. Some were embedded in her hand and with a grimace of pain, she plucked them from her flesh, watching the skin heal over nicely as the jagged pieces bounced onto the floor.

Another one broken, she thought bitterly. *I don't know why I bother to replace them.*

Snatching up her blade as a distraction, she slipped it inside her belt and slid a long black jacket over her body, hiding the weapon from view. She was preparing to patrol, and tonight she was feeling a great need to find a bad-guy to pummel.

*

Sweat and perfume.

It wafted thickly through the air. But it wasn't the saltiness of human sweat that the aroma manifested from. Not exactly. It was the natural scent of someone nearby. Their entire *essence* reeked of b.o.

Some people are born with a smell that they carry as a

genuine feature. The natural scent of a person can often be linked to something nice, like strawberries for example. There can be earthy aromas, fruity aromas or sometimes foul smelling aromas. And tonight, Serenity was picking up the scent of someone who had once smelt delicious, and had somehow been tainted with something disgusting.

What is that stench? she queried inwardly, reaching cautiously beneath her jacket for the blade concealed within.

She followed the scent along a dark street, keeping her eyes peeled for movement until she came upon an enticing sight.

Two bouncers were standing outside a building labelled 'The Sword and Stone;' both vaguely aware of their surroundings as they nodded along to the banging beats from within.

The smell of sweat and perfume remained in the air as Serenity slid into the shadows like a prowling beast and watched in fascination as a familiar face exited the miraculous building alongside a *very* handsome young man.

"Phoenix's sister," she mouthed.

She could smell the flowery scent that drifted from Atlanta's perfect, creamy skin and realised how intrusive she was being as the blonde haired male spoke in heartwarming tones- proceeding to give his girlfriend a kiss.

Serenity averted her gaze.

When the loved-up teenagers had decided to move their conversation *away* from the building, she made sure her presence remained unknown- waiting patiently like a cat in an alley of rats, until the coast was clear, before emerging. But as her foot touched the concrete parking lot- something shifted unexplainably from behind her.

Swifter than a Samurai in battle, she drew her blade and held it against the white throat of the creature shadowing her steps. In awe, she met the eyes of a young man, whose face bore no resemblance to anyone she had ever met.

Their chests rose and fell rapidly from a shared sense of surprise.

"Excuse me," the young man said smoothly. His breathing had become more relaxed a lot quicker than her own, even though a cold, steel point pricked at his flesh.

Serenity's nostrils flared. The stench of sweat and perfume was strong now.

She returned her blade to her side.

"I was just going to the club," the boy informed her, his eyes dull black pits in the night.

She scanned his appearance. Tall, pale with greasy

black dreadlocks in his hair that showed white-blonde roots at the top of his head. This boy- whoever he may be- was a natural blonde, masking his true colours with a gothic dress sense and a typical 'heavy metal' hairstyle.

"Keep moving," she growled.

The boy nodded and continued towards the club.

"Hey!" he called suddenly.

Serenity turned- the lingering smell of sweat and perfume tampering with her thoughts.

"What's your name, sweetheart?"

Sweetheart?

"Sarah," she lied quickly.

"Right-o," he replied. "See you around, *Sarah*."

She shivered. Something about the way he had said 'Sarah' gave her the impression he *knew* she wasn't telling the truth about her identity.

Forget him, she thought, leaving the club behind her.

After seeing Atlanta with her new Prince Charming, her heart had begun to swell. She wanted to see Phoenix- knowing he would be the kind of guy to welcome her into his home if she showed up unexpectedly, but she was positively sure it was a bad idea. Completely out of the question!

But the least she could do was see to it that his twin

sister made it home okay.

With a sharp inhale of oxygen, she picked up Atlanta's flowery scent and took off at a run.

And *still* the smell of sweat and perfume lingered.

- Chapter Twenty Five -

Knock, Knock

"This is where you live?" Atlanta's jaw hit the floor as Julian led her along the garden path to a house of incredible beauty- ivy running up its brilliant white walls and rose bushes growing beneath its lower front windows. "I've never even seen flowers like these before, except in the history books at school. How do they grow so beautifully in the dead earth of Meridion? It's impossible! "

Julian touched the largest rose he could find with his soft hand and sniffed its spectacular fragrance. "Love makes them grow. Like most things I suppose-"

Atlanta watched tentatively as Julian plucked the rose from the bush and broke the thorns from its stem, handing it over to her with a smile. She returned his grin and lifted the flower to her nose, wishing that she could keep it alive for the rest of her life, but knowing it would soon wilt and die.

"Shall we?" Julian crooked his arm for her to link onto and led her over the step into the elaborate front passage of his household.

"Should I take my heels off?"

He glanced around as if the answer was on the floor.

"Oh…um… no it's okay. We have a cleaner that works his magic on this place twice a week. I've never seen a spot of dust or dirt, so if you left a mark, I'm sure he'd just see it as a challenge." Julian's face was turning red as he spoke and his eyes were flitting to the ceiling nervously.

"Is there someone here?" she asked worriedly, putting a hand on his arm.

"Not at all. I just have a headache. The music at the club… guess it's the aftermath right? I'm not used to rock and roll. Here…make yourself at home."

Atlanta followed Julian into the living room where her eyes feasted upon walls of the richest red and furniture that looked golden in colour. On the floor, her heels were cushioned by the softest cream carpet she had ever set foot upon and the cushions on the sofas were almost as big as herself.

"This is amazing," she whispered, admiring the extravagant chandelier. She had truly believed luxuries such as these no longer existed. The house was just full of antiques!

"Glad you like it," Julian replied, using a dimmer

switch to set the mood.

Suddenly, Atlanta was aware of her situation. She was alone at last with the hottest, sweetest guy she had ever met and the pair of them had access to a free house for the evening.

Who knows what might happen? she thought.

Julian disappeared briefly, returning with a bottle and two glasses balanced between his fingers.

"Wine?"

She blushed, knowing she probably shouldn't accept the alcohol.

You only live once, her mind pointed out.

"Just a little."

He nodded and poured the red liquid, tasting his own. Clearly, he thought the wine was heavenly.

"Good?" Atlanta laughed, sipping her own. The taste didn't appeal to her at all, but she didn't want to hurt Julian's feelings. At timed intervals, she sipped a little more, feeling relief as the glass gradually emptied. He must have gone to great lengths to obtain the wine and it would have been rude if she wasted any.

The pair of them sunk into the folds of the deliciously large sofa in silence, touching thigh to thigh as they basked in tipsy states of mind.

"Can I ask you something?" she spoke up eventually.

"Ask away," Julian insisted, propping his head against the palm of his hand.

"How can you afford something so grand if your mother is in hospital and you're still in school? A weekend job wouldn't cover this place."

Julian's cheeks gave away his embarrassment.

"I'm sorry," Atlanta gushed. "I shouldn't have been so nosey."

"It's okay," he mumbled. "If you must know, my father provides me with everything I need."

"Oh. I see. And do you ever get to see him?"

Julian sighed. "It's been a long time, but I know he's just a prayer away if I need him. I'll see him soon I should imagine. He's not one to desert the ones he loves."

Atlanta had grown accustomed to the taste of the wine now and swallowed the last mouthful with a numb tongue and a shiver.

"Re-fill?"

"No. That's quite alright." As she moved to place the glass on the gold tinted coffee table, she lost her balance and dropped it to the floor.

"Shoot!"

"Don't worry," Julian assured her, putting a hand on her leg as he bent to retrieve it. He then picked his own glass up and left for the kitchen, placing everything in the sink.

"So are we watching a film tonight?" Atlanta called after him, looking about idly for a collection of dvd's she could scrutinise as she waited.

Julian stood in the doorway for a moment on his return, his face a picture of perfection beneath his long blonde hair.

"I was thinking, if you permitted it, that we could do something else instead…"

Atlanta stifled a giggle as he approached, tall and handsome in the soft lighting- seeming a lot older in his own home. He undid the top button of his shirt as he slid onto the sofa next to her.

Their eyes met.

"Kiss me," he said.

Atlanta pressed her lips to his obediently.

Her hands gripped his shirt front as their tongues touched and their lips began to hurt from the urgency of their desire to connect. Julian's back bent with time, until he was lying flat, and Atlanta was led across him, thighs either side of his waist.

His hand touched the back of her neck as he pressed her to him gently, keeping their kisses rhythmic and always hungry for more.

"Julian," she whispered raggedly.

He moved a palm over her thigh and pushed her skirt higher to reveal a blood red thong with gold stitching and a scarlet bow.

Atlanta's shoulders shuddered, but she had little time to consider what was happening as he flipped her onto her back. He was above her now- all that she could see in her line of vision.

The kisses became slower and more relaxed.

The anticipation thickened.

Julian left her lips and trailed his mouth over her neck, listening to the encouraging sound of her low moans of enjoyment. Moving further down, he kissed the exposed skin at the top of her breasts and then arched his back to plant his lips against the inside of her left thigh.

The heat between them was becoming unbearable.

"Take off your shirt," Atlanta suggested daringly.

Julian shed his upper garments to reveal a breathtaking six pack.

"Better?" he asked, as he dived upon her thigh again.

Atlanta sighed in pleasure, feeling Julian's hands fumbling at her thong.

"Do it," she said. "Hurry-"

The thong slid away at her command and the breeze between her legs made her sober-up instantly.

"We can wait if you're not ready," Julian offered, noticing her reaction, but already hard and aching for her.

"I really want to, Julian. I swear. I've never felt this way about a guy before, and it sounds crazy because I've only just met you, but it just… it just feels so right when I'm with you."

He nodded and kissed her lips, before unbuttoning his jeans and lowering the silver zip.

Atlanta bit her lip. She had never gotten this far before with anyone.

There was no turning back now. Julian was ready for her…

Suddenly, there came a loud banging.

"What the hell is that?" she breathed in fear, sitting up automatically.

Julian's face wrinkled into a frown of concern.

"Front door," he mumbled.

"Is it your mother?"

He shook his head.

"It wouldn't be her and I don't get any visitors. Nobody knows me well enough to stop by."

The banging sounded again- impatient and frightening.

"It's probably just a neighbour wanting to ask the good looking new guy for some teabags. Put your shirt on and go answer the door."

Julian turned to her and smiled lasciviously. "Just as long as you'll still be here when I get back, ready and eager for me?"

"Of course," she purred and then licked her top lip sexily. "Don't keep me waiting."

Julian snatched up the discarded shirt and hopped over the back of the sofa, running into the passageway like a child expecting a package in the mail. Giving her one quick look before disappearing, he closed the living room door behind him and ventured to discover who was disturbing the romance.

The banging sounded for a third time.

"Alright!" he cried. "I'm coming!"

As soon as the latch was lifted, the door burst in on him.

Julian's mouth gaped open.

"Am I too late?"

Before he could question the visitor, a fist collided with his nose, knocking Julian clear across the passageway with unfathomable force.

"I fucking hope not…"

- Chapter Twenty Six -

Angels

Julian had barely caught his breath before the intruder had a hold of him by his shirt front, throwing him through the wall; smashing it to pieces and blasting plaster all over the living room floor.

Atlanta screamed hysterically as a young man, with filth encrusted dreadlocks dangling from his scalp pounced into the room in pursuit of her fallen boyfriend.

"Don't even think about moving," he instructed, in a tone that sounded full of satanic intent- thrusting a finger in her direction.

When Julian had found his feet at last, scarlet rivers appeared to pour from his nose and the wounds in his arms and back. Bits of plaster and dust were clinging to his hair and shirt, which kept flapping open in the fray to reveal his bare flesh.

Without a thought to the consequences of further enraging his new enemy, Julian threw a punch at the dark coated stranger, knocking him back a few meagre steps.

Laughter dripped from the dreadlocked intruder's mouth disdainfully and his eyes began to dance with mischief.

He sucked in a deep breath and tutted loudly.

"Look at the state of you," he boasted. "And I thought *Angels* didn't bleed! Perhaps *Father* has turned His back on you, winged one?"

Julian stopped in mid punch.

"How do you know about my Father?" he asked in complete bafflement.

Atlanta was looking from one young man to the next, wondering in a state of sheer horror what was unfolding before her. The intruder seemed to know Julian. Were they long time enemies? Was Julian really who he said he was?

Why are they fighting like madmen? Oh Lord, help me!

"*Hmmm*. I can smell that sweet smell of Heaven *all* over your pretty body."

The intruder kicked Julian in the chest, knocking him into the fireplace with staggering speed. Coals tumbled to the carpet as Julian tried to clamber to his feet, and as he did so, something about his appearance altered.

Atlanta became faint and disorientated.

Two large wings, made of the whitest feathers the

world had ever known, burst from Julian's back with a flash of silver light that lifted him from the ground.

"Run!" he suddenly screamed at Atlanta, for she was just sitting dumbstruck and incoherent on the sofa. "Get out of here, NOW!"

Julian's shirt floated to the floor, torn in two. His wings beat the air around them, wafting the increasing heat against Atlanta's goose pimpled flesh.

"No!" the intruder screeched in response. "Stay there, my little virgin. You're my ticket to youth and there's no *way* I'm leaving here without you."

Julian dived at the intruder, enfolding his wings around his enemy to keep him imprisoned, but the winged boy hadn't bargained on him bearing a knife. With sharp explosions of pain that took his breath away, Julian stumbled to the floor- the shiny knife plunging into his chest three times in succession.

The intruder eventually fell to his knees and stroked a leather gloved hand over the Angel's beautiful bleeding face.

"I remember you," he said derisively, sweating at the brow. "I remember your hair and those big blue eyes. You were there at my judgement day, like all the rest of them. And you mock me by pretending to have never seen my face before?!"

Julian coughed blood from his mouth. Speckles of red flecked against his attackers cheek.

"Go Atlanta!" he shouted helplessly. His main concern was getting her away safely, for it was his utmost desire to keep her protected.

The intruder pushed Julian's head to the floor, keeping him from looking in Atlanta's direction.

"How sweet," he spat. "Do I detect warm *fuzzy* feelings for the human girl? Is it possible that I've discovered an Angel in *love*? What would Father say?"

Behind them, Atlanta made a move towards the kitchen, but she screamed in agony as something pierced her arm. A small dagger, the size of a spoon, was embedded deep within her flesh.

"Move again and the next one will penetrate your spine."

She gagged at the sight of her bleeding skin and felt her legs fold beneath her, hitting the floor unconsciously.

"That makes things a whole lot easier for me," the intruder drawled appreciatively.

Julian lifted his legs up and pushed them against his attackers chest, tossing him backwards with the last of his energy. The carpet was more red than cream now- having been drenched in his own blood- and he was feeling increasingly woozy.

"Some Angel you are," the intruder laughed, after flipping back onto his feet. "I should have known you were sent by *Him* as soon as you turned up at Meridion High with looks to *die* for." He advanced on the winged creature, producing a second dagger so that each hand was armed. "I'd hoped you were just another human, wanting to have sex with all the pretty damsels, instead of a self-righteous asshole with wings. Guess you let your heart rule over everything else in the end, because if He knew you were getting cosy on the sofa with that whiny virgin, he would have tossed you from Heaven by now... like the best of us."

Julian shook his head.

"You know nothing of our plan and what I feel, filthy one."

"Filthy one! *Ha!*"

He threw both daggers at once, pinning Julian to the walls by his shoulders and before the Angel could break free, threw another pair of blades to keep his wrists pinned to his sides.

"That's better," the intruder smiled. "Now you can

watch me walk out of your *charming* home with your girlfriend."

A sob escaped Julian's mouth. He wriggled and writhed, trying to release the daggers from the wall, but to no avail.

"I'm going to find you and kill you just as soon as I get free," he promised, becoming light headed as blood ran thickly down the walls. His wings disappeared at will, for they were becoming uncomfortable in his current state of pure agony.

"You've obviously been on earth for too long, brother. You're feeling pain. You're showing fear. And soon, you'll grieve."

Julian watched in despair as the intruder bent over Atlanta and gave her a kiss against her unresponsive lips.

"Tasty," he said. "I love a virgin, me."

"Get your filthy fucking hands off her!"

"What?" he asked shrewdly. "These hands?"

He bent down and ran his gloved fingers between Atlanta's legs.

Julian was seething with anger and disgust. "You bastard!"

"Jealous, friend?"

With ease, he slung Atlanta over his shoulder, stopping in front of Julian before exiting. Slyly, he raised his fingers beneath the Angel's nose.

"She was ready for you," he rasped in delightful wickedness. "Ready to make love for the first time. But don't worry... I'll see to it she still loses her virginity before she dies."

Julian spat at the young man.

"Now, *now*. No hard feelings I hope? The best Angel won after all." He chuckled to himself, and just as he disappeared, said. "I promise the sex won't be *too* rough. Although, I do have a tendency to get a *bit* carried away."

- Chapter Twenty Seven -

Tarian

Isaac was groping Natalie when his phone rang in his back pocket, trailing a tongue over her cheek and forcing it into her mouth before she could cry out in disgust.

"Damn it!" he cursed, keeping one hand on her left breast as he fumbled for the vibrating mobile.

"Tarian, what's up?" he asked, closely observing the bound beauty at his feet.

"I have her. Leave now and meet me half way. And be quick about it."

"Can't you just drive here and dump the car in the lake later?"

Tarian's anger simmered uncontrollably. "I don't want the car to be traced. Just stick with the plan, okay? I helped you select your Karanthian bitch. Now help me get my sacrifice away from Meridion like we agreed."

Isaac sighed. "Of course. I'm sorry. I've just been a little preoccupied."

Tarian grit his teeth. "I know you, brother. Is Natalie

still actually *usable?*"

Isaac looked down at his aching crotch and shivered at the thought of penetrating the kidnapped teen' before him.

"She's good to go. But I've been growing impatient."

"It won't be much longer now. The anniversary of our fall from grace isn't that far away-"

Isaac licked his lips and felt a tooth dislodge from his gum. His body was decaying fast now that the spell cast from his last sacrifice was fading. He spat the tooth to the floor and swallowed the blood that was pooling inside his mouth.

"See you soon."

The conversation ended.

- Chapter Twenty Eight -

Wings

Once again, Serenity was too slow.

The smell of perfume and sweat hit her so suddenly that before she could twist into a defensive stance, something large and jagged smashed into the side of her scalp, knocking her into oblivion.

If she had been human, the blow from the tree branch- wielded by a darkly clothed stranger- would have surely killed her, but thanks to the extraordinary genetics she had inherited from her father's demonic side, she was only rendered unconscious.

All she remembered when she stirred from the blackness was that she had been watching Atlanta enter a glamorous domain with a handsome young man- a person she knew very little about and desired to investigate.

Her sharp senses divulged that a lot of time had passed since she was last conscious, and on scanning her surroundings, she noticed the front door to the young man's home was now left wide open for anyone or *anything* to gain access.

Something didn't smell right, and the ache in her head backed up her suspicions.

Wasting no time to gather her thoughts, Serenity charged into the house, side-stepping into the living room through its demolished wall. She came to a halt instantaneously.

There, before her, stood Atlanta's boyfriend impaled to a wall- drenched in blood that teased her senses. His eyes were closed, his mouth slightly parted, and his head hung limp.

"Shit!" she cried, rushing to his aid.

Serenity touched his face with her hands.

His flesh was cold.

"Wake up!"

Was he dead? Did she fail to protect an innocent? Was Atlanta dead too?

His eyes fluttered ever so slightly, giving Serenity a spark of hope.

"Wake up!" she yelled, tapping his cheek with the palm of her hand.

Suddenly, two glorious white wings exploded from the

teenager's back as he jolted awake, knocking Serenity back in alarm. She lay on the floor, breathless and afraid, observing the boy's struggle against the knives that held him prisoner.

He growled in agony.

"Atlanta!" he shouted, looking up towards the ceiling "Lord, help me! Free me, *please*!"

It was as if Serenity didn't exist.

He was talking nonsense- babbling and sobbing to the Almighty, by the sound of it.

"Stop flapping your wings," Serenity commanded, finding it hard to reach him.

He stopped and looked at her, his eyes penetrating her soul for the first time since he had woken.

"Who are you, stranger?"

"I'm...here to help," she said apprehensively. "What's your name?"

"Julian," he quickly stated. "But you're...you're not even-"

"-human?" she said for him.

He blinked the tears from his eyes. He wanted her to help him, but didn't know if it would end in his untimely death.

"No. You're right, I'm not. Well, not *completely* at

least." She held his gaze. "I'm a half-blood. A Dhampir."

"A *vampire?*"

She shook her head. "Not a vampire. A *Dhampir*. I have a human mother, but I carry the vampiric gene of my father. Even so, I'm a good guy, I promise you."

Julian winced as she put a hand to the handle of the weapon deep within his flesh and with a great tug, she ripped it free from his shoulder.

"I take it those wings aren't part of a fancy dress costume?" she queried, trying her best to keep his tired mind off the pain she was causing as she gradually released him. Even though she was trying to remain calm, her mind kept screaming, *He's an Angel! A big, beautiful* Angel! *This is so incredibly surreal!*

"You weren't meant to see me like this," he explained, with a look of failure. He was shaking visibly. "No one was."

"And no one is meant to know about *my* darker truths, but now you do. So we'll both keep each other's secrets right?"

Julian nodded, right before he screamed as the second knife left his body.

"D...Deal," he panted.

"Now tell me, what the hell happened here and where

is Atlanta?"

His eyes became moist once more as he spoke of the Fallen Angel that had taken the girl he had been sent to protect.

"The Lord had foreseen that Atlanta would be used as a sacrifice, but someday, she will bear a child that will hold a great importance in the lives of many people.

"He didn't know who would take her, but He sent me- her Guardian Angel- to watch over her in the form of a physical being so that she could interact with me. I was meant to stay with her for as long as necessary…until the Lord asked me to return to His kingdom."

"Atlanta has been *taken*?"

"Yes. And I don't know where exactly. They have a two hour head start."

When the last knife came out, Julian tumbled into Serenity, his wings flapping uselessly in his state of weakness.

"I'm sorry," he mumbled, blood smearing across Serenity's front.

She looked at the blood, felt her eyes flash silver momentarily with a searing warmth to match, and dipped her head to shield her face from Julian.

"You… you have a good soul you know. I can see it."

Serenity choked on a smile. "Are you sure?"

"Yes."

"Thank you," she sighed. "I was beginning to wonder if I even had a soul… being a Dhampir and all that."

"You do. I'm sure of it. Thank you for freeing me."

Julian made to get up, but fell to the floor once more.

"You have to stay here," Serenity instructed, thinking with rationality. "I'm going to Atlanta's house to speak with her brother. If Atlanta returns, get her to call her brother's mobile. I'm going to find her I promise."

"I think they're heading outside the city. How will you be able to find her?"

Serenity tucked one of the knives into her belt, after examining the cold beauty of its blade. "I have a few perks to my species, just as you do."

"I can't just wait here!" Julian protested. "The Lord has spoken! I am to protect her at *all* costs."

Serenity laid a hand on his bare chest.

"You're no use to anyone in this state. Run a bath- soak your wounds. Patch yourself up. I assume you're immortal?"

"So I'm told," Julian muttered.

"If that's the case, your body will heal faster than a

human's. So sit tight. If you haven't heard from me in two days, do as you wish."

She moved to the front door.

"Wait!" he called. "What's your name?"

Serenity looked at her feet and announced her identity to the most curiously handsome and purest creature she had ever met.

"Find her, Serenity. *Please.*"

"I'll try," she whispered, and set off at a sprint.

- Chapter Twenty Nine -

Box of Secrets

Phoenix looked at the door to the basement and then at the hair grip in his hand. If it worked in the movies, then quite possibly, it would work for him. So determinedly, he bent his knees, peered through the keyhole and began wiggling the grip around in hope of unlocking the door.

Ten minutes passed.

Still no access.

"Why…won't…you…open?!"

He kicked the handle and made a face at the dirty scuff mark he had left on the paintwork next to it.

"Oops," he grumbled, tossing the crippled hair clip into a bin.

Boredom began to sink in.

He read a chapter of his book. He switched the channels on the television, but settled for nothing. He walked from one room to the next, hoping something would trigger some interest. He did twenty press ups. Finally, he looked at the clock mounted on the wall.

Shall I just go to the Sword and Stone regardless? he thought. Atlanta would give him an ear bashing if he did. And what if she wasn't around? He would look like a right *loser* if he went alone, *for sure.*

He thought about Serenity.

That's when there came a knock at the front door.

Siren was his first guess. His father was bound to have tipped the Chinese Slayer off that his children might be causing havoc with their new found freedom. He would have to lie and say Atlanta was sleeping in her room if that were the case.

But on the front step stood the girl he had moments before envisioned; beautiful, breathless and covered in blood.

"Holy shit, are you okay?"

Serenity pushed into the house without waiting for an invite.

"We need to go, *now*. Where are the keys to your sister's car?"

Phoenix closed the front door behind his visitor and followed her into the front room. Serenity was pacing impatiently, her body language suggesting something serious was wrong, and it scared him to his wits end.

"What…what are you talking about?"

"Keys!" she snapped. "Now! We have to go."

"I'm not giving you anything until you explain yourself."

"Atlanta is in trouble."

Phoenix's mouth dropped open.

"What do you-"

"-I mean she's been taken by someone *bad* and we need to hunt them down before they seriously hurt her."

A tremble threatened to disturb his facial muscles.

"Whose blood is that?" He pointed to her breasts.

Serenity looked down at her clothes. Julian's blood had soaked into the material, oddly adding some colour coordination to her hair and eyelashes.

"It's not hers."

"Is it *yours*?"

"No. It's the new boys."

Phoenix raised his hands to his head. "Did you kill him?"

Serenity approached Phoenix and put a comforting hand on his arm. "No. Julian's fine. He got hurt trying to protect your sister. I've told him to wait at his house in case she returns to him. But in the meantime, you and I have to get out of this city."

"I... I don't know where she keeps her keys. She hides them from me."

Serenity sighed. "We need transport. Now! We can't chase them on foot."

Phoenix clicked his fingers.

"The Harley."

"Excuse me?" she frowned. *Whatever a Harley is, it had better be fast.*

"Come with me."

Phoenix entered his parents' bedroom cautiously, flicking the switch to illuminate the neatly made bed and the array of furniture that kept their belongings safe.

Beside the double bed lay a dish in the shape of an open hand, and within it lay his father's keys.

"You need to arm yourself too," Serenity breathed into the room, keeping her distance by positioning herself on the landing.

"The weapons are locked away," he explained, with a sinking heart. "Except for..."

His heart jolted.

There were many things his mother had refused to talk about when the 'past' had been brought up. The only thing she ever really spoke of was her marriage to Kieran and the life she had led when raising the twins, though they were all aware she had briefly participated in some slaying during her life.

One night, when Phoenix had come home late from a chess tournament, he had caught a glimpse of his mother slipping her hands beneath her bed and pulling out a red Samurai sword with a well-polished blade. He had watched how she'd lovingly stroked the steel, and how she had distinctly shook as she held it. But before she could catch her son staring at her, he had disappeared into his bedroom- full of ideas that his mother desired to fight like she had done years ago, before he was born.

"What is it?" Serenity asked, disturbing his thoughts. "We need to hurry or I won't be able to track them."

Phoenix reached beneath the bed and pulled a box out, then again he reached underneath and felt the sword brush against his fingertips.

"Got it!"

In his haste to pull the sword free, the lid of the cardboard box beside him flew off.

"Let's go!" Serenity hissed, entering the room in hope of encouraging some pace to his actions.

"No wait-" he said, shrugging himself loose, for his

eyes had caught sight of something that paralysed him.

There were newspaper clippings, with his mother's name and face all over.

He picked one up hurriedly.

The headline read: *'Nightmare Unfolds as Police Agent tells Rycan White's Clueless Lover of his Crime;'* and the accompanying picture expressed a younger Kiya in pyjamas, standing on the doorstep to an unfamiliar house in the company of an attractive police woman.

"What the-?"

Phoenix picked up another, this time bearing a picture of a man. The breath caught in his throat.

"He...he looks just like me-!"

'The Execution of Rycan White:' Only one woman mourns the death of the guilty one...'

Another picture of his mother.

"Phoenix!" Serenity pleaded.

"No! Just look at these!" he yelled, brandishing the newspaper articles. "This man looks like me! And my mother was involved with him. Some sort of murderer-"

He picked up another and another.

Pictures of his mother stared back at him. Some a tearful sight, others of her bearing a sword on her back.

'Out for Revenge? Infamous Kiya seen at West Meridion Mall bearing a deadly blade. Who Is She Hunting? Read more on page 5...'

'Woman with a Death Wish or Lady on a Mission for Revenge? ...A crazed woman, identified as the murderer 'Rycan White's' fiancé, jumped from the balcony at the West Meridion Mall in pursuit of a man...'

'Man sobs at the loss of his arm. Has the infamous Kiya lost her mind...?"

"Leave them," Serenity commanded. She dragged Phoenix to his feet effortlessly and pushed him out of the room. "They'll be there when we get back."

He tried to protest, but knew she was right.

His sister was all that mattered now.

With the sword on his back and Serenity at his side, he made his way to the garage and quickly presented her with their mode of transport.

"Perfect," Serenity whispered as the plastic sheet that covered Kieran's motorbike fell away.

Phoenix swung his leg over, started the bike up and offered his hand to the Dhampir.

"Just tell me where to find her."

- Chapter Thirty -

Escape

Tarian dumped his prize in the passenger seat of a vehicle he had prepped for the getaway a few streets away, and slid into the driver's seat beside her, putting a seat belt on for safety in case the escape got a little messy.

He was ecstatic.

The thrill of wounding one of God's Angels and stealing away into the night with a pretty little miss was the ultimate adrenaline rush. Just another payback he had been waiting to set in motion since the night he had arrived in Meridion. Especially after the dreary few days he had spent scoping out the high school for virgin meat.

And it had been so *easy* to find what he was looking for…

Tarian had noticed Atlanta Nightly arguing with Deacon Price, and later overheard Deacon discussing Atlanta's lack of 'experience' in certain things. He'd seen the wicked high school bully putting the 'Virgin' note into Atlanta's locker as a cruel joke one morning. Also, he'd seen just how *fragile* Atlanta appeared to be- hiding away from the boy that had once been her partner- making her easy prey.

He had been convinced Atlanta's kidnapping would be a walk in the park, until the boy-wonder- *Julian*- had arrived just in time to try and protect her. How *obvious* it had been that she would fall for his charms instantaneously! He *was* a blonde after all, and not to mention perfect in face.

Tarian had looked like that once.

Atlanta mumbled in her sleep.

He cast a wary eye upon her pale beauty and weaved a hand through her hair, touching the warmth of her scalp and smiling to himself.

Yes. She was a fine prize indeed. The perfect sacrifice for another blissful year on earth; drinking booze, eating the greasiest foods, lazing about all day at the church or a strip club and his all-time favourite activity- sleeping with as many bitches he could convince to get naked and dirty with him.

Ah, the sins of the Lord's people, Tarian thought to himself as he pushed the car to its limit. *How I enjoy them so!*

In the rear-view mirror, he caught sight of a fleshy patch upon his brow, pussing and oozing from what appeared to be a terrible burn. Deterioration was kicking in now, thanks to their *merciful* God.

"Lucifer's gonna get his sacrifice tomorrow night," Tarian promised, touching the patch of disgusting skin on his once handsome face and flinching at the pain. "The Great One will prolong my life for another year. And you, my dear old friend, will have to watch as I spread misery amongst your lands."

The dark night sky clouded over.

"You'd have to send an army to stop me now."

Fat drops of rain began pelting the window, blurring his view of the road; the windscreen wipers were apparently broken, so his driving became dangerous.

"Damn it!" he yelled, crashing into some rubbish bins that bounced off the hood of the car and cracked the windshield before sliding off onto the road.

Atlanta jerked awake as the car swerved.

"Phoenix!" she shouted, half dazed.

She had thought for a split second that she was in her own car and that her brother was driving her home.

"No, sweet heart," Tarian replied, biting his lip as he dodged the curb moments before clipping it. "I think you'll find I'm nowhere near as nice as your brother."

She spluttered in horror, looking into the dark eyes of a young man she recalled stabbing her boyfriend. Frantically, she tried the handle of the car door.

"How stupid do I look? Of course it's locked. Now sit down properly, or you'll feel my fist in your face."

"Not before you feel mine!" Atlanta bellowed back, using newfound bravely to punch Tarian in his left temple.

The car skidded across the wet road, mounted the pavement and narrowly missing a lamp post. An old lady, shuffling as fast as her tired legs could carry her, screamed as the side mirror of the vehicle clipped her arm, knocking her to the floor in a wail of agony.

"Stop this damn car!" Atlanta screeched, punching him again and again until the pain in her wounded arm rendered her powerless.

Tarian dropped the arm he was using to shield himself from her blows and reached for the dagger embedded in Atlanta's flesh, giving it a nudge and a twist.

She visibly gagged and her eyelids fluttered.

"Painful, huh?" he wheezed, with a hint of joy. "Well, keep it up little miss and I'll put a couple more blades between your ribs next time."

Tears streamed from Atlanta's eyes.

"Where are you taking me?"

He chuckled to himself.

"You're sadly mistaken if you think I'm one of those villains who stupidly brag about their evil plans before they're even complete! It screams failure, and I am *not* about to jinx what has been running smoothly over the past few days."

Atlanta hit the side of the car as they took a sharp right, crying out uselessly. When it finally straightened up, she tugged the seatbelt around her.

"That's better. A little cooperation is all I ask."

She continued to sob.

"Shut the hell up!"

"Please…"

"*What*?!"

"Please, could you take the knife out. I c…can't sit pr…properly."

He glanced at her awkward position, nodded curtly and ripped the knife from her arm. Blood splashed out of the open gash in fascinating rivulets, making the gear stick shiny and wet.

"Tie a rag around it quickly. You're messing up my ride."

Without a word, she obeyed, tearing a shirt that Tarian had left on the back seat. There were a few other items he'd stashed there- cans of lager, so that he and his buddy Isaac could crack open a few after the ritual; packets of cigarettes; a pile of jeans, jumpers and shirts and amongst the mess, a long sword and a variety of knives.

"How about a little music?"

He turned the radio on swiftly, discovering a station that specialised in heavy metal music- or what Atlanta preferred to call 'loud grunting noises with ugly drums banging in the background.'

"You can't beat this shit," Tarian mused, and put his foot down on the accelerator.

*

Across the South Meridion Bridge and off into the desert they went, leaving the only city Atlanta had ever seen behind her.

She sank her head into the palms of her hands and wept, thinking about Julian.

She had seen the knives cut into him; seen the way he had cried and yelled in agony.

Surely he was dead now, or dying- alone.

But those wings…

He had proven to be of an inhuman race. An *Angel*! Perhaps- she prayed- Julian would still be alive, when she returned to Meridion? *If* she ever returned…

"You're quiet," Tarian pointed out.

"Well pardon me for being shit scared in my current dilemma. And anyway, I thought it's what you preferred?"

He shrugged. "I didn't say you couldn't make conversation. Just don't cry on me. I can't deal with chicks that get all weepy. I've seen enough of them in my line of work to last an eternity."

"Oh, I do apologise," she muttered scornfully. "So, let's talk about how you're a murderer shall we?"

Tarian kept his jet black eyes on the road ahead.

"You *killed* Julian!" she shouted. "How could you?!"

Her voice pierced his eardrums painfully, enticing a twitch from his right eye.

"He'll survive."

"How could you possibly know that? You stabbed him countless times! You're a murderer, you evil bastard-"

"We Angels cant be killed *that* easily. I'm sure wonder-boy is just licking his cuts and bruises whilst sitting in wait for the good Lord to show up…which will never happen I might add. Mr High and Mighty doesn't much care for our kind. Only you."

Atlanta's nose wrinkled in disgust.

"You're lying. You're not an Angel." She gave his dyed black hair a furtive glance. It was hideous in comparison to Julian's perfect, glossy blonde locks.

He nodded. "You're right. I'm not. But I was once, and let me tell you something babe, it's the worst job you could possibly imagine. Listening to humans whine and beg night and day is not my idea of a fulfilling existence."

"Perhaps you're just bitter because you weren't very good at what you did."

He scowled. "I could have been good. I just chose not to be."

Silence passed between them.

"Where are we going?"

"Will you never learn?" he laughed, humourlessly. "I'm not telling you jack-shit. So shut up!"

"I really need to go to the toilet. You're going to have to pull over."

"Yeah, sure you do. Try 'no.'"

"Stop the car!"

"Go to Hell."

Atlanta slumped in her seat, turning her face so that she was looking away from the Fallen One. She couldn't bear to see his face for much longer, blistering and flaking disturbingly. Chunks of hair seemed to fall from his head with every movement he made, slithering like worms to his lap. And Atlanta had almost vomited when she had caught sight of a fingernail falling from his hand.

"Ah ha! Here's my boy now. Right on schedule too."

The car came to a sudden halt, throwing Atlanta forwards against her seat belt.

In front of them, a rusty old truck was parked at the side of the road, and from it came a boy, similar in age to herself, with scraggy dyed black hair. Blonde roots were pushing through at the scalp and his attire consisted of dark denim jeans and a long black jacket that almost brushed the desert floor.

"Isaac," Tarian called, as he opened his door.

The young man approached hurriedly, giving Atlanta a peek before shaking hands with his friend.

"Any problems?" he asked.

"A Guardian."

"Still alive?"

"Unfortunately, yes. I didn't have the time to behead the bastard. It was fight, snatch and *run*. But unless he can find the strength to pull himself off a wall with several blades pinning him there, I think we'll be good for a couple of days."

"You'd better hope Gabriel doesn't get involved in this."

"Gabriel loves the comfort of Heaven too much to come down here and rescue one measly virgin."

The boys glanced Atlanta's way.

"Damn," Isaac grinned, "How'd a pretty little thing like that keep the men out of her knickers?"

"She's a bitch."

The boys laughed raucously.

"Come on, let's get going. She has a twin brother and he's probably wondering where she is."

"A twin you say?"

Tarian nodded. "He's no threat."

Isaac drew courage from his partner's determined expression and together, they shifted Tarian's belongings from the car to the truck, including the very reluctant Atlanta.

"Get off me!" she screamed.

"Why? Are you going to walk by yourself like a good girl?" Isaac mocked, pushing her sharply. She stumbled as he shoved her between her shoulder blades, hitting the mud and sand face first.

"I've always liked my women dirty," Isaac said, picking her back up by the hair.

Atlanta cried out in pain, and ran to the truck as soon as she was on her feet.

"An eager beaver," he laughed, climbing into the driver's seat. It smelt of sweat inside.

Whilst they got comfortable, Tarian was immersed in burning his 'ride.' He splashed petrol over the seats and set them aflame, closing the doors swiftly and running away as fast as he could- the last bundle of belongings in his arms. He had seen the movies and if they held true, burning cars could explode at any given moment.

As he entered the truck, wedging Atlanta between himself and his Fallen friend, a chunk of his right ear fell, bouncing from his arm onto her lap.

"Whoops!" he giggled in an hysterical manner, showing a glint of madness in his eyes. "It appears I'm falling apart."

She squealed in horror, swatting the fleshy mass onto the floor and feeling a fresh burst of tears rising with her increasing despair.

- *Phoenix! Where are you?* -

Silence, except for the hyena like guffaws that came from the young men on either side of her.

-*Find me*!-

Her heart prayed for one word from her brother, but it never came. They were too far out of range from each other. Unless he was nearby, he would never tune into her thoughts.

Lord, I'm praying to you now because I need your help. I'm being kidnapped! They hurt Julian and now they're going to...to kill me. Please...if you could... save me.

But still, there was nothing.

- Chapter Thirty One -

Crashing

If it wasn't for the urgency of their mission, Serenity would have enjoyed gripping onto Phoenix's torso as they tore through the desert on his father's motorbike, chasing car tracks in the wet dirt and sand.

The rain was falling hard, as if God's Angels were sobbing in anticipation of the events that were unfolding.

Fear had set in long before now.

"Just keep following this road," Serenity yelled, over the sound of the wind in their ears.

"It's hard to see!" Phoenix screamed back, his glasses becoming cloudy and rain spattered.

Suddenly the bike swerved.

"Phoenix!" Serenity bellowed in his ear, holding onto him tightly until her hands were white and aching.

"Take my glasses off my face!" he called.

At the speed they were travelling, he knew he should slow down and take them off himself, but his determination to save his sister kept his hand on the throttle, sending them speeding through the desert at a heart stopping rate.

"What?!"

But it was too late.

The bike's back wheel kicked out and threw the vehicle into a wobbly descent, tossing both Serenity and Phoenix onto the sand.

They rolled for a while.

Serenity hit a dead tree, smashing her cheek against the rough bark.

That was when the lights went well and truly out.

*

"Serenity?"

When she managed to open her eyes again, she discovered her head was propped up against Phoenix's leg.

"Don't move for a second. You're bleeding."

Gingerly, she touched her cheek. A mixture of rainwater and blood dripped from her fingertips as she pulled her hand away. It didn't feel particularly painful in comparison to some of her past wounds, but there was enough blood to cause an onlooker concern.

"Shit-" she grumbled, lifting herself up regardless of

his order to stay still.

Her body was drenched and her hair stuck to her head in a thick blood red mass of dripping rainwater and sand. Her clothes felt heavy and her bones clicked and clacked in discontent.

"Your glasses," she whispered, touching Phoenix's cheek. They were missing from his handsome face.

Bright blue eyes flashed back at her, full of concern and fear.

"I'm sorry," he whispered back.

"For what?"

Tears were springing to his eyes.

"I lost control of the bike-"

"Well, we were going a little too fast for people without crash helmets. But it's understandable-"

She twisted her body so that her back was propped against the rough tree trunk. How typical it seemed that she would hit the *only* tree in the *entire* desert during their frightening fall. *A Dhampir's luck,* she thought.

"Is the bike okay?" she asked, glancing around the open plains.

"I didn't check," Phoenix said, his voice breaking a little. "When I saw you lying there, I thought I'd... I thought

I'd...*killed* you."

Serenity smiled weakly. "It's harder to get rid of me than you make think."

He looked at the floor in shame. Serenity reached up and touched his cheek once more. Rain from his hair fell over her hand and their eyes met with fierce emotional intensity.

"When a warrior falls, he knows he has a chance to pick himself up again. You can chose to die, or you can chose to fight, because if you truly wish to survive in this world, you'll pass over only when *you're* ready to. We have a reason to keep moving on, right? So let's show the world we can keep fighting," she sighed. "It's what I do every day of my life. *Don't give up on me.*"

"I'm not a warrior."

"I'm sure after this your parents will say differently. As will your sister. And right now, she needs us."

"I hurt you... the only girl I've ever..." He paused.

Serenity's heart did a somersault.

"Ever-?" she pressed nervously.

The wind didn't sound so loud now.

"...had feelings for."

Her heart lurched violently, but it felt sensational.

"Say that again," she breathed. Feelings? What kind of

feelings? Was she hearing him right?

"I think I…" he forced his gaze to search hers. "…love you."

Suddenly, her body took on its own life and flung itself onto Phoenix, drawing his body to her own and touching his face with a newfound sense of 'rightness' to it.

"I never imagined you'd say that," she smiled through her words. "We've barely spoken in school…"

"I think I've been so wrapped up in all my books about heroes and daring situations ending in romance, that I didn't realise I had a beautiful girl right before my eyes… who wanted me." He paused. "You do want me, right?"

She nodded. She always had, and always would.

He coughed, but it turned into laughter. Sweet happiness warmed his body through and he lightly kissed her lips.

"Well, it feels good to say it out loud," he said, "But in the current circumstances, I have to apologise for the ill timing."

Serenity climbed to her feet and dragged Phoenix up with her. They kissed hungrily before parting.

"Get the bike," she instructed suddenly. She could feel the wound on her cheek healing and in a panic, she wanted

Phoenix to get away from her. He still didn't know what she was...

He ran off without any more prompting and with a sigh of relief, kicked the bike back into life.

Serenity jumped onto the back once more, feeling the vehicle moving forward before her right foot had even left the ground.

*

"What the-?"

There was a car, in the middle of the desert, burning from within. Black smoke billowed upwards, like dark souls escaping into the stormy sky.

"Atlanta!" Phoenix screeched in a burst of pure terror.

Serenity hopped off the back of the Harley with ease as Phoenix braked and came to a stop, leaving the bike behind the second he had the chance.

"Wait!" Serenity yelled after him "It might-"

And before she could finish her words, the engine exploded, throwing bits of debris all around them.

Part of the car's flaming bonnet almost collided with Phoenix's head.

"Atlanta!" he screeched in desperation, for a second

time.

Serenity ran to his aid. Her nose was telling her that another creature, emitting the formidable smell of sweat and perfume, had met with the kidnapper at this point- and mingled with their disgusting scent was Atlanta's distinct aroma, flowery and pure.

"She's still alive!" Serenity informed her sobbing partner. "They changed vehicles. It's okay-"

Phoenix tugged his arm free from her grasp.

"It's not okay!" he yelled. "This is *not* fucking *okay!*"

She stood dumbfounded for a moment.

Phoenix walked over to the bike- his mother's Samurai sword glistening wetly on his shoulder.

"We shouldn't have done this alone," Phoenix said, barely audible.

Serenity saw this as a sign to approach him.

"We should have told Siren and he could have sent the troops out to find her."

She shook her head.

"I'm stronger than they are…"

He snorted. "What can *you* do?"

His words cut into her, but in understanding, she let it go without comment.

"If an army went after your sister, then the guy who took her would leave her for dead and run off. I promise, the less people involved in this matter, the better chance we have of finding your sister still intact."

It took him a while, but eventually, Phoenix nodded.

"I hope you're right."

I hope so too, Serenity thought.

- Chapter Thirty Two -

Temper

"So you made it then?"

The two Fallen Angels carried Atlanta into the church- one holding her legs, the other, her spindly arms- and dropped her next to a cringing Natalie onto the dust encrusted wooden floorboards.

Atlanta was unconscious- punched violently in the head by an agitated Isaac when she had taken up screaming for help. But the people of Karanthian were a lot like the people of Meridion. As much as she'd shouted and cried hysterically from the front seat of the truck, nobody even glanced their way.

"Barely," Isaac mumbled to himself, kneeling before Natalie and giving her a sharp kiss on her mouth- though a rag was tied there, preventing the sensation of his touch.

"I've been patient," Tarian implored to the old man, who sat scrutinizing them with a critical gaze in his rocking chair- the usual mound of newspapers at his feet. "I had to be sure she was a virgin. I couldn't risk bringing a worthless slut all this way could I?"

"Hmm. Don't you think she's far too pretty to be a virgin-?"

Tarian looked at his Fallen comrade, who had shared a similar view in the beginning. Isaac just smiled in response.

"Ask a boy called Deacon at Meridion High and he'll tell you how she squirmed out of his car one night, after he'd pulled his dick out in front of her. I'm telling you now, that bitch is untouched."

"Correct me if I'm wrong," the old man said, scowling at the pair of them. "But when you carried her in, I could have sworn she wasn't wearing knickers. Did you two…?"

Tarian crossed his arms over his chest and laughed mirthlessly. "Like *hell* did we, *Gramps*."

The old man threw his newspaper to the floor and pointed his finger at the arrogant Fallen One before him. "There's something you aren't telling me *boy*. Now spill it, or else I cut your guts open and spill *them* instead."

"What makes you think that?" he asked coolly.

"I've been on this earth for eleven thousand years, watching over little pricks like you, and I can smell a liar when I see one. You can't keep secrets from me. Give me one good reason and I'll call upon Lucifer and have him throw you in the fires of Hell, where you belong."

Isaac glanced nervously at his partner, trying to remain in the shadows of the Godless church they had been squatting in for almost two years now. Tarian had always been the loud-mouthed one, and at times he feared the old man and Tarian would one day come to blows. If he had to put money on it, he'd bet the old man would annihilate the young Angel with powers they'd never even known he had-

"She was protected."

"By whom?"

"A Guardian," he divulged reluctantly.

"A Guardian! You kidnapped a girl that the Lord Himself had sent a Guardian to watch over? Are you mad? Have I taught you *nothing,* you dumb *shit?*"

"I didn't think it would matter-"

"Well of course it fucking matters!" He clambered out of his chair, standing taller than everyone present. "Because of this, you've brought a whole load of trouble on our heads as well as giving the Lord a fix on our location." He threw a half eaten apple across the room, smashing it to mush against the stone wall. "I've been using all my damn energy to mask this place from His sight and now you've probably led His fucking army to our door!"

"He won't send Gabriel for one girl."

"You don't know *what* the hell He *will* or *won't* do."

"*You* may have been stuck on earth for eleven thousand years, but *we* were in Heaven just as long! Gabriel *will not* come for her."

The old man shook his head.

"But you forget… he doesn't have to send Angels to do his bidding." He paused for effect. "He can influence any creature on Earth to carry out His orders. Human or not."

Tarian's thoughts flashed to Atlanta's brother. He was a worthless human. A nobody. What could he do? And on stalking Atlanta, he had discovered her parents were away on holiday. She was an easy catch for sure.

"We're still safe here."

"Give it a day or two and we'll see, my boy. And I'll have you know that if someone does show up at our doors- even if it's a fucking Jehovah's witness trying to convert us- I'll rip your spine out and throw it at the poor bastard."

Tarian tried not to show any discomfort or fear. He'd learned long ago that the old man had a temper, and he wasn't about to let any threats ruin his triumphant day. With a sniff and a scratch behind his non-existent ear, he slumped into a chair and put his feet up on the table.

"Couldn't you have grabbed a homeless girl? There's plenty of them around."

"Most of them are prostitutes, or have been raped."

The old man wrinkled his nose. "A fair point. But still-"

Atlanta stirred in the corner or the room, beside the other hostage, turning the heads of the squabbling men.

"Wonder why she's so special any how-" Tarian said.

"Doesn't matter. She'll be dead soon," Isaac piped up from the darkest corner of the room.

Tarian was glad his Brother had said so. The old man didn't need to hear pessimistic remarks at this point. It would only set him off on another of his rants.

"Why don't you two go out?" the old man suggested, lighting his pipe and sampling its taste between his parched lips. "I'll watch over the girls."

Tarian dropped his feet from the table. "I'm not sure if you've noticed, but our faces are falling apart," he complained. "Do you think *any* barman is going to let a freak with patches of skull showing through, sit at his bar? We'd scare off the customers."

Isaac laughed freakishly, picturing his nose dangling from a thread as he requested a pint, but he silenced himself when the old man shot him a disdainful look.

"There are plenty of clubs that allow *freaks* such as yourselves to enjoy the nightlife."

"I know of which clubs you speak, but I don't fancy mingling with vampires and werewolves in the early hours of the morning. All they want to do is start fights-"

Atlanta was sitting up now, making noises of puzzlement and eventually let out a howl when she saw Natalie.

"Be a doll. Tie her up," Tarian asked of his friend.

But Isaac was already at her side, white rope and rags in his hands.

Atlanta grabbed the first thing she could as he approached- a handful of the boy's hair- and let out a scream as a chunk of his fleshy scalp came away in her hand, gooey and moist.

"That hurt, bitch!" he cried, slapping her across the face.

She fell into Natalie with force and gave her a look of apology as the mound of flesh and hair fell onto the poor girl's lap.

Tarian was chuckling at the display of madness before him.

"Will you knock it off!" the old man demanded. "You're playing on my last nerve!"

"Ha ha!" Tarian continued to hoot, watching as Isaac pounced on Atlanta and attempted to tie her hands behind her back.

"Help!" she belted out. "HELP ME SOMEONE!"

He hit her again.

"HELP ME, *PLEASE!*"

At last, he got the rag around her mouth.

"Hush now," Isaac cooed, stroking her face. "My two pretties. *Hush.*"

"Fuck it," said Tarian suddenly. "I think I will have a drink. Dusk is but a few hours away. We shall go out under cover of darkness and find ourselves a corner to hide in."

"I think I'll stay here," Isaac spoke up, sat between the two young ladies with his arms wrapped around their delicate shoulders.

"You won't raise a pint in the name of our Brotherhood, the eve before the sacrifice?" Tarian asked, looking hurt.

Isaac kissed Natalie on the cheek and proceeded to kiss Atlanta.

He sighed. "Fine. But I'm not walking. You can book

us a taxi this time."

"Consider it done."

"And don't forget," the old man chipped in. "Any trouble, due to your stupidity, and you'll find Lucifer waiting for you when you get home."

"Yeah, yeah," Tarian waved his threat aside. "You know you love us really."

Behind the newspaper he had reclaimed from the floor, the old man smiled.

- Chapter Thirty Three -

The Toll Booth Test

"This is the city of Karanthian?" Phoenix queried as they approached the bridge to a city that looked almost identical to their own rundown home. The only difference was they had taller buildings because the population was apparently greater, and a bigger graveyard on the outskirts to bury their dead. From within, factories appeared to be billowing black smoke into the stormy sky and the rain felt sticky on their skin- like oil.

At the toll booth, the pair of them skidded to a halt and gave the overweight individual within- filing her talons and chewing gum unappetisingly- a desperate smile to show they meant no trouble. She gave them both a once over- long black bushy hair surrounding a podgy face with shiny red boils- and returned their smiles with a look of uncaring.

"All visitors have to be checked over," she muttered churlishly. The speaker through which she spoke was on full volume, making Phoenix's ears vibrate painfully.

"We're kind of in a hurry-" Phoenix replied. "Did a

vehicle come through here with a teenage girl and-"

"Place your hand through the window, Sir," the obese lady instructed, ignoring his apparent need for urgency and any questions he might have.

"Would you *listen* to me?!" he said irascibly. "My sister is in trouble!"

"This won't hurt...much," she ploughed on, bringing forward a hand held device that looked like a large stapler with little bulbs on its top. Clamping the device down, a sharp needle point bit into the top of Phoenix's hand.

"Ouch!"

"Just wait one moment please, Sir,"

Phoenix glanced back at Serenity, who's face was rigid, a crease frozen on her brow.

A light on the little device flashed green.

"Okay, that's fine. Now, would you like to put your hand forward, Miss," the lady asked, making popping noises with her gum as she wiped the needle point clean with an antiseptic wipe.

Serenity bit her lip. "I don't like needles," she informed the lady. "Is there something else you could-"

"Hand forward, or no entry," the lady snapped.

Phoenix was sighing furiously- losing his tether with

the stranger.

Reluctantly, Serenity placed her hand through the gap in the window. The bite of the needle made her wince, but she didn't move her hand away in alarm like Phoenix had.

A bulb lit up, and to Phoenix's surprise, it was the red light that flashed.

Unexpectedly, the woman in the booth reached out of sight and retrieved a crossbow, pointing its deadly arrow at Serenity's heart as she remained perched on the back of the bike in confusion.

"Are you aware, Sir, that you're harbouring a vampire?"

He scowled. "Don't be so absurd! Does she look like a vampire to you?"

The lady chewed vigorously. "Blood red hair. Purple eyes. Something ain't right about her *that's* for sure. And the device is indicating she's a vampire."

Serenity gripped tighter onto Phoenix's back.

"But it's daylight!" he argued. "Vampires burn in daylight. Check again."

The lady frowned. "Are you undermining my authority, Sir?"

"What? No-" he babbled. "I'm clearly pointing out

that this girl can't be a vampire and that your device may have malfunctioned when it read her DNA."

"It's never lied to me before," the female said calmly. "Now either you move on and leave her behind, or both of you head back the way you came."

Phoenix killed the engine and climbed off the seat of the Harley.

"Listen to me you fat cow," he said, hammering his hand against the glass. "You check her one more time or I'll come in there and rip your teeth out."

The lady choked on her gum at his remark and lowered the crossbow unintentionally.

Serenity quietly put her hand through the window once more.

The lady glanced from the hand, to the device, to a very angry Phoenix standing in wait and with a silent unwillingness, clamped the strange device onto Serenity's flesh once more.

She held her breath as the red light flickered for a second, but to her relief, the green light decided she was a-Ok to enter the city.

"Thank you." Phoenix jumped onto the bike as the barrier lifted and left the toll booth behind, performing a wheel spin that blew dust into the booth window, making the woman cough painfully.

"I'm sorry," Serenity mumbled as they entered Karanthian.

"What are *you* sorry for?" he retorted, picking up speed for the sake of lost time.

If only you knew, she thought.

As half an hour of street-weaving flew by, Phoenix soon realised they were getting nowhere and pulled over into the car park of a run-down supermarket called 'Bucket-loads of Bargains!'

An old man walked by, just as he killed the engine, talking to himself about 'damn motorbikes' and 'the damn rain,' without any concern for the ears of those who might hear and take offence.

"Why are we stopping?" Serenity asked.

"It's extremely late."

"So?"

"We don't know where we're going."

"I told you on the way here, I can find them. We just need to drive around for a bit."

She watched as he paced beside the bike. Her backside was aching unbearably and no amount of shifting around eased the discomfort. Eventually, she joined him on the solid ground. A short break wouldn't hurt.

"Have you ever been to this city before?" Phoenix asked hopefully.

"I've passed through once, but I was never one for sight-seeing-"

"And you think we'll find Atlanta if we drive around in circles?"

Her brow furrowed. "I told you, *I can find her*. We just need to keep moving."

"Somehow that doesn't quite fill me with confidence," he replied sarcastically. "Plus the bike won't run on air if we keep burning fuel for much longer."

Serenity opened her mouth, but closed it again.

Phoenix's hard expression melted.

"I'm sorry," he said, kissing her gently on the forehead and brushing her damp red hair aside to gain a full view of her amazing purple eyes. "I'm just cranky."

"I would be too, if it were my sister."

"But that doesn't give me an excuse. You came all this way to help her. To… help *me*."

"Who wouldn't?"

"You're just so brave," he admitted. "I only ever saw

you reading in the library and yet you've proven to be this amazing person who…who doesn't sit back like most of us when people are in danger."

"Stop it," Serenity whispered, averting her gaze.

"But it's true!"

"Get on the bike, Phoenix."

"What?" he noted her change in expression, just before she stepped around him and drew a glistening silver blade from inside her coat.

A man, roughly six foot six in height with brilliant white hair and a body like a bull, came barrelling towards them from behind the supermarket trolleys.

He went for Serenity first, believing her to be the easiest kill, and aimed for her unflinching face with a balled up fist.

Phoenix tripped over in his haste to back away, hitting his head on the foot peg of the bike- almost missing the moment that Serenity side stepped the beast and plunged her knife into its back.

"Serenity!" he called in complete astonishment. He hadn't expected her to try and stab the guy! Runaway maybe, but not-

The man was twisting in agony, opening his jaw and

letting a howl escape his throat. He was trying to pull the blade from his back, but couldn't get his arms around far enough to reach it.

Whilst her attacker was in a state of disorientation, Serenity took the opportunity to take the blade she had extracted from Julian's body hours ago into her cold hands and smashed it deep into the man's front- piercing his wildly beating heart.

"Serenity, you're killing him!"

She pulled the knife free, splattering blood all over her bone white face, and felt the icy bite of her irises flashing silver.

The man fell forward suddenly, like a tree severed at its base, and hit the concrete forehead first where he then began to convulse.

Moments passed and with a final yowl, the man stilled at last.

"Get on the bike," Serenity repeated, aware of her fangs disappearing back into her protective pink gums.

"You-"

"He was a werewolf in human form. He wanted to kill us."

"But-"

"No buts. Just ride."

He obeyed shakily, leaving the car park behind with the image of that great hulking corpse in his mind's eye. She hadn't even hesitated. That's what scared him the most. She hadn't even thought about it- just had a 'kill and be done with it' attitude.

Serenity sniffed the air.

Sweat and perfume filled her nostrils.

"Follow this road."

Phoenix was still quivering from the shock of seeing someone die- whether it was a werewolf or not.

"Shouldn't we at least call the police?"

"And have them call us in with the body? We don't have time! Just keep your eyes on the road."

Phoenix squinted, feeling naked without his glasses. Faces passed them in a blur- with accusatory looks he began to imagine.

"We need fuel. The bike is on its last legs."

Serenity closed her eyes slowly. She had hoped it wouldn't have run out on them before obtaining Atlanta.

"Stop here," she said.

Phoenix did so without question, braking alongside a group of punks that were dressed in leather and bearing a whole museum's worth of piercings and tattoos that would boggle the mind. Each one of them looked up as the bike stopped. The tallest of the group, with scars either side of his lips that gave the impression of an extra-long, clownish grin, clomped over in his metal capped boots- an air of importance about him.

"First time buyers?" he asked, opening his leather jacket to reveal a selection of small plastic bags. Each contained a mind altering substance.

"Oh- oh no," Phoenix stumbled over his words. "We're…we're looking for a station to fill our tank. Is there-"

"Sorry. We don't give away freebies in this city, and helpful words fall into that category."

The punk turned his back on them, revealing a large white skull with a snake leaving one of its eye-sockets on the back of his jacket. He sparked up a cigarette as his followers leant coolly against a brick wall, all showing signs of being stoned or drunk.

"What do you want?" Serenity spoke up.

The punk turned to them once more.

"That Samurai sword."

Phoenix scowled.

"No deal."

"Then fuck off," the punk hissed, blowing smoke into Phoenix's face. "Before I get nasty."

Serenity slid off the back of the bike and stepped forward. The punk sized her up instantly.

"Don't do something stupid little girl," he threatened, flicking the smouldering cigarette to the ground in a haste to free his hands.

A girl from his gang stepped forward also- a live snake trailing around her thin neck. She had jet black hair with silver streaks and a chain that ran from her nose to her ear.

"Tell me where the station is."

"Fuck me and I'll tell you," he grinned mischievously, receiving laughter from his cronies.

Serenity brought her knife out and watched the smiling faces change before her eyes. "Do I have to ask you again?"

Her eyes flashed silver.

They all saw it, except for Phoenix, who had no view of her face.

"She's a-"

Before he could finish those words, she lunged forwards with her knife hand, chopping the head clean off the snake that was wrapped around the paper white flesh of its owner.

"You bitch!" the girl screeched as the snake's body coiled up around her, blood pouring from its missing face. The punk helped free the girl from its tangled, scaly body, and while he worked, he gave Serenity directions- cursing between most of his panicked words.

"See. That wasn't so bad, was it?" she asked, winking with one silver eye and smiling with her gradually receding fangs.

Phoenix sped off with Serenity before the group could retaliate.

"That was too risky!" he cried, as a fresh layer of rain splashed down around them. "You can't keep *killing* things."

Her heart pumped wildly in her chest.

"Watch me," she breathed- too quiet for him to hear.

- Chapter Thirty Four -

Strip Club

Tarian gave a friendly nod to the bouncer, standing as tall as he possibly could so that his age would not be questioned, and felt his chest deflate as the balding human shook his head- denying him and his pal access.

Isaac's spirit sunk. It happened *every* time they went somewhere. And when they were told to stop darkening doorsteps, Tarian would get 'funny' with people-

"You kids can piss off back home to your mummys," the bouncer said, placing a red rope across the open door to the strip club. "Unless you have valid I.D. of course?"

Tarian clenched his jaw.

Isaac blithely put his hands in his jeans, tinkling the coins within his pockets. He had nothing to say on the matter. If they couldn't get in, they could always try again at the next club. Some places didn't require I.D. They let anyone and *anything* drink as long as they were paying. But he knew his partner wouldn't let this go. Not without a fight.

"I was born a little after the world began, and you're

telling me I can't get in to watch some whores dance? My dick has been in more women than you've had cooked dinners!"

The bouncer's face creased with anger, but he stopped in his tracks unexpectedly.

"Hey...," he mumbled, in a state of bewilderment. "What... what happened to your faces?"

"What this?" Tarian pivoted on the spot- his coat billowing out around him like Joseph in a performance of his techni-coloured dream coat. "The doctor says we have just one day left to live," he laughed hysterically. "This flesh eating virus will have consumed us both by tomorrow night. But don't worry- it's not contagious."

"Shouldn't you be at a hospital-?" the bouncer suggested curiously.

"I'm sorry, what?" Tarian cupped his hand around the ear that was missing, allowing the bouncer to see the gaping, fleshy hole where it should have been.

"Jeez-" he gagged, putting his hands up protectively. "You boys need to clear off now. You're freaking me out."

Tarian pouted. "But my friend here wants to see what a naked lady looks like before he dies." He struggled to bite back a giggle. "You wouldn't deny a virgin one glimpse of beautiful *womanly* flesh?"

"I could lose my job-"

Tarian stopped smiling and put on his meanest face, with eyes like the darkest pits of hell. "If you don't let us in, you could lose your fucking *life*."

With a disconcerting glance behind him, the bouncer gave a curt nod and allowed the two Fallen Ones entry.

Strangely, Isaac had never seen things pan out this way. It usually ended in a tussle and with a body he'd have to dump in a shadow encased alleyway.

"You made a wise choice tonight friend," Tarian insisted darkly.

"Just don't draw attention to yourselves," the bouncer hissed.

Tarian patted Isaac's back and led the way, rushing up the steep red stairs of the strip joint, where he was greeted first by a lady of oriental heritage; her large breasts on display and a tiny silver thong barely concealing her private parts. Her lips sparkled with silvery gloss and her eyes were caked in mascara. For a moment, she broke out of her seductive pose at the sight of Tarian's deformed face, but with a stern look from her manager, she hurriedly flashed him a broad and welcoming smile.

"Table, Sirs?"

"Yes please, you sexy bitch," Tarian exclaimed, slapping the stripper on the backside.

She squeaked in discontent and the manager shook his head at the Fallen One.

"Couldn't resist." He winked as he strolled on by.

At their table, Tarian relaxed more- waving his hand at a skinny blonde in red bikini bottoms that was serving drinks. She acknowledged his gesture and quickly wiggled over with legs long enough to use as oars on a rowboat.

Isaac grinned, just as a tooth dropped from his gum.

The blonde's eyes bugged out of her head at the sight of it spinning on the tabletop.

"G...Gentlemen?" She tried hiding her repulsion.

"I'd like you to get under this table and suck me off if you wouldn't mind," Tarian asked, none too politely.

Her light brown eyebrows lowered over dull blue eyes. She did *not* look impressed.

Isaac snorted back a panicked laugh.

"Either buy a drink, or get out. We're a respectable club and we don't provide sex for money."

"I didn't say I was going to pay you," the Fallen Angel smiled crudely.

With a flick of her lush blonde hair, the beautiful waitress in her gold stilettos stormed off towards the bar, where she could be seen speaking animatedly to a barman.

Isaac glanced around nervously as the lights in the room dimmed. It was plush inside- as luxurious as it could get for a Karanthian club- full of cigar smoking, pockmarked faced men that liked to pretend they watched strippers purely for their love of dance and finely sculpted, picturesque bodies, when really all they wanted was to whip out their erections and masturbate.

"Go get the drinks," Tarian demanded. The smell of cigarette smoke and cheap perfume wafted up his nose, making him feel even thirstier.

"You go get them. You're the one that's making people look at us."

Tarian put his hands behind his head comfortably. "I don't know if you noticed, Brother, but we would have received 'looks' even if I *hadn't* pissed off that stuck up, anorexic cow. Your nose is missing for Christ sake!"

Isaac let out a long breath that he'd been holding in.

"Cheer up. This could be our last night on earth."

"Stop saying that!" Isaac shot back.

"Why?"

"Because I've got this creepy feeling Gabriel or Michael is going to walk through that door."

Tarian sat up straight. "Not you as well?" He cursed and slammed his fist on the table. A nail flipped off in the process. "If you keep saying their names, they probably *will*!"

"Sorry."

"Now get me a double shot of something strong and a bottle of beer."

Sullenly, Isaac skulked off.

The barman did *not* look happy to serve him, and when Isaac walked away, he noticed their shot glasses were still a bit dirty from previous drinkers.

"Now, let's enjoy the show."

Isaac downed his absinthe, shuddering pleasantly, and for a moment, he thought he could feel the sensation of the wings he had once carried on his back.

Often, he had wondered if there was a way he could return. If it was possible to keep living a life of rapid decay and yearly renewals then surely- if he proved himself worthy- he could return to the good Lord?

When the strippers began their routine on stage, he forgot about Heaven and remembered why he enjoyed being human so much.

A familiar ache for sex washed over his blistering exterior and he moaned low in his throat as the naked women strutted through the crowd.

One- a strawberry blonde with blinding white teeth and breasts the size of melons - approached their table with a lascivious smile, licking her lips as she moved. But as she got closer- seeing the Fallen Angels mutilated faces- she turned sharply, until all they could see was the jiggle of her backside and her slender shoulder blades. On her back, a large black cross had been tattooed.

"He mocks us," Tarian said miserably, referring to God.

"He hates us," Isaac whispered back. "It is why we suffer."

Tarian downed his bottle of beer.

"I think I'm going to need another drink."

- Chapter Thirty Five -

Corpse in the Alley

Like a body that had been relaxing in a bathtub full of hot soapy water for *far* too long, Phoenix's skin was becoming wrinkly and soft. It hurt to keep his fingers curled around the handlebars of the Harley and his face was stinging from the rain and cold that kept hitting it.

We're going to have to fill the tank again at this rate, he thought miserably. Then…

- Atlanta!- he called out with his mind. -*Atlanta speak to me! Tell me where I can find you*!-

He could tell she was still alive. If she had been killed, he would have felt her connection to him being severed completely.

"Slow down a moment."

Phoenix sighed inwardly. A few times since the hunt had begun, Serenity had commanded him to 'slow down,' with no real explanation as to why. She just kept promising she knew what she was doing, but he was completely baffled as to how that could be the case. There had been no definite sign of Atlanta so far. And what if the kidnappers had carried on through Karanthian into another town or city? They'd *never* catch up to her.

"They went down that way-" She pointed to a narrow road leading away from the heart of the city, "But have more recently doubled back and headed that way."

Phoenix's eyebrows lowered as he gazed from the small road, to the road that was signposted as 'city centre.'

"Which way do we follow?"

Serenity paused a moment in thought, her blood red lashes shielding her intense purple eyes.

"We go where we are more likely to find them, and if we don't, we'll just double back and take that road."

"Okay," he agreed halfheartedly.

They sped off yet again.

*

"I think you've had enough now, Brother," Isaac hissed, tugging the bottle from Tarian's limp hands and placing it on the tabletop.

"Who are you to tell me when I've had enough? Give that back!" he leant forward to snatch it back, but felt gravity pull his head down, and as a result, he hit the tabletop- staying there.

Isaac placed a hand on his partner's back and waved at the onlookers who were watching curiously from the bar and the surrounding tables.

"We're fine," he mouthed. "He's okay."

The smoke in the room was thick and revolting now and the dancers had stripped till nothing remained but the necklaces draped over their heads and the hair pieces in their luscious locks, sparkling enticingly- richly- from the small stage.

The waitress that had endured Tarian's insults earlier that evening suddenly approached as Isaac continued to caress Tarian's back.

"The manager would like you boys to leave," she explained bluntly. Her lips shone with a tantalising gloss that made Isaac salivate at the sight of them- plump, juicy, *inviting*.

"I'm not causing any trouble!" he replied in mild outrage.

She stamped her foot. "Get the fuck out of our club!"

Tarian peered up at her from beneath his ragged dreadlocks. "Excuse me, Miss," he said. "But I think I'm going to throw up."

She scowled at him and turned to give the barman an oppressive look.

"Just leave, would you?"

Tarian climbed unsteadily to his feet.

"Show me the back door and I will gladly get the Hell out of this hole full of tramps and whores."

Slamming her cleaning rag onto the table, the waitress spun around and with a flick of her wrist for them to follow, she led the young men in the direction of a side door.

Through this side door- opened with a four digit number on a small grey pad- she brought them to an emergency exit for staff that led out into a quiet alley full of rubbish cans and big industrial sized dustbins.

"There you go," she said, holding the door open for the young men to take their leave. "Now you can go puke your guts up in the alley with the rats; away from our customers and the front doorstep."

Tarian tumbled into the doorframe, then paused.

The waitress gave Isaac a frown of impatience.

"Would you get this idiot out of he-"

She stopped in mid-sentence.

With her eyes focused on Isaac, she had failed to see

Tarian's hand dart out, suddenly taking a grip of her fragile neck- crushing her wind-wipe.

His eyes, she saw, swirled faintly with the same colouring as oil on water. And like mirrors, she saw her face staring back at her, beautiful, yet petrified.

With admirable strength, Tarian carried her by the throat into the alley, signalling for Isaac to close the door to the club.

She couldn't scream. She couldn't speak out. Her voice box was rendered useless as Tarian's hands squeezed the life out of her.

"Thought you could be a cocky bitch and ruin our fun, didn't you?" he asked her, without even desiring an answer.

"Tarian-" Isaac said, giggling nervously at the thought of being caught toiling mercilessly with a staff member of the club. "If the bouncers notice she's gone too long, they'll come looking for her."

Tarian noticed hope flash in the woman's eyes.

"Then we'll make this quick-" he promised, trailing his tongue over her lips. "Hold her."

Isaac ran to his aid, placing a palm over the woman's mouth and pressing her hands into her back.

Tarian bent at the knees and trailed his pink, blistered

tongue over her right breast, stopping to suck at her nipple.

The waitress squirmed desperately.

Tarian persisted.

He ran a hand over her thong, tugging it down to reveal his goal.

Eyes wild with fear, she twisted her body violently, dragging Isaac to the floor with her. In the fray, he managed to keep his hand over her lips, but she was wriggling about too much for him to keep her still.

"That's perfect," Tarian whispered, as she turned until her back was to him. Her firm backside was on display to the stars and a smiling half-moon.

Tarian released his hard-on from his restricting jeans and knelt behind the waitress.

Three minutes past from the time he had entered her.

"Hurry the Hell up!" Isaac screeched, observing the alley for any sign of witnesses.

Ecstasy washed over the Fallen Angel's face finally, and he ceased thrusting. With a shake of his head, he reached forwards and twisted the woman's neck until it snapped.

The body flopped face down into a puddle.

"Don't look so bloody worried," Tarian laughed, zipping his trousers back up. "She can't tell anyone now."

Together, they left the alley and its violated corpse behind, returning to the main street and gave the oblivious bouncer a friendly smile on passing.

"I've had my fun for the night." Tarian breathed in the damp, fresh air, enjoying the feeling of sexual satisfaction. "What say we order a pizza and head home?"

Isaac grinned. "Sure thing. But if we find a pretty little someone on the way home, you're doing the holding this time and I'm doing the *thrusting*."

Tarian shook his partner's hand. "It's a deal my friend."

*

"They're either inside this building, or have been around here recently. I can't tell which."

Serenity could smell the vile stench of sweat and perfume all around a nondescript strip club that she had no doubt they'd be incapable of entering- even if they asked nicely.

"So what do we do now?"

The bouncer was giving the pair of them a puzzled glance. He didn't like the way the Harley had been parked opposite the club, with its riders showing no sign of moving.

"If we wait…we waste precious time," Phoenix said.

"But if we go, we may regret it," she counter-pointed.

The rain had eased off, at last, and the street sparkled wetly beneath the dim lamplight. A fat rat was mincing its way down the road at a casual pace, sniffing bits of litter and examining every drain. It stopped by the Harley and gave it a curious examining before moving on in disinterest.

"I don't know about you, but I'm freezing."

Serenity was cold- yes- but probably not as cold as Phoenix. She was half vampire, and vampires didn't feel much of anything, besides bloodlust.

"I'm going in."

"Give it a minute."

"Serenity-" he stopped. *What was the use in arguing?*

Half an hour passed.

Laughter and cheers from within the strip club floated on the foul smelling air.

"That's it. I'm asking the bouncer a few questions-"

Born with impatience, Phoenix displayed this trait by boldly strolling across the street; his mother's sword proudly on display. He had hoped the sword might give the bouncer the impression he was old enough to carry a permit for such a weapon, hence getting him inside for a quick look around.

"Good evening," he said coolly, with a little nod.

The bouncer lifted a single eyebrow, but said nothing. The rope remained across the doorway.

"I'm...I'm in pursuit of a young girl. My sister actually. She was taken by a young man, and I was wondering if you could grant me access so that I might search for them?"

The bouncer grunted. A laugh.

"And why would he bring her here of all places?"

"I'm not quite sure. But my partner over there," he signalled in the direction of the bike, "assures me that he came in here and she's equally positive that there is another man working with the person who kidnapped her."

"Is your sister an exotic dancer?"

Phoenix scowled. "No! Of course not-"

"Well then you won't find her here."

"But how can you be sure? Please, Sir-"

"*Listen*. The only people I've let inside are horny perv's and beautiful women that strip for money. If your sister isn't a dancer, then she's not inside."

"But can't I-"

The bouncer pushed Phoenix in the centre of his chest, sending him flying backwards off the curb of the pavement and onto the road.

"Clear off-"

A rat poked its head up from a drain at that precise moment, squeaked in alarm and disappeared once more beneath the city.

"Hey!" Serenity exclaimed suddenly. She was at Phoenix's side before he could protest or advise against it. "Don't you *dare* touch him."

She took Phoenix's sword from its sheath and advanced on the man that had hurt the boy she loved. The bouncer's face dropped at the sight of her and his hands reached for something beneath his coat.

"Please," she spoke firmly. "We just want to have a quick look around-"

"Auditions for dancers are held at nine a.m. on Tuesdays," the Bouncer grinned, bringing his hand forward and stroking a strand of her blood red hair.

"Serenity, just leave it. He won't let us in."

Phoenix's blood was running cold. He feared she would kill another man and didn't want to return to Meridion with the Karanthian police force at their backs for murder. His father would *never* let him see the light of day if he had a criminal record and he'd *never* get into university. So much more could go wrong if they weren't careful. Murder was punishable by execution.

"Let. Me. *In.*"

Her eyes erupted with silver light.

Damn it, she thought furiously. She could never quite control it…

"Hey, wait a second-!"

The bouncer saw the change in her eyes and backed off, bringing a weapon from a holster at his hip.

Serenity was poised to attack, bringing the blade up- planning to harm him without a second thought.

Phoenix saw everything happen in slow motion and ran faster than he ever imagined he could move- knocking Serenity unthinkingly to the pavement before his mother's blade could sever the man's arm.

The bouncer dived with him, pressing his weapon to Serenity's throat.

"No!" Phoenix shouted, panic engulfing him.

He had thought the bouncer bore a knife and that Serenity would surely die, but it appeared the weapon emitted bolts of electricity, not bullets or a blade.

Serenity shook sickeningly, her eyes- now purple- were wide and full of pain.

"Stop it!" Phoenix screamed, hitting the bouncer in the face. Pain shot up his right arm on impact and he fell to the floor as the full grown man tripped him slyly.

Serenity's eyes half closed.

The bouncer straightened up.

Everything fell silent.

"What did you do?" Phoenix sobbed when the shock had faded slightly. He touched Serenity's pale cheek, feeling a jolt of electricity jump onto and *through* his cold hand.

"Put a few bolts of electricity through her." Calmly, the man returned the taser-gun to his hip and brushed the dirt from his knees. "She'll wake with a headache, nothing more."

Phoenix retrieved the sword beside Serenity's body and sheathed it safely.

His world was crumbling around him again and his mind was whirring with thoughts of failure and fear.

Without Serenity, he didn't know how he would find Atlanta.

"You have no idea what you've done!"

The bouncer thought about Serenity's frightening silver eyes as he stared fixedly at her sleeping body and replied, "I've just saved your life mate. Now I suggest you get as far away from here as possible before either I, or *she*, kicks your ass."

He shook the cobwebs from his mind, ignoring the warning.

"How long until she's conscious again?"

"A good while yet. So get moving."

Phoenix paced madly.

"I...I need a hotel room."

"And I need a strong drink-"

"Please! Just tell me where I can find a cheap hotel-"

The man smiled an unfriendly smile. "You're parked right outside one."

For the first time since they'd pulled over in the city's despicable heart, he noticed a sign with only one of its letters lit. Heartbreak Hotel it read in the dim light. How unimpressive.

"They get a lot of trouble with drunkards and vampires," the bouncer's eyes flitted to Serenity, "So she'll probably feel right at home."

Phoenix scowled. "If my sister dies," he spat. "I'm coming back here, so that you may taste my blade in your big *fat* gut."

"Ha!" the bouncer laughed. "Like I'm afraid of a kid like you! Teenagers today- mouthy little bastards the lot of you."

Phoenix ignored the laughter as he scooped Serenity up and clutched her to his chest, walking as hastily as his body would allow towards the blackened and un-inviting doors of the hotel. Inside, he noticed the mauve coloured carpet consisted of rips, tears, blood stains and burn marks and at the counter sat a big juicy cockroach, sitting comfortably beside a silver bell.

"Hello!" Phoenix called out, his face beginning to show the strain of keeping Serenity in his tired arms. He couldn't quite reach up to give the bell a ring, and hoped his voice alone would summon some help.

An old woman appeared moments later, hunched and clothed in grey rags, using a walking stick for support. She was smiling at him with black, crooked teeth- happy for the company at such a late hour.

"We require a room, if it's not too much bother," Phoenix asked politely. He tried to focus on her grey eyes instead of the peeling wallpaper and the lack of furniture the room displayed. The blood and vomit stains on the carpet made him want to throw up.

"Payment upfront," she announced, running a wrinkled finger lovingly along the back of the cockroach.

Phoenix unwillingly placed Serenity at his feet and fished for some notes from his pockets.

"This is all I have-"

The old woman scrutinized his small offering.

"That will buy just one of you a place in my hotel." Her smile broadened- a thin slither of drool escaping between the gaps in her teeth.

"Fine. Let her sleep and I'll wait outside."

The woman laughed. "You'd leave a sleeping beauty alone in one of my rooms?"

Phoenix frowned. "Are you threatening us?"

She cackled. "My, my! Not me young man! But my customers are renowned for bearing hearts full of darkness and she may find herself waking with nothing- not even a soul."

He looked down at Serenity- his heart beating wildly and his eyes stinging with the threat of tears. From beneath her coat, he saw the glint of a dagger. It had a crimson handle, bearing gold tentacles that curled fashionably around it. Carefully, he abstracted it from its sheath and presented it to the old woman, who was crooning over the cockroach in the palm of her hand.

"What about this? It would fetch you a fair price if you

were to sell it on the market when the gypsies come to the city during the trading season."

She gave the blade an excitable grimace, and stroked its sharp edge. Blood pooled from the tip of one yellow finger. Lifting the cockroach to her ear, she whispered back, "Yes. My husband agrees to the trade." From the wall, she lifted a bronze key and rested it on the counter top. "Take your girl and find peace in room thirteen."

Phoenix didn't bother to thank her. He pushed the key into his pocket and returned Serenity to his arms, following the revolting old woman down a dark corridor, deeper into the Heartbreak Hotel.

- Chapter Thirty Six -

Room Thirteen

Room thirteen was abysmal.

The unmade bed suggested ill-happenings and the roof leaked rain water onto the filthy carpet in visible puddles that squelched beneath Phoenix's feet.

Stripping the bed of its sheets, he tossed everything he deemed unhygienic into a random corner and ended up with nothing but one pillow and a bare mattress.

Serenity, in her unconscious state, didn't murmur as he lay her down- fetching a clean towel from the bathroom as a substitute for a blanket- draping it over her cold, wet body.

He considered taking her clothes off and hanging them to dry, paused, then began pulling her jeans from her unresponsive legs. It was a challenge, but eventually he got her down to her undergarments without 'seeing' too much beneath the towel.

She'll complain about this when she wakes, he assumed, *but it's better than seeing her die of pneumonia.*

Now it was his turn. With a quick glance in the

cracked mirror at the bags under his blue eyes, he shed his own pair of jeans from his frozen legs, followed by his dripping wet shirt. Without a blanket, he was sure he would suffer from frost bite, but nothing could tempt him to retrieve the bedding from the corner of the room- not even if the Grim Reaper was standing two feet away, pointing a bony finger at his chest.

When he was positive the door was locked, he sunk into a chair beside an empty, old wooden desk and dropped his head into his hands. His stomach growled loudly as he sat defeated in the silence of their enclosure.

Sleep, he thought. *Sleep and forget.*

He tried to slouch comfortably in the chair, but felt his back beginning to ache within the first half hour.

And so, mechanically, he walked to the bed, lying beside Serenity.

What if someone tries getting into the room? he thought suddenly, his eyes shooting open in fear.

Reaching out, he sleepily picked up the Samurai sword and clutched it to his bare chest.

Finally, his mind darkened with the passing of time and the steady drip drip drip of the rebellious rain water ceased to play on his last nerve.

*

Serenity jerked awake the instant her mind detected a foreign warmth across her stomach and she threw herself off the bed- breathing heavily.

She stood completely in awe of what she could see.

Phoenix- in nothing but a pair of boxer shorts- sleeping peacefully on a strange and unfamiliar bed!

Sunlight was pouring through the holes in dusty mauve curtains, and she was aware suddenly of her half-nakedness- her clothing hanging from a radiator.

"Phoenix!"

He jumped up instantly, still gripping his mother's sword.

"What did you do?" she asked incredulously.

He blinked a few times, patting his jet black hair down until it resembled its usual state of straightness, flopping across one eye.

"I had to get us a room."

Serenity kept the towel to her chest, covering her purple bra and knickers.

"At what point did I agree to this?" she cried testily.

Then, she clicked on. She recalled there had been a bit of a tussle outside the strip club. The bouncer…he had electrocuted her with a weapon of some sort. A weapon she'd never seen before. After that, she remembered *zilch*.

"Did we…?"

Phoenix frowned in a state of confusion, until she pointed at his boxer shorts.

"Oh!" he gasped. "Oh no…of course not…I wouldn't…!"

She nodded. "Good."

Hurriedly, she slipped into her jeans and pulled her top over her goose pimpled flesh.

"What time is it?" she asked.

Phoenix glanced at his watch.

"Shit-" he hissed. "It's almost one!"

Her heart sunk. From the warmth of the sun's rays, she had guessed as much.

"You know we may be too late."

Phoenix couldn't bring himself to make a noise.

"But we won't give up yet, ok?"

Silently, he dressed himself.

"I'm sorry," she muttered. "Sorry for getting us into this mess."

He sighed. "You didn't know that man was going to render you unconscious Serenity-"

Her head sunk, and her hair fell like a bloody curtain across her milky white face. *A beautiful contrast*, Phoenix thought.

"You should have left me in the street."

"Don't be stupid," he said icily. She knew very well that he wouldn't leave her and it angered him that she would even suggest it.

They left as soon as they were ready, dryer than they had been when they'd entered the building, but feeling just as peckish.

"Wait-" Serenity paused as Phoenix closed the door behind him, the key tinkling against a key-ring with the number thirteen embossed onto a piece of metal. "My favourite dagger!" She checked her sheath and found it missing. The expression on her face appeared crestfallen.

"Oh... right," Phoenix said. His face paled. "I had to use it as payment for the room. I didn't know what else to do."

"You could have used your mother's sword," she pointed out, a little selfishly.

He said nothing in response, leading the way down the

corridor.

And as she watched the back of him, she wished she had kept her mouth shut.

- Chapter Thirty Seven -

Past Grievances

The Watcher put his head in his hands and clenched his teeth in irritation.

"Will you *stop* that!" he exploded, jumping from his chair when he couldn't take it any longer. The wood of the rocking chair scraping noisily along the floor alarmed the two young women even further, and their little hearts beat rapidly in their chests liked stunned birds.

He overshadowed Atlanta- eyes hidden beneath dark lashes- and struck her face with the back of his hand. "I'm trying to read my papers and I can't think with you making all that racket!"

Lighter than he imagined her impressive and attractive frame to be, he picked her up with ease, jostling her about cruelly and led her into an adjoining room. Inside, there was a bed, its covers all bunched up and the pillows askew. Other than that, it was relatively bare, besides a small desk with no chair to sit at and a cross on the wall that somebody had turned upside down for their own amusement.

"We're back!" came a cry from somewhere within the old church. The words echoed off the stone walls.

Atlanta looked horrified at the Watcher's face- expressing animosity- and he left the room, not before tossing her effortlessly into the bed post where she fell to the floor, curling up weakly.

When the Watcher entered the main room again, he noted the state of the Fallen Angels faces making 'tutting' noises with his mouth.

Tarian shed the coat from his broad shoulders and smiled a crooked smile.

"Any phone calls while I was out, old man?" he joked.

The Watcher approached Tarian slowly and reached out to touch the young man's face, examining the blisters and dark patches. "You should put some ointment on it. Stop the pain-"

"What's a little pain? It reminds me we're human."

The old man's eyes darkened at his words.

"Did you have a pleasant evening?" He looked to Isaac as he said this.

"Not as pleasant as it could have been. But finding a willing partner to sleep with when you look this monstrous is never an easy task." Tarian spoke for his friend, whose mouth hung open speechlessly- words stolen from his lips.

"You should rest up," the Watcher suggested, returning to his rocking chair.

"I am, just as soon as-" Tarian stopped, his heart in his mouth suddenly. "Where's my sacrifice?"

Isaac followed his partner's gaze.

"Don't panic yourself, boy," the old man chuckled. "She's in your room."

Tarian scowled. "She'd better still be a virgin."

The old man laughed heartily. "Don't worry, she's not my type."

"And what exactly *is* your type?"

His eyes flashed a brilliant red as he said, "You just wait until you see some of the bitches in Hell, my boy. You'll never want a human female again-"

Hell, Tarian thought with a shiver up his spine. Hell was the last place he wanted to go for sex.

"I'm going to lay down," Isaac decided, bending to press his lips to an obediently still Natalie on passing. The soft tickle of his eyelashes falling out made him shudder as he entered his room, wanting painfully for the new day to begin so that he could perform the ritual to renew his youth. Luckily for him, he had fallen from Heaven *before* his partner, meaning he would have the privilege of sacrificing his virgin first.

"Me too," Tarian yawned.

By the time I'm finished with Atlanta, he thought, *I'll sleep like the dead.*

*

She was awake, even at such a late hour, and he welcomed the warmth of her skin as he picked her up into his arms and dropped her onto his bed.

"Let me get that for you," he smiled with false kindness. Slowly, he untied the rag from her mouth. "Better?"

She said nothing. Looking hopefully at the door, but she felt his hand touch her face- turning her head in his direction.

"It's locked," he told her.

Her eyes fell to the floor.

-Phoenix. Come and find me, please! I'm in a church. An old church somewhere in Karanthian. Tell Siren! Tell Daddy! Tell someone!-

"You won't have to wait much longer now." Tarian trailed his hand over her face, stroking her cheek and touching the delicate details of her nose and lips. "I'm so glad it's you," he purred lustfully.

She looked into his shiny black eyes suddenly.

"I can't believe how beautiful you are," he continued. "No wonder he was falling in love with you."

Her heart fluttered briefly. There was only one person he could be speaking of, surely.

"It's not unheard of," Tarian said.

In a broken voice, Atlanta whispered. "What isn't?"

She saw the spark in his irises at the sound of her response. It seemed he *wanted* a proper conversation with her. For the moment...

"Love. Between Angel and human." He sighed. "We are weaker than we look. Suckers for love. Born to worship and obey God, it becomes tiresome for some and we fall ever so slightly in love with the people we guard. Someone as fascinatingly beautiful as you would be like a forbidden fruit to one of us, if we were to become too involved."

"You speak as if you-"

"I told you," he cut her off. "I told you I was an Angel. Do you not *listen*?"

She flinched as he spat the last word, but his face soon softened.

"When I went to Meridion High, I had first targeted a girl who I assumed would not be missed."

Atlanta didn't want to know who, but Tarian's description triggered a familiar image in her head. She'd gotten off lightly it seemed.

"She had blood red hair. An intriguing shape to her body and eyes like the purple fires of God's great kingdom. I knew she would be a virgin after a brief study period. I can smell loneliness from a mile away and this girl reeked of self-pity and pain."

No wonder she just stared at Phoenix like a zombie, Atlanta thought.

"But then I saw you and you reminded me so much of a girl I once lusted for when I was still in His good graces. She didn't know me of course. She never even saw me. But I watched her whenever I had the chance, until the day she overdosed and died."

Atlanta avoided his gaze now.

"That was when I changed," he whispered. "That was when I rebelled. Because I couldn't have her. I couldn't bring her back. I wanted to touch her hair and know that her smile was because of me, but instead, God took her from me." He sniffed. "A human male would never have loved her as much as I did."

"Can't you speak to her now…in Heaven?"

Tarian blinked. "She killed herself with drugs-"

She sat in confusion as the silence lingered for three heartbeats.

"People who take their own lives don't go to Heaven," he pointed out bitterly.

"Oh…," she muttered.

He stroked her face again, harder than before.

"It's okay. I have my life here and its pretty good. I was thrown out for rebelling and now I'm going to kill you and be done with it for another year."

A little sob escaped from Atlanta's mouth and Tarian looked at her angrily.

"Something the matter?" he snarled.

She glanced at the door, took a deep breath then bolted across the room, grabbing the handle and wrenching at it.

"I told you," Tarian grinned wickedly, displaying a key in the palm of his hand. "It's locked."

Banging furiously at the wood, she screamed and screamed until her lungs ached, barging her shoulder into it to no avail.

"Help me!" she bellowed. "Please help me. Julian!

Julian, help me!"

"He can't hear you. This place is masked from His sight."

"No! No, you're lying. He sees everything. *Everyone*. Help me! Someone please help!"

"You're giving me a headache," Tarian growled. "And if the old man comes in here ranting and raving, I'll see to it you suffer greatly for your misbehaviour."

She stopped banging at last, and slid to the floor in defeat.

"Get over here."

"No," she whispered defiantly.

Tarian sighed and rested his head against a pillow.

"Fine. Sleep on the floor."

And with that, the lights went out.

- Chapter Thirty Eight -

Blind

When the sunlight blindingly hit Phoenix's eyes, it hurt. The world had been dark and dreary for so long now that he had grown accustomed to the gloom, but the weather was improving a little, drying the streets out at last and emphasising the colour of certain buildings and signs.

To his immense relief, the Harley was still outside and untouched as he left the hotel with a curt nod from the old woman and her husband- the cockroach. There appeared to be no sign of an attempted theft at least.

But fear hit him like a fist to his stomach when he saw *beyond* the motorbike.

A cluster of people wearing various outfits and uniforms were hovering in one area, with a large white ambulance and three vacant police cars parked at the side of the road.

"What's going on?" he asked Serenity. He didn't think his heart could take much more of this.

He could just about make out the bouncer from the

strip club, standing uncomfortably besides a woman in an officer's dark blue uniform who was writing in a notebook, whilst other police men were trying to keep a small group of curious bystanders from pushing forward towards the yellow tape that cordoned off an alley.

Serenity could smell death on the air.

"Someone's been hurt," she whispered.

Phoenix's eyes widened and he took off across the road, calling out Atlanta's name, too fast for Serenity to verbally discourage him.

As he raced between two police vehicles, a man in uniform stepped into his path and brought him to a sudden halt.

"Atlanta!" he exclaimed distractedly. "Please, you have to let me see her."

The officer, old and visibly tired, placed a hand on Phoenix's chest.

"Slow down, son. Please remain calm."

Phoenix couldn't see much. As far as he could tell, a body lay within the shadows of the alley and a man with a camera was taking photographs, whilst speaking his mind to an officer overshadowing him.

"Do you know the victim?"

"I think it's my sister-"

The officer frowned. "The manager of the club informed me that the victim has no living relatives…"

Phoenix stopped breathing so heavily.

"Now tell me, son. What makes you think this could be your sister? Have you reported her missing?"

Phoenix wasn't listening to the officer though. The photographer had shifted position and he had caught a glimpse of the corpse's face.

It wasn't her.

"Son?" the officer pressed, glancing at a paramedic, who watched the young boy with distinct suspicion written across his face. "Does your sister work at this club?"

"No…no she doesn't."

He backed away slowly.

"If you have concerns regarding the disappearance of another young woman, then please speak with another member of my team or head directly to the station. Thank you."

He turned and indicated to the paramedic to bring a stretcher through. "Let's hurry this up, before out of town press arrive and start stinking up our crime scene," he instructed crisply.

Phoenix approached Serenity.

"It wasn't her."

She already knew this. If it had been Atlanta, she would have recognised her scent. The woman that had died had a natural smell of grapefruit about her. But she'd let Phoenix run off so that she wouldn't have to convince him that his sister was nowhere near them.

"We can't stay in this city for another night, Seren,'"

She nodded. "I know."

"We have to find her today, and if we don't, I'm calling Siren. He can come and take care of this."

Her eyes darkened. "If you get the police involved, I'm afraid I'm going to have to leave you."

He looked surprised.

"Only for a little while," she added.

"But why?"

She gripped him tightly as he started up the bike. "I just don't want them to start asking questions."

"Whatever," he grumbled. He just didn't understand her!

"Head to that road we skipped yesterday. It's our last hope." She piped up, realising miserably that the scent she had been following all along was now too old for her to track after sleeping half the day away. The rain hadn't helped prolong any familiar smells that may have lingered.

They were searching blind.

*

"I think…I think I can hear her!" Phoenix screamed in exaltation.

They'd found the road, which had gone on for miles, surrounded by dead trees and even crustier bushes, and as an old graveyard and its weathered little church came into view, he was one hundred percent *sure* he'd telepathically picked up on Atlanta's sobbing.

"She's here. Inside that church!"

Serenity inhaled the air around her and caught of whiff of Atlanta's scent.

"Kill the engine," she said quickly. "We'll walk the rest of the way."

"When we get her out, how will the three of us get away? We'll be pulled over if we're all on it at once and with your hatred of the police force…"

She nodded. "I know. That's why you're going to leave me behind and ride as if there's an army of vampires at your back. I'll be okay here for a few days."

Phoenix parked the bike as close to the bushes as he possibly could, then slid off the seat. He turned to Serenity, who appeared deep in thought, and cupped her face suddenly.

A little gasp of surprise escaped her lips, just before he kissed her passionately.

"I'll come back for you. You know that right?"

She smiled lopsidedly, not feeling at all happy about having to stay behind, but trying to be supportive of her partner, who had travelled all this way specifically to save his sister. Not her.

"I know." The smile faded. She was beginning to think that it would be for the best if she just stayed. Stayed in Karanthian to help clean up some of its mess and leave Meridion's problems to the capable slayer team. And then, of course, Phoenix could forget about her- perhaps find a girl to love who didn't have the blood of a vampire in her veins...

"Phoenix-"

He was already walking the winding, dusty road to the church, with his head held high and the Samurai sword bouncing against his broad back.

"Phoenix, there's something I need to tell you."

He stopped, looking uneasy. It was plain to see he was eager to reach his sister.

"What is it?"

Her mouth hung open stupidly.

Tell him you're a Dhampir, she thought.

"I wanted to tell you that-"

Tell him!

"That...I love you."

An awkward silence descended upon them.

"As much as I adore hearing you say that, you must understand that we have more important things to worry about right now. I know she's not your family, but-"

"I understand," she cut in. "Let's move."

She overtook him with a determined stride.

The sooner they saved Atlanta, the sooner they could end this.

- Chapter Thirty Nine -

The Angel of Death

He heard the footsteps *long* before any human or Fallen One could have detected them.

Two sets, approaching the church via the old dirt road that very few people had opted to take over the years, since he'd decided to become a Watcher for the cursed.

He had hoped that his boys would have performed the ritual *long* before anyone found their hideout, but it appeared God had influenced people that were far more resourceful than he could have anticipated. Even with his magic protecting the area, they'd somehow made it.

As much as he had pretended to know nothing, he had always had an inkling of the events that were to come, for God wasn't the *only* being with the gift of foresight.

He had been fully aware that the Fallen Angels were going to have to fight for their freedom this year, but had kept his lips sealed so that they wouldn't over-think their plans and make a mess of it.

Instead, he had sat back- reading as many newspapers

as he could lay his wrinkled hands on; feeding off the stories and searching for signs. Any signs, like the second coming of the messiah, or the blessed judgement day.

It's what he did for fun.

When you're the Angel of Death in a world so full of killing, deadly diseases, terminal illnesses and suicide, you didn't have to fly around, influencing humans and demons to do your bidding anymore.

He was taking a vacation. A permanent one.

A mouse disturbed the silence.

The Watcher- *Death*- glowered at its fragile body and crushed it beneath his boot, leaving a bloody mass of bone, flesh and grey fur beside his chair.

"Damn rodents," he mumbled, scraping the excess mush from the leather sole. He then moved to a cupboard, where he pulled from its shadows a shotgun loaded with bullets. Sure, he could use his hands to make a heart stop forever, but something about gun power made him feel human, and he liked that. The use of his powers always drained him anyhow, especially after the lack of practise over the millennia.

The girl's were locked away with the Fallen, and he had no reason to stir them all from their sleep. Instead, he aimed the gun at the door, placed his smoking pipe in his mouth and sat down to do what he did best. Watch.

*

Phoenix drew his blade and held it tightly in his hands, just how Kieran had taught him. They'd practiced many nights, and he was confident he could battle without losing any limbs- but it was hard to mentally prepare himself when he wasn't sure what they were up against.

"If a fight starts, I think it's best you leave the killing to me," Serenity offered, twirling two daggers in the palms of her hands expertly.

They were in the graveyard now, passing a sycamore tree with wide spread branches and a pitiful amount of half-parched leaves. Weeds folded beneath their feet and the faster they moved, the more it felt as if they were disturbing the lifeless bodies beneath the earth.

Serenity caught a whiff of Atlanta, but also the smell of tobacco.

"Be careful," she warned, inching closer to the door.

"We're not going through the front door are we?"

She shrugged. "I've always preferred the hastiest

route."

Quietly, she pressed her shoulder against the wooden door and nudged it open a crack.

Phoenix flanked her, his breath caught in lungs that felt fit to burst.

"Ready?" she mouthed.

He closed his eyes.

- *Atlanta-* he thought quickly. *-Atlanta we're here!-*

-Phoenix!!- came an excited scream inside his mind.

His sister was here! Hallelujah! It felt so uplifting to hear her voice again…

-We're coming in-

-Phoenix wait!-

Serenity went in first, signalling sharply for Phoenix to remain outside, but he couldn't bear to stand there with nothing but old tombstones for company.

He stopped dead in his tracks.

Something made a crashing noise- like wooden furniture hitting a wall- and he felt his body creeping closer to the open door automatically.

"Come in, boy!" came a loud voice.

Phoenix held his sword aloft and tiptoed into the old church where he found a tall, greying man holding a gun to

Serenity's head.

"Call yourself a gentleman, do you? Letting a woman go in first?"

Her bright red hair stood out vividly against the man's dark grey suit as Serenity twisted in the grip of his hands. For an old man, she had not anticipated such inhuman strength. She couldn't smell any true or natural scent about him… as if he were neither human nor demon, but something entirely different. Although the smell of tobacco choked his clothing enough for even *human* noses to detect.

Death pointed at the door and it closed without the assistance of physical touch.

"Come into the light."

Phoenix, lips tightly shut and teeth clenched, edged forwards.

"So you're the twin?"

He didn't answer.

Serenity's eyes pleaded with him not to try fighting. The moment she had lifted her own dagger, it had disappeared into a murky black substance that had disintegrated into the stale air. In complete bewilderment, she had then tucked the second dagger into her belt for safe keeping, just as the old man had kicked his rocking chair aside and lifted her from the floor by her neck.

"Where's my sister?"

Death looked amused by this.

"She's dead," he lied.

If the boy had nothing to fight for, he'd lose all his determination to win. Who liked fighting if there was no prize at the end of their troubles?

"You're lying."

Death lifted his eyebrows in further amusement.

"You sound confident about that."

- *Atlanta?*-

-*Yes! I'm here! I'm locked in a room. If I move around, Tarian will wake-*

"I don't know why you've taken her and I don't really care for details right now. Just hand her over and we'll be on our way."

A chuckle.

Serenity made a strange choking sound as Death squeezed her throat harder. If he so wished, he could summon his gift of killing with a stroke of his fingers against her milky skin at any given moment-

- *Find a weapon and kill him if you have to*-

-*There's nothing in here! He's too strong. This guy*

used to be an Angel-

"Phoenix-" Serenity managed to squeeze out.

She didn't know why she said it, she just didn't like the silence. Her senses told her she was going to die here, and she didn't want it to happen without having his eyes on her, one last time.

"Are you aware I can kill you quite easily?"

"So why don't you?" Phoenix queried.

Death had his reasons. If too many innocents were slaughtered at once, God's gaze would fall upon his hideout and he'd be finished- forced to live in Hell with his bastard neighbour, Lucifer. Sure, Hell had some perks, but it was always too hot for his liking-

"Let's make a deal shall we? One that involves you still walking out of here alive."

"I'm listening."

"You and your sister can go back to your home right now. You have my word. But... *she* stays," he shook Serenity to prompt him.

"Why?" his voice quavered slightly. "Why must she stay? What are you people doing here?"

"My boys need a virgin's blood," he laughed suddenly. "But wait. I haven't even thought to check if she's pure-"

Closing his eyes, he let his mind reach out, touching Serenity's thoughts. He knew what he was looking for, so he was able to push aside the memories that were of no use to him and located just the thoughts of passion and love.

He saw Serenity on her first day of school, leaning against a wall alone with her folder clutched to her chest as Phoenix strolled by- the first time she'd felt a spark of love for him.

The colours blended together and when they rearranged, Death saw Serenity once more, sitting in the library waiting for Phoenix to enter, hoping that he might notice the new earrings that dangled from her earlobes.

A new scene. Serenity kissing Phoenix in a Religious Studies classroom, quickly followed by a scene involving a motorbike crash and the pair of them holding each other, bloodied and beaten.

But there was no sex. No images of two bodies becoming one in an act of incredible ecstasy. Just the distinct desire for such an occurrence one day in the future…

"How touching," Death spoke openly. "It almost brought a tear to my eye."

"Phoenix, do what he says!" Serenity shouted, the

second Death had loosened his grip.

"Serenity-" Phoenix replied. "How could I leave you here... with *him*?"

Death was intrigued. This female was willing to sacrifice herself so that her true love could escape with his sibling. It was uncommonly noble.

I'll never understand human relationships, he thought.

"So we have a deal. You take your sister and leave this place and the feisty red-head stays with me."

Phoenix pondered over Death's offer. He could take Atlanta home and return with the police. Siren and his father would never allow such a thing to happen. But what if it was too late when they returned? What if she'd...

"Do it Phoenix. Just say yes. I won't...I won't hate you for it."

Hate. Such a strong word.

His stomach churned at the thought of having his girlfriend's blood on his hands. But he seemed to have no other choice.

"It's okay," Serenity whispered softly.

His eyes darted around the room. Sweat beaded at his forehead. His vision blurred.

Nothing made sense anymore.

-Phoenix! What's happening? Please get me out of here! PLEASE-

"Alright!" he exclaimed.

Death nodded his approval.

He clicked his fingers and a bemused and frightened Atlanta hit the dirty floor at his feet magically.

"Take her."

It didn't take Atlanta long to climb up and dash to her brother's arms, crying salty tears into his shoulder and holding him so tightly that his flesh bled where her nails had penetrated his skin.

"I can't do this," he sobbed, over his sisters shoulder to Serenity.

Death liked the fact they were looking longingly at each other. It was rather entertaining after all.

"Get out of here," Serenity instructed firmly.

"But I love you!"

Atlanta was tugging on his arm, eyeing her freedom with desperation and eventually, he succumbed to his sister's needs.

The door slammed behind them on the way out.

And Phoenix sunk to his knees at last, in heartbreak.

- Chapter Forty -

Replacement

Her breath came out in ice cool clouds as Death trailed his fingers over her bottom lip.

Serenity was in a state of shock, held in the arms of a strange man who had traded Atlanta for her instead as if their lives were nothing- just simple possessions with little significance.

"Such fascinating eyes," he said, "And hair-" He brushed a wrinkled hand through her scraggy, windswept locks, bringing his hand to rest at the nape of her neck. "You have the same colouring as majority of the women in Hell."

Suddenly, the sound of a door swinging open broke the spell he was casting upon her quivering body.

"She's gone!" Tarian shouted. His face showed more of his skull now than muscle and flesh. It was as if one of the skeletons from the science department at school had donned some clothing and escaped. "How did she-" He stopped when he saw Serenity.

"I let her go with her brother," Death explained demurely. "It was easier than killing them all."

Tarian's jaw clenched at the news.

"Here is the replacement."

The Fallen Angel approached slowly, his eyes boring into the new 'sacrifice.'

"This is just too much of a coincidence...," he said, after pondering over her appearance for a few seconds. "Didn't I leave you for dead once?"

"The blow wasn't powerful enough I guess," she replied quietly.

"So it may seem," he murmured sceptically. "You were following Atlanta home the night I hit you-"

She didn't feel the need to speak during his pause.

"Why were you doing it? I mean, I was right behind you, but I couldn't figure out why-?"

"I had a crush," Serenity quickly lied. It wasn't like she could tell him the truth- that she protected humans in her spare time. That she was part *vampire*. "I had a crush on Julian and I wanted to find out where he lived."

Death was frowning. He hated hearing about teenage frivolities and tales of petty jealousy.

"Well, I guess you'll do, although I *was* looking forward to screwing the Nightly girl," he threw an angry scowl at the old man, who disregarded it breezily.

Serenity was shivering. The cold had finally bitten deep enough for her to feel it and she could hardly stay still.

"Fetch her a blanket," Death suggested. It was making him cold just looking at her.

Tarian laughed. "I'm a maid now, am I?"

Death touched Serenity's cheek, and the moment she felt the physical connection, her body grew unbearably weary and her vision darken.

Just before hitting the floor, Death caught her in his arms and lifted her off her feet.

"What are you going to do with her?" Tarian questioned.

"Taking her to your room of course. What else?"

He followed Death like a puppy, watching as he placed Serenity on the bed, then taking the rest of her daggers from her clothing and tossing a blanket over her lifeless torso.

"You've got about four more hours," Death said, before leaving the room.

"I was aware of that, thanks."

They were going to be the *longest* four hours of his sinful life!

*

Walking away was hard.

Atlanta was judiciously leading Phoenix on with sealed lips, keeping one arm firmly on his bicep. He had pointed her in the direction of their father's bike and had said nothing more as they put the old church behind them.

He had done one thing for Serenity before leaving, although he was unsure as to whether it would help in any way.

Kiya's Samurai sword was now sticking in the soft, mushy earth; red tang easily noticeable, like a polar bear in a rainforest.

He knew his mother would be heart broken when she found out, but he was willing to pay the price for the theft of her precious keepsake.

When they reached the bike, he sat there for a while in quiet reflection.

They had come for Atlanta and here she was, bruised and bloody, but safe at last.

Serenity had done exactly what she'd promised- found his sister and helped her get away safely. And for that, he owed her everything.

- Chapter Forty One -

Sacrifice

Serenity didn't move. In fact, she was so still, any given person would have thought she had frozen to death.

The Angel of Death's sleeping spell had lasted a mere hour. She had woken to find a disgusting, fleshless *monster* beside her, playing with her hair like a child would a mother or sister's. In sensing his presence, she had kept herself rigid so as to avoid a reaction from him.

"There's something not quite right about you."

It appeared her nefarious roommate could not be fooled.

"You aren't like normal girls, are you?"

Any words she thought she might speak remained dead on her lips.

"You haven't whined and fussed like the rest. Strange that you should be so strong willed after the exchange that was just made. As if *your* life meant far less in comparison to Atlanta's."

She opened her eyes at last, an unobtrusive predator

feigning defeat.

Tarian lightly kissed her neck.

"It baffles me why you hid yourself in school," he continued, conversationally. "I saw you, those few days I watched from the shadows, and you were one of my first choices- 'the invisible girl,' whose appearance was the most unique of all the girls in Meridion." As he spoke, he planted a hand on her thigh and buried his face in her hair to breathe in her scent. "If a human could be crafted with the likeness of a rose, you would be she. Like mother nature herself- beauteous and untouched. Your hair reminds me so much of blood that I feel compelled to drink in the sight of you."

Serenity was careful not to turn and bite the young man as he spouted out his flattering, yet unnerving dialect. The thought of tearing his throat out made her eyes flash silver.

Not yet, she thought.

She couldn't kill Tarian with the old man outside and Phoenix still close enough to be hunted down.

She had a plan.

But whether it would be a successful plan or not, only time would tell.

*

"It's time, my boy,"

Isaac received his calling two hours before Tarian, for he had been the first to fall from God's grace. Dragging his patchy torso from his bed, he took Natalie by the hand and began to pull her to the door.

"No-" she screamed through her rag, a tone of distinct desperation seeping through in muffled outbursts.

He lifted her off her feet to pick up the pace a little- her legs flailing all over the place- and exited the church, heading determinedly across the graveyard to the sycamore tree. Isaac remembered it well; how he had come crashing through its branches before smashing into the earth, wingless for the first time in his long existence. A few of his ribs had broken and his legs would not respond to his pleas for movement for a while, but he had made it to the church with the old man's help, just in time to see Tarian fall a couple of hours later.

"Here-"

Death presented him with a sacrificial dagger- shaped like a crucifix, with a deadly, cold, silver point.

"Make it quick."

Isaac grinned toothlessly.

"I've waited a long time to play with this one, so forgive me if I take my time."

Natalie kicked and screamed as Isaac ripped her clothing off unceremoniously, pausing once in a while to kiss parts of her naked flesh.

Death left the young man to the foul necessities that were taking place, giving Isaac the freedom to do as he wished- slowly taking the teenage girl's virginity as her eyes filled with pain and revulsion.

"It's your first and *last* time babe, so at least pretend you're enjoying it," Isaac said, his skeletal frame moving between her forcibly parted legs.

When his heart filled with readiness, he cast his eyes to the Heaven's, took the dagger in his sweaty hands and proceeded to cut Natalie's throat.

Lightening streaked the sky, illuminating the graveyard with its awesome power.

As blood bubbled from Natalie's fatal wound, Isaac's eyes glazed over, now scarlet in colour. His mouth gaped open as his body pulsed with renewed life and for no more than three brief seconds, his brilliant white wings burst from his back, then dissolved once more into nothingness.

Natalie's eyes glared up at him as her last thoughts drained away with the blood that freely pumped out, gradually shutting off the portal that had been created to transfer energy into the Fallen Angel.

The light that flooded the graveyard faded.

Isaac slumped against Natalie's body, shaking with adrenaline and laughing as he admired the return of his good looks and healthy skin with probing fingers.

"Did that feel good, babe?" he whispered in the dead girl's ear, nibbling her earlobe and giving her motionless lips one last kiss.

The rain came, pummelling against his back.

He stared at Natalie for a minute, lying in eternal slumber beneath the dying tree.

Isaac would have to do this all over again. Every year, another victim. How tiresome it was!

Part of him hated his life. His sanity was slipping with every day that passed, for he missed the light of God against his face and the feeling of accomplishment when influencing a human to do good.

And he would never fly again. Never see Heaven.

This was all he had…thrills of a high cost and Hell waiting when he was ready to give up.

How lucky you humans are, he thought, rising to his feet. He stretched his back and arms before moving towards the church. *He asks so little of you. He gives you choices. And then He keeps you safe in His great kingdom for all eternity.*

The same went for Angels- in a way- but Isaac chose not to think about it.

*

Serenity could smell blood. *Lots* of blood.

She looked at Tarian for answers, but he just glared back with a wan smile across his face, unaware of her heightened senses and what they were picking up on.

Someone was either dead, or dying.

"Is it just you and the old man here?" she asked suddenly.

The sound of her voice alarmed Tarian, for she had been silent since she had woken.

"Why do you want to know?"

Her nostrils flared. It was human blood. Had Phoenix attempted to come back and save her? Had the old man killed him on his untimely return?

"Tell me, please?"

"You look like a deer in headlights. Why so panicked, love? You've been real quiet up until now-"

"Please. I just... I just want to know."

Tarian scowled at her. "There is another, yes-" he said, unsure of what she might 'do' with this information. "He's probably performing his ritual right now."

She paled.

Another ritual?

She hadn't bargained on there being another innocent on the premises! And to think, she'd been laying there *all* this time, thinking about her own escape when another human was in danger just doors away!

"Why are you crying?"

She placed a hand over her mouth and felt the warm tears streak down her cheeks.

Failure. It was a real bitch.

"Overwhelmed," she mumbled through her fingers.

"Overdue," Tarian retorted. He scratched at his neck, pulling a chunk of skin off in the process. His spine was clearly visible.

A knock came at the door.

"It's time," the old man announced, giving Serenity an icy glare of acknowledgement. She was too calm for his liking. "It's raining outside."

Tarian shrugged, gripping Serenity by the back of her neck and forcing her ahead of him.

Death followed, as he always did- a tall, wrinkled bodyguard. He was using all of his strength to keep the barriers up for his charges. God was quick to plant His gaze over areas when blood had spilt, so he had to mask the graveyard from sight. With what little power he possessed, Death made the old church and its graveyard appear as a small, neglected lake on the outskirts of Karanthian- full of toxic waste and dead fish.

"On your knees!" Tarian commanded, throwing Serenity down.

Her forehead struck a root from the sycamore tree, dirtying her brow, but the rain soon washed it clear.

"Your dagger," Death interposed.

Tarian tore his eyes from his sacrifice to snatch the dagger from the old man. He then waved his hands to urge Death's leave of absence.

"Good luck," he said, on parting.

The sky came ablaze with lightning and thunder clapped in the distance, shaking the earth with its hungry growls as Serenity was forced onto her back.

Tarian, virtually devoid of skin now, pressed his hard skull against her lips and began nipping at her flesh, peeling her coat off.

"Get off me!" she screamed, wriggling an arm from his hold and forcing his head back with her palm.

Tarian laughed mirthlessly.

As she pushed him off her body, he watched in a daze as she ran across the graveyard.

He giggled nervously, unzipping his trousers and shedding the shirt from his back.

At a backwards glance, Serenity could see that his private parts still bore muscle and skin and that his chest was relatively intact, besides a rib that poked through a thin patch of dying flesh.

It made her gag at the sight of him and she slipped in a puddle of mud, falling to her knees.

On the ground before her lay Natalie- the human she had failed to detect in the church and who had suffered a grotesque fate.

"I'm so sorry," she whispered shakily, keeping her eyes averted from the wound in the teenager's neck. Her sense of smell wasn't *completely* reliable, so it seemed. She may have detected the girl's presence *sooner*.

Serenity clambered to her feet and ran onwards, aware of Tarian in hot pursuit, stark naked and howling at the sky like a rabid dog.

Suddenly, she paused.

Something red and silver stood out vividly against a tombstone, in the dirt.

It couldn't be, she thought. *He didn't, did he-?*

"Look what the girlie found-"

She hadn't realised she'd been frozen in place for so long, and as a result, Tarian was a hairsbreadth from her.

Lunging forward, she wrenched Kiya's Samurai sword from the ground, pirouetted on the spot and jabbed the blade towards Tarian's chest.

The smile on his lips faded as the tip of the weapon punctured his right lung.

Rain mingled with the dark flow of blood that began pouring from his chest.

His footing faltered, and in Serenity's state of bewilderment, the blade slipped from her grasp.

He lurched, regained his balance and slowly pulled the blade from his body.

"You have... no idea... how *painful* that was," he breathed raggedly.

She turned to run again, but felt her face hit something solid.

Death grabbed her by the throat and lifted her from the ground- something he was growing accustomed to doing.

"Stop fucking around!" he shouted, over the sound of the thunder. "Finish this now. You're running out of time."

Tarian nodded dubiously, clutching his chest in clear agony.

Death sighed and waved his hand over the gaping wound, sealing the patch with what little flesh was left on Tarian's body. The bloody streaks vanished with it.

"Hurry."

Serenity found herself at the base of the sycamore tree once more, shamefully unclothed and bound by an invisible force. She couldn't move her legs or her arms and had to suffer the abhorrent descent of Tarian against her milky skin.

Tears filled her eyes.

This wasn't how it was meant to happen, she cried inwardly.

And even worse, the old man watched as it happened, calm and collected on the sidelines as if the disturbing foulness of the ritual stirred no part of his morality.

Tarian's face screwed up in ecstasy as he finished at

long last and Serenity bit her lip as he raised the sacrificial dagger.

Lightening reflected from its point, stinging Serenity's eyes, and in that split second she turned away, Tarian cut her throat in one fluid motion.

- Chapter Forty Two -

Failure

Tarian waited for the rush of staggering energy.

But it never came.

The clouds were breaking up overhead, the thunder had quieted and the lightening had petered off. All that remained of the storm were a few fat drops of rain that bounced off the leaves of the sycamore tree and onto his hairless head.

He looked down worriedly at his sacrifice.

Her throat was indeed cut and bleeding all over the place.

"What's happening?" he asked testily.

The old man moved to Tarian's side, crouched and touched Serenity's ice-cold face.

"Is this some sort of *trickery* on your part, old man?"

Death's lip curled. "Don't go pointing the finger at me, *boy*."

Tarian was ready to argue some more, when an almighty lurch in his stomach made him bend over double in pain.

"Ow!" he screeched. "Oh shit... Oh..."

Death looked on in bemusement as Tarian's skin blackened.

"What's...what's happening?" His mouth opened and closed; the sides of his body felt as if crowbars were wedged between every rib, bending and forcing them apart agonisingly. "But I... did the... *ritual*!"

His eyes went milky in colour and Death grabbed his face, summoning power to heal the creature before him. Nothing changed however, and the Fallen Angel continued to break apart helplessly.

What had gone wrong? This girl was a virgin, he had no doubt! But the ritual had failed-

"Tarian-"

Tarian screamed and gagged and then screamed some more.

He was blind now, as well as crumbling to pieces in Death's hands.

Suddenly, movement from the body beneath Tarian's legs alerted both men.

It appeared the wound in Serenity's neck was shrinking- shrinking to nothingness until fresh, milky flesh replaced any sign of there *ever* being a slash in her throat.

"What the-?" Death whispered.

Serenity's eyes shot open, silver and cold.

"She's a vampire!" Tarian bellowed, between gasps. "You brought me... a fucking...*vampire!*"

Death shook his head, eyes glued to Serenity as she smiled back at him.

"Surprise," she said, and with a flattened palm, smashed the stub of Tarian's missing nose.

His disintegrating face exploded into ash as the wind whipped his final screams of despair away, leaving nothing but a withered, naked torso at Death's feet.

How had he not known? How had he not detected the vampire gene within her?

"You walk in daylight!" Death stated, in disbelief. "How is this so?"

"Dhampir," Serenity explained smugly, and raised her fist quicker than he could anticipate. The blow from the punch knocked him backwards and he tripped over a root, hitting the ground backside first.

"Hey! What's going on?"

From afar, Isaac waved madly, now the embodiment of pure deliciousness. The ritual had made him perfect again-a blonde haired hunk with eyes like the bluest regions of the vast ocean and a finely sculpted body to die for.

When he had made it to the sycamore, Serenity already had the Samurai sword in her hands and Death at her feet.

"What's going on?" Isaac asked, just as he noticed Tarian's headless corpse. "Oh shit- No! No... Tar'...*how*...?"

The Angel of Death gritted his teeth and turned to the Dhampir with rage burning in his blood red eyes.

"Try it," he encouraged, ignoring the weeping Fallen One.

She didn't need telling twice.

With a steady swish, she brought the blade down on Death's skull and felt the sword leave her hand, ricocheting off unexpectedly. They both watched it hit the trunk of the tree, where he then summoned it to his own hand and snapped it in two effortlessly.

Serenity gaped at the old man's strength.

He laughed heartily.

But it didn't make her panic.

In the heartbeat it took for Death to close his eyes in exhilaration and triumph, she slid behind Isaac's back and bit down into his neck with her elongated fangs.

Her eyes flashed purest silver as she tasted his life, draining every drop in view of the gawping old man.

She'd vowed never to take a life this way, but she'd never felt so pissed off with a bunch of low life's before.

Isaac crashed to the floor- not dead, but unconscious.

And then, using the sharpest half of the broken sword now wallowing in mud, she hurriedly severed the boy's head from his neck, ending his useless existence completely.

"NO!" The Angel of Death screeched like a mother whose precious first born child had been taken from her.

"That's for the girl," she said, a vision of Natalie filling her tired mind. "And for any girls previous to this."

The Angel of Death stood up and after many years of neglecting his scythe, summoned it to his hand.

Serenity blinked in fear.

But just as he raised the scythe above his head, he vanished in a cloud of thick silver smoke.

- Chapter Forty Three -

Caught

"Found you at last," God said.

"*Shit,*" grumbled Death.

- Chapter Forty Four -

Empty Spaces

-Please, Phoenix. I have to know-

Atlanta had grown weary of shouting over the sound of the wind in her ears and thought it wise to save her parched throat the trouble by using telepathy instead. The South Meridion Bridge was up ahead, as well as the toll booth, and she had been pleading with Phoenix to take her to Julian's house for the past two hours. Her mind could not rest until she knew he was okay.

Phoenix knew his sister was lovesick for Julian and it hurt hearing her cries, especially after he had just done the dishonourable thing of leaving his own partner with twisted kidnappers, likely to kill her.

"I'm dying for a shower, sis," he mumbled unenthusiastically.

"What? I can't hear you?" she called back, a little hysterical.

As the Harley slowed to a stop at the gate, he turned to his sister.

"Is it really so important that you can't get out of your wet clothes first and take the car later?"

Her eyes twinkled with sadness. "Please, Phoenix. He could be dead! I need to see him. I need to know if he's...if he's still around."

"Well-," Phoenix replied reluctantly. "I guess we can make a quick stop, if we have to."

She hugged his back. "Thank you," she breathed in relief, pressing her cheek into his jacket. "Thank you so much."

There was no blood sampling to be done at the gates of Meridion. The Mayor could not afford the fancy equipment Karanthian had displayed at their gates. A simple nod from the old man, with a bushy brown beard, granted them access and they sped across the bridge faster than was legally advised.

"It's on this street," Atlanta directed, twenty minutes after entering their home city. "Just before that red van!"

Phoenix braked and allowed his sister to climb off, but her eagerness to find Julian seemed to die the moment her feet touched the concrete.

"What the-?"

A giant gap between two houses- the very place

Julian's grand domain had once stood, just days previousleered back at her.

"This can't be."

The lawn was an uneven smear of rocks and mud and the foundations of the house stood in ruins- depicting only a rough outline of its four outer walls in patchy towers of brick and rubble. There was no hint of a fire breaking out and no sign of any furniture and belongings being destroyed.

"I don't understand," she whispered. "He was here! This is where he lived, I swear it."

Phoenix joined her and picked up a squashed red rose, its petals covered in dirt and brick dust.

There was nothing he could say to comfort her, for he didn't understand what was happening either. None of it made sense to him.

"Take me home," Atlanta quivered, her eyes fixated on the dying flower in her brother's hand.

"I'm sure everything is okay. Perhaps he packed up and moved on. If he likes you as much as you say he did, he probably feels heartbroken that you were taken. Being helpless can really hurt."

She shook her head. "But why would his house disappear with him? I don't understand any of this. Just take me home. I can't bear to look at this gap any longer. It's as if he was never here."

Phoenix put a hand on her back and led her away.

*

As they pulled onto their driveway, it was as Phoenix had feared.

A car was parked right outside their door and inside sat a lady wearing the extremely familiar uniform of a 'Meridion Slayer.'

"Siren, this is Steevie. Come in please," she radioed through to base, the moment she laid eyes on her targets.

The car window was rolled down, and the twins could hear every word their Godfather was saying in response to his colleague.

"Receiving you," Siren said.

"The twins are home." Her expression was unreadable to them.

"Don't let them out of your sight! I'll be right over!"

The transmission ended.

The Slayer unbuckled her seatbelt and stepped outside the vehicle- silver stake at the hip sparkling in the patches of sunlight that lit up the front garden.

"I hope you pair have a *Hell* of a good story," she spoke up, "Because Siren and your parents have been hitting the roof since they discovered you were missing."

Phoenix looked back at Atlanta. Her head was down and her eyes averted.

"We need to warm up," Phoenix explained.

"By all means, get inside. But don't think I'm not going to be watching your *every* move from now on."

Atlanta was shivering behind him and he caringly grasped her hand. His telepathy was detecting her despair and it was mingling with his own grief for Serenity.

"There's something I need you to do," Phoenix said suddenly.

Steevie folded her arms across her chest in wait.

"My girlfriend…she's being held captive in a small church on the outskirts of Karanthian. She needs help immediately."

Steevie's hand reached for the walkie-talkie pinned to her breast pocket. "Description?"

Phoenix blinked. "Um. Red hair, the colour of blood. Purple eyes. Very pale. About five foot eight in height and eighteen years of age."

She nodded. "Get inside and help your sister. I'll get in contact with the Karanthian police force right away."

But Phoenix never made it inside the house. His weakened state of mind and the effect of Atlanta's solemn thoughts linking to his own made his head spin. Before he could cushion his fall with his hands, he hit the pavement- swallowed by darkness.

- Chapter Forty Five -

Lectures

A healing kiss. That was all it took for Kiya to coax her son back into consciousness and he shot up like a rabbit from its hole- almost blacking out again from the speed of his awakening.

"Slowly does is, son," Kieran said, his hand spread across Phoenix's chest.

He lay back down on the sofa, a fluffy cushion beneath his head.

"Dad?" he whispered. At a glance, he could see the faces of his parents, Siren and the Slayer that had witnessed his arrival. All of them had looks of concern as he tried to get his bearings.

"Where's Atlanta?"

Had he dreamt everything? Had he really rode across the desert with Serenity and rescued his sister from a strange old man in a church?

"She's taking a bath. I've healed most of her wounds, but she's desperate for a good wash," Kiya clarified.

"Did she tell you?" he asked them nervously.

Kieran looked at his wife before giving Phoenix a nod. "You're a stupid boy," he said, unexpectedly.

Kiya gripped Kieran's hand, but he refused to back down without justifying his statement.

"Your sister was kidnapped and you think stealing my bike and riding off to her rescue is the *right* thing to do? Have I taught you *nothing*? Is there no ounce of common sense in your body?"

Phoenix kept his eyes on his hands as he twisted his fingers around, clearly uncomfortable.

"I'm waiting for an answer," Kieran demanded.

The heat in the room increased as the people present became tense. It was plain to see that Kieran was disappointed with his Son. He'd never imagined that Phoenix could do something so irrational! His book-smarts were obviously clouding his common sense. *Must be reading too many stories about bloody super heroes and warriors rescuing damsels.*

"I guess I wasn't thinking, dad."

"You're damn right you weren't thinking! When Siren came over here and found the both of you missing, he turned the whole of Meridion upside down trying to find you! He even had people from your school handing out flyers and marching the streets calling out your names! And, let's not forget your mother and I in all this-" He paused. "Our first holiday alone together in over eighteen years and we had to come straight back here in a blind panic, thinking our kids had been murdered."

Phoenix's head throbbed painfully. Regret radiated off his skin in the form of a building sweat.

"A phone call. A note. Anything to make every minute less torturous would have been a real blessing!"

The walkie-talkie on Steevie's pocket buzzed suddenly.

"This is the Karanthian station."

"Go ahead," Steevie said, turning to leave the group.

"Stay!" Phoenix called, alarming his father with his newly directed attention. Steevie stopped shuffling away and leant closer to the device on her shirt front.

"We have the girl."

"Roger that," Steevie replied.

"Two of our boys are driving to Meridion as we speak. She'll be home within the next few hours."

"We'll be waiting."

The transmission ended.

Phoenix couldn't believe it.

He really could not fathom what he had just heard.

"Is it really her?" he begged. "Is she really alive?"

Kiya grabbed Phoenix's hand. Her son was all starry eyed. What had happened to him? Why did this 'girl' have such an effect on her little boy?

"Why did she go to Karanthian with you?" she questioned. "Who is she, Phoenix?"

Phoenix had tears in his eyes. He wanted to jump up and down and scream in delight. He wanted to hug his mother and father and dance about the room. He wanted to find an ocean somewhere in a faraway land and dive beneath its cool waves. Anything that could express his pure relief on hearing she had survived.

"I love her mum," he cried joyously. "She saved Atlanta and somehow she's saved herself. And I love her immensely!"

Kieran's face had softened now. He'd seen that look before, in the faces of the people he worked with and the faces of friends long past. Love. Powerful and all-consuming. He now understood that Phoenix had let his heart lead the way instead of his head. It was a silly thing to go by, but thank the Lord, his children were home safe and sound.

He ruffled his son's hair. "Get some rest. We'll talk

more later."

"How can I rest now?" Phoenix asked, his body tingling with excitement.

He couldn't wait to hold Serenity in his arms again.

"At least lay down and close your eyes. You look terrible. Your sister too-"

"I'll soon sort that out with some nice homemade cookies," Kiya smiled, winking at her child- all grown up now. It made her want to weep, seeing how much he'd changed. If Kieran ever suggested leaving the twins again, she knew her answer would only ever be a two letter word. At least until the children have families and homes of their own...

- Chapter Forty Six -

Secrets Revealed

"She's here," came a whisper at his door.

Phoenix lifted his head from his pillow and smiled uncontrollably.

"Send her up."

Two minutes later, Serenity was sitting beside him, crying tears of joy as he kissed her cheeks and forehead.

"I was so afraid I'd lost you," Phoenix sobbed. His happiness was clear, but his remorse for leaving her was still *very* strong.

"Phoenix-" she gripped the hand that touched her cheek.

"How did you manage to get away?" he asked.

She had been about to open her mouth and speak, but he was too excited about her physical presence to notice she was hesitant.

"I will never leave you again, I promise."

A sigh escaped her mouth unintentionally, and he moved back so that he could see her face more clearly.

"What's wrong?"

Silence.

This was it.

He *had* to know.

Now or never.

Never sounded good, but it wasn't wise in the long run.

"Phoenix. There's something I've been meaning to tell you."

His palm dropped from her face, and she folded her hands onto her lap.

"The reason I can track people down and fight the way I do is because I'm not what you think I am."

The atmosphere felt stuffy and Phoenix's head whirred with possibilities.

"You are…human…right?"

Her eyes widened and she allowed the question to linger between them.

"Would it change anything?" she asked quietly. "If I told you?"

She looked saddened by the thought of losing him, and he reached out once more to lay a comforting hand on her leg.

"I…I don't know," he admitted. "Unless you come out

and say it, I guess I don't know what I'll feel. All I know is that the person I've grown to love over the past couple of days has been there for me from the very beginning and that I feel as if she could be…my soul mate."

A smile curled her lip, but it faded just as fast.

"Give me your hand," she instructed.

He lifted his palm trustingly.

She fished inside her coat for the sacrificial dagger shaped like a crucifix, which she'd stolen from the crime scene in Karanthian- a painful memory she had desired to keep. Blades were expensive to replace and she'd lost many over the years.

"What are you-?"

Before he could finish, she pricked his palm, until a small bead of scarlet fluid appeared against his soft skin. He tried looking at the little cut in wonderment, but Serenity proceeded to lift his chin with her hand- revealing her identity at last.

Silver eyes.

Sharp fangs.

He didn't know whether to call for help, or ask her if she was faking it somehow.

"I'm half vampire," she explained poignantly. "A

Dhampir."

He blinked a few times.

"You…drink blood?"

A nod.

Phoenix rose from the bed sharply and began pacing the room.

"I knew it!" he exclaimed. "I knew it had to be something like that! It was too much of a coincidence…the way all those people feared you and warned me away."

Her head sunk at the words 'feared' and 'warned.'

"This is why we can't be together."

Phoenix paused, mid step.

"Are you afraid you might kill me?"

A feeble laugh escaped her lips.

"I'm afraid of loving you too much and then losing you. But I could never kill you Phoenix. I wouldn't. I have more self control than that, I promise you."

A knock came at the door.

Kiya entered with a plate balanced in her hand. "Hi," she said, as warmly as she could without seeming like she was nosing into their business. "I thought you guys might be hungry, so I've made you some toast."

Luckily for Serenity, her eyes had returned to their

natural colour and her fangs had slipped back into her gums on Mrs Nightly's arrival .

"Thanks mum," Phoenix mumbled, still in a state of shock.

"Are you okay?" Kiya pressed.

"We're fine. Just have a lot of catching up to do. It's been a hell of an ordeal for us both-"

Kiya nodded. "Well, the police need to ask you a few questions before they let you relax. There's a lot of things that still need investigating and only *you* can help get them started on the case. Your father has agreed to take you both to the station."

"I understand." Phoenix replied.

"Well, just come down when you're ready." She left the room, but kept the door open a crack.

Serenity looked into Phoenix's blue eyes and felt her body shiver all over. He was so handsome. So incredibly handsome. She didn't deserve him.

"We can save this conversation for another time perhaps," she offered, as loud as her broken voice could muster.

Phoenix slid closer to her and wrapped an arm around her shoulders.

"What are you really afraid of?" he asked.

Her nose wrinkled in confusion. "I told you-"

He shook his head. "You *think* that's what you're afraid of. But let's be honest here Ser'-" He caressed her arm as he spoke. "You thought I wouldn't like you anymore if you allowed me to see the real you."

She was silent.

"But you see, I'm not a traditionalist. I like the idea of you being different. It's wild and fun and I love you all the more for telling me."

"How could you love a person that drinks blood?"

"How could you love a person that left you at a strange church to *die*?"

She shook her head vigorously.

"You were just doing what I asked of you!"

"But still-" he grumbled miserably.

"Let's forget it all," she said suddenly. "Forget any of this shit happened and start over."

She twisted on the bed to face him properly.

"Hello." She cheerily held out her hand for him to shake. "My name is Serenity Heller. I'm eighteen and I'm half vampire, although I only kill bad guys and drink the blood of animals, which I purchase at a butcher shop. I love to read. I love to slay. And I'm in love with *you*."

Phoenix's eyes sparkled and his smile broadened at her bravery.

"Hello Serenity," he replied, trying not to laugh at the stupidity of their 'play.' "My name is Phoenix Knightly and I'm *almost* eighteen. I prefer drinking a cup of tea, to a glass of blood and I love to read also. I have a twin sister who can communicate with me telepathically and parents that are slayers too, although one has quit to become a Healer. I like high school, though many people despise it and I enjoy singing when there's no one around to hear me." Serenity chuckled at this. "And one last thing-" He leant forwards and caught Serenity's lips with his own. "I've fallen madly in love with the sexiest red-headed vampire chick on the planet."

He kissed her again and again.

And *again* just to be sure he'd got his point across.

"Don't ever stop loving me," she whispered in his ear, tears of happiness in her purple eyes.

"I promise," he grinned. "As long as I live."

*

Kiya found Atlanta crying in her bedroom, lying with her long brown hair across her tear streaked face and both arms folded beneath her head.

The curtains were closed and the music from her CD player drifted dreamily from the speakers at the far side of the room, filling her with *more* sadness as the lyrics spoke of true love and togetherness.

Kiya perched on the edge of the bed and touched Atlanta's shoulder. She hated seeing her little girl in so much pain. When she'd first rushed into the house, Steevie had already dragged Phoenix to the sofa and Atlanta had been curled up in a ball on one of the armchairs- a knife wound in her arm and her face a picture of nasty purple bruises. It had traumatised her a little.

"It's okay," Kiya cooed, stroking her daughter's hair lovingly. "Everything's okay now."

Sniffles came from beneath Atlanta's arms.

"It's *not* okay, mum. He's gone."

"Who, honey?"

She wiped her nose against her wrist and came up for air- her hair sticking to her cheeks in random places.

"It doesn't matter. Just forget I said anything."

Kiya pulled her into a hug. "I love you, sweetheart. You have no idea how happy I am to have you safe in my arms right now."

Atlanta allowed her mother to grip her as tightly as she wished.

"And if I ever find the people who took you-"

She doubted they ever would. Phoenix had telepathically informed her that Serenity had made it back alive and that she'd slaughtered both the young men who were involved in the kidnapping. The old man however, had disappeared without a trace.

"It's over, mum. I don't want to think or talk about it for a long *long* time, if that's okay with you?"

"Okay," she promised. "You can tell me whatever you want when you're ready."

Atlanta felt more at ease than she had in a while and when her mother eventually left her to her own thoughts, she wandered to the bedroom window and opened it as far as it would go.

The wind made the curtains flutter and her hair flap around her face, but she liked the feeling of it cooling her skin.

"Julian-" she uttered. "Come back to me."

The wind whistled louder.

"Come back to Meridion so I can see that you're

alright! I never thanked you for everything you did for me."

An hour passed in silence, before she returned to her bed to cry some more.

*

When Phoenix returned from the police station, Kiya was in a state of unease, twiddling her fingers around and looking for things to clean so that she could take her mind off what was about to happen.

"Everything okay?" she asked, her voice a little high pitched.

Phoenix nodded and began to head to his room.

"Wait!" Kiya called, alarming both her husband and son, for Kieran was now closing the front door behind him. "I need to talk to you about something."

A feeling of dread washed over him.

"Shall I call Atlanta?"

Kiya shook her head. "That won't be necessary." She motioned for him to sit down. Kieran gave his wife a confused stare.

Nervously, she sat beside her son, and struggled to find an opening statement.

"Phoenix-" she began apprehensively. "I know you've seen the newspaper clippings."

Shit, Phoenix thought. He'd forgotten to pack away the junk he'd dragged out from beneath his mother's bed.

"Oh, mum. I swear I never meant to go through your private stuff, it's just dad forgot to leave the keys to the basement and I knew you had a sword under there-"

"My sword?" she said, eyes widening. "Yes. My sword. Where is it? I had a feeling you might have borrowed it."

Serenity had given him the bad news just before they'd left for the station. The sword was long gone. Broken in two and left in the dirt- now bagged up as evidence at the Karanthian police station.

"It's gone."

Her jaw dropped.

Kieran moved behind her and placed both of his large hands on her shoulders.

"It's...*gone?*"

He nodded meekly. "I kept it safe the whole time, until Atlanta and I were freed. Serenity was unarmed. I had to leave her something to fight with and it kind of got...snapped in two."

"No human, vampire or werewolf could destroy that sword!" Kiya protested, with a glimmer of hope. Perhaps her son was mistaken?

"Serenity isn't lying, mum. It broke. It's gone."

Kiya's head collapsed into her hands, and Kieran massaged her shoulders. Phoenix felt unimaginable guilt as he watched her sob.

"I'm sorry."

"No. It's… It's okay. It doesn't matter."

"But it does matter! I know it meant a lot to you and I should never have taken it without your permission."

Kiya stopped crying and reached out for her son. "You mean more to me than anything," she said fervently. "Your safety is all that matters."

Phoenix squeezed her affectionately.

There was an awkward pause, followed by another hesitant mutter from his mother.

"Do you have any questions, about what you read upstairs?"

He glanced at his father, who looked rigid.

"Yes."

Kiya understood completely and allowed Phoenix to speak his mind.

"Is the man in the pictures my...*father*?"

Kieran had known this day would come sooner or later.

"Yes, he is."

"And he died before I was born?"

"That's right. Kieran was there from the moment you were born and has loved you like his own. Rycan may be your father by blood, but Kieran has been a great father to you."

"As far as I'm concerned," Kieran spoke up. "You *are* and always *will* be my son. As Atlanta will *always* be my little girl for as long as we live."

Phoenix admired the passion in Kieran's voice.

"Did you know my real father?"

Kieran looked at Kiya. "No, Phoenix. I knew your mother after Rycan's execution."

"So, forgive me for asking, but..." he struggled to phrase the question without hurting his mother, "...was he a bad man? Because the papers didn't paint a pretty picture of him."

"No. He wasn't bad at all. Rycan was wonderful and caring. He would never harm a soul and was wrongly accused of murdering a young girl."

"He was innocent?"

"Yes."

"And you loved him?"

"Very much."

Phoenix paused.

"I don't think we should tell Atlanta about any of this."

Both parents stared back at him in awe.

"These memories…this 'past'… is what made you who you are, mum," he said bravely, "But it is both you and *Kieran* who made me who I am, and Atlanta too. So keep your secrets. Don't let her see any of the newspaper clippings. I don't want anything to change."

Kieran smiled. "That's a very adult decision, son- one that I heartily agree with."

"Mum?"

She looked shaken from her thoughts.

"Of course," she agreed. "She doesn't need to know."

"Well, if you don't mind, I'm going to get some rest. It's been a rough few days."

Both parents nodded and watched their son rise from the sofa.

"I love you both," he announced.

"We love you too," Kiya replied.

- Chapter Forty Seven -

A Visitor in the Night

Three weeks later and the Knightly twins were back in Meridion High on the brink of exams, and suffering a strange new popularity since their disappearance.

Rumours had circulated. Atlanta's friend Nerys had been ripe with ideas about selling their story to magazines and allowing the Meridion News to do a special programme on them both. It would have raised a small about of cash to get them started at university and increase their popularity further, but the twins had begged her to keep her mouth shut, to which she had unwillingly obeyed.

"Deacon seems to have been tamed," Phoenix pointed out as they walked away from the food district eating ham salad rolls. The bane of Atlanta's life gave her a meagre wave as he drove by, a few friends brandishing burgers in the back seat of his car.

"He apologised to me," she justified. "When he'd heard I'd disappeared, he freaked out a bit. Now, he's practically faultless- carrying my books when he thinks I'm struggling and buying little cupcakes and cookies at the bakery for me to eat."

Serenity snorted, dropping the bottle of blood conccaled in a flask from beneath her parted lips. Phoenix had been kind enough to go to the butchers with her every lunch break since he'd heard about her dietary needs and he seemed completely at ease with her lust for 'the red stuff.'

"Did you say he brings you *cupcakes?*"

Atlanta blushed. "I thought it was rather sweet."

They laughed.

Deacon had never given anyone *anything* other than a black eye, previous to her abduction.

"You've certainly made an impact on him," Phoenix piped up.

"But for how long?"

"Would you ever get back with him?" Phoenix cut in.

Atlanta shook her head. "Of course not."

"Even if he brought you a bunch of roses, shipped in from exotic lands?"

The word 'roses' made her shudder, remembering the wonderful bushes outside Julian's once fabulous domain.

"No," she mumbled. "No, I wouldn't."

That night, she left the window open as usual and

cried deep into the early hours of the morning, wondering whether she'd ever see Julian again. Her father had found no records of a body fitting his description and she'd had no luck in discovering the 'ill mother' he'd mentioned was staying at Meridian's hospital.

He was gone. Flown right out of her life with those big beautiful wings of his.

"Julian," she whispered mournfully into her pillow. His name had become a broken record. Even *she* was getting sick of saying it.

Suddenly, a vivid scraping noise made the hairs on the back of her neck stand on end and she watched in pure disarray as the lock on her bedroom door slid into place all by itself!

She was ready to scream her lungs out, until a warm hand touched her mouth- drawing her gaze to something breathtakingly beautiful.

"Julian?" she cried, reaching hurriedly for the lamp beside her bed.

But the Angel before her was not the creature she had fallen in love with.

Standing at six foot seven, with long blonde hair and emerald eyes- the winged man at the foot of her bed was unashamedly naked and watching her with curiosity.

"Who are you?" she breathed, as the Angel moved closer.

He slid onto the bed and wrapped his muscular arms around her slim body. Atlanta's cheeks flared scarlet in colour as his distinctly unclothed parts came into view, and she tried her hardest to keep her eyes focused on the neck up.

"Sweet girl," the man sang. "You must stop mourning for Julian."

Her heart skipped a beat.

"Julian! You know my Julian?"

"I am Gabriel. The Archangel. And yes, I know all the Lord's creations by name."

She grabbed his arms in desperation.

"Where is he? I must speak with him!"

"He is in Heaven. As long as you worship the Lord and live a sinless life, you will see him one day. Repent and be saved young one. It is the only way-"

He rose from the bed, tall and elegant- his wings the colour of goose feathers.

"No, wait. Tell him I must see him!"

"He has been forbidden to come here. He failed to protect you. You are no longer Julian's charge."

"But I love him!"

A flicker of pity teased Gabriel's facial features.

"You can love another in his place," he suggested plaintively.

Atlanta stood up, furious. *As if it's that easy, you insufferable jerk!*

"You sent him to me and now you think you can take him away?! What happened to his home?"

"It was temporary for the purposes of your protection."

"Can't you take me with you? You have wings! Fly me to him."

"That is *not* an option."

Atlanta fell to her knees and grabbed hold of the Archangel Gabriel's left leg.

"I'm begging you! Please let me see him."

"It is *forbidden*."

"You must!" she screamed.

And as she lifted her head to see Gabriel's reaction, she realised the room was now empty. His foreign presence a mere memory.

But at her knees lay two feathers, soft and delicate. Carefully, she plucked them both from the carpet and slipped them under her pillow.

I refuse to believe it, she thought tiredly. *If Gabriel can visit me, then Julian can too.*

He will come.

He will.

- Chapter Forty Eight -

Giving Up

A month later; Atlanta was still shrouded with grief.

She could not let Julian go.

Her mother was frantic, trying to keep her daughter occupied with outings and encouraging her to move on. But Atlanta was becoming impossible to live with- bursting into tears at the sight of Serenity and Phoenix holding hands; launching into fits of tears when Deacon asked her politely if she would like to go for dinner with him sometime; paling at the sight of Malcolm and Nerys kissing after a night at The Sword and Stone.

-You have to move on - Phoenix proclaimed. *- It's not healthy, sis -*

-What do you know? You're all content with your girlfriend and mum's wrapped up in dad. All around me I see couples, whilst I'm still struggling with losing my Julian-

-But he's not your Julian anymore- he replied bluntly. *-You have to forget about him now -*

-When a person falls in love with someone, all they

can think about is when they might see or speak with that person again. It dominates almost every waking moment. I even dream that Julian has returned to me, only to wake and find I'm alone. I can't bear it, brother. I'm empty inside and I hate it-

-You have me. You have your family-

-Sometimes family isn't enough-

The conversation ended.

That night, dinner was laced with anxiety as Atlanta swirled her pasta around her plate. Serenity was at the table, as she so often was now, drinking spoonfuls of blood from a steaming bowl as if it were soup.

"How were your exams?" Kiya asked pleasantly.

Serenity swallowed her mouthful before speaking. "All over and done with, thankfully. English Literature had some brutal questions, but I think I did well. As long as you have your own opinions on the text, it makes up quite a bit of your overall mark. And I've always been pretty opinionated on the writings of others!"

Kiya smiled.

Phoenix reached beneath the table and gave Serenity's knee a squeeze. His father had found it hard to believe that his girlfriend was a 'Dhampir' and he almost had to physically stop the Chief Slayer from gawking at her the first night she came over for 'dinner'- her meal picked from a *whole* different kind of menu. But all was well now. His mother had even taken to picking up pig's blood from the butchers and kept it in the fridge-freezer for when she visited.

"When do you plan on going to the opticians, Phoe'?" Kieran asked.

"Oh- um. Well, I gave them a ring and asked if they could provide me with contact lenses instead from now on."

Kieran nodded and smiled. "Not hiding that handsome face any longer, eh? You'll be beating the ladies away I'm sure."

Phoenix grinned. "There's only one lady I care about." He turned to Serenity and winked.

Atlanta put her knife and fork down loudly.

"May I be excused?" she asked with curtness.

"Surely you can eat some more, honey?" her mother practically pleaded.

"I'm not hungry."

"But you're losing so much weight. It's not healthy."

Atlanta cringed inwardly. If she heard the words 'it's not healthy' come from *one* more mouth, she thought she might explode. Even Nerys was bringing extra sandwiches to school so she could dump them on her at break times, none too subtly.

She wanted to curse, but wisely opted for silence, leaving with all four pairs of eyes on her.

When she made it to her bedroom, she had to pinch herself- and then pinch herself again even *harder*.

Met with a flash of brilliant white light, she stood aghast- eyes resting upon the body of the one person she had prayed every hour of every day to be near.

The pain of the pinching made her flinch, and it was enough to convince her she was far from dreaming.

Shuddering visibly at her feet was Julian- naked, but crouched protectively so she could see very little of him besides his creased brow, sweaty arms and quaking kneecaps.

She tried to speak, but her words came out in incoherent little squeaks.

"Blanket-" Julian said, his voice raspy.

She tossed him the pink throw she kept tucked away on the top shelf of her wardrobe and watched breathlessly as he stood up at last.

"You're okay!"

He turned and smiled. It was warm, friendly and full of relief.

"I couldn't stand seeing you in so much pain."

She moved an inch closer, went to put her arms around him, but thought better of it. He looked delicate- suffering. He was standing, yes, but his back was arched ever so slightly as if it hurt to straighten his spine.

"Are you okay?" she asked, barely above a whisper.

"I'll be fine in a moment. The fall takes a bit of getting used to. We Angels aren't used to feeling this…human."

She put a hand against his back and led him to the bed. Tears sprung to her eyes as his powerful gaze fell upon her face- distinctly pleased with the sight of her.

"Now that I'm here, I can't stop smiling," he laughed, displaying his pearly white teeth.

Atlanta laughed with him, dropping her hand to his leg. His palm rested over her fingers affectionately.

"Is this just…a visit?" she asked. "Because Gabriel told me you weren't allowed to see me, but I have so much I want to tell you! After I was taken, I thought you were-"

He placed a hand on her lips and swiftly kissed the words from her mouth.

"I don't think you understand," he said, their kisses becoming more passionate as the towel dropped from his back and his front became completely visible to her. She blushed, but allowed the increasing desire to touch him guide her lips to his.

"I fell for you," he told her raggedly.

She touched his hair and he picked her up, placing her on his lap.

Atlanta didn't quite understand him.

He stroked a hand through her hair.

"I told Him I wanted to be with you, so He allowed me to fall from Heaven."

"You mean, you gave up your wings for me?" she asked incredulously. Her eyes were wide with fear for him. "No Julian. You can't! I won't let you!"

"It's too late," he tried to kiss her but she pulled away.

"I saw what the last Fallen Angel went through. His body fell to pieces before my very eyes! You'll die—"

He shook his head. Was there something she was missing here?

"It's not quite the same," he explained, admiring her concern for his wellbeing. "If an Angel is banished from Heaven, they are punished with deterioration- as you witnessed. But I have done nothing wrong. Not really. So I asked Him to withdraw me from His services and fell- for you- with no drawbacks besides aging naturally like a human and dying when my body is ready to give up."

Atlanta couldn't believe what he was saying.

It was magical, but it was also wrong.

"You can't give up something so amazing, for love."

"I wanted to. And I have."

The tears flowed freely from her now.

"I missed you so much," he confided. "I could hear you calling my name and it killed me inside that I couldn't be here for you."

She kissed him gently and nestled her head against his shoulder. "I missed you too."

There was silence for a while, until Julian broke the spell.

"Don't ever feel guilty. I don't mind losing my wings. Being human is a gift. I can still serve Him by making you the happiest girl in the world."

She smiled. "I'm okay with that."

"Now, I think you'd better have a word with your brother."

She frowned. "What's Phoenix got to do with *us*?"

Julian allowed his gaze to fall to the part of him that was not rightly meant for public display.

"Oh-," she replied, blushing madly. "You need some

of his clothes."

"And then, perhaps an introduction to you mother and father wouldn't go amiss, since I'm going to be keeping their daughter company for many years to come." He winked playfully.

Atlanta was smiling. Smiling so much her jaw hurt. But it felt good to be this happy.

At last, she had him back.

- Epilogue -

Many Years Later...

The graveyard was cold and wet.

Father Lucas had completed his recitation of Bible passages a good hour ago and had left eagerly when the rain had started to fall down.

But many still remained in silent reflection- overlooking Kieran Nightly's resting place with much sorrow in their hearts.

Phoenix stood beside his wife, Serenity, who was clutching the hand of their ten year old boy, Micah.

Atlanta huddled against her husband Julian- their six year old daughter Faith keeping her grandmother company at the foot of Kieran's grave.

And Siren had lingered also, eyes closed in silent prayer for the man who had provided him with employment, a decent home and Godchildren he could care for, since he had never settled down to raise a family of his own.

Kieran had died just as he'd always said he would... pushing himself too far in a fight. He had never been one to sit back and relax, and at the age of seventy one, a vampire had barrelled into him as he left the station one night. He had died of a heart attack, which doctors had warned was likely to occur soon if he didn't leave the overly demanding job he cherished so much. But he didn't listen, and now he was gone.

Kiya brushed a tear from her eye and smiled at Faith, who was staring at the coffin with curiosity. She was so proud of Phoenix and Atlanta- blessing her with two healthy grandchildren; full of life and happiness. It seemed Kieran's funeral was the first occasion she'd ever seen Faith dumbstruck. There had never been a time she hadn't had *something* to say since the moment she had learnt to speak.

"You okay, sweetheart?" she asked softly.

Faith nodded with enthusiasm.

"Why don't you go give your mummy a big hug?" she whispered.

The little girl, dressed in a long red skirt, matching jacket and black shoes ran to Atlanta, leaving Kiya to talk with the *other* young lady at her side.

"I wish daddy was going to be around for my Prom next month," Rose sighed, stepping closer to her mother. She was clothed in a long black dress that billowed out behind her in the wind, dragging a little in the dirt. "I never showed him my prom dress. It was going to be a surprise on the night."

"Hah! Can you imagine his reaction if he ever saw how low cut it is?" Kiya joked, attempting to be humorous, though spirits were still low. She imagined Kieran trying to drape a thick woolen cardigan over her shoulders, but if it hadn't worked for Atlanta all those years ago, so it wouldn't work for Rose.

Kieran's daughter- by blood- had grown to be a spectacularly beautiful girl with hair the same shade as his and eyes to match. She carried a similar passion for life and every day, Kiya thanked the Lord that her husband had blessed her with another child.

"Daddy doesn't mind me wearing nice dresses as long as they're tasteful, Mum. He knows I won't let any of the guys go near me, so it doesn't matter what I wear or how I choose to express myself."

She was telling the truth of course. Rose refused to get close to *any* guy. Her plan was to finish high school- free and single- then pursue creative writing in university. If all went well, she then desired to travel the world in search of cities less dire than their own, whilst writing for children. Rose had the 'brains,' and put them before frivolous relationships with boys. They were all imbeciles according to her.

Kiya winked and left her to talk with Siren, who was looking rather lonely as he trailed behind. They had all delayed long enough and the rain was making Kiya's old bones ache.

"Let's get all warmed up shall we?" she said, as handsome little dark-haired Micah ran past her in hot pursuit of his cousin.

Suddenly, Atlanta came to her mother's side and offered her arm for support, which she took without a fuss.

"There's something I wanted to tell you," Atlanta announced, checking her brother was at a distance and that Julian was keeping an eye on the kids.

Kiya felt a pang of fear creep up her bent spine.

"Is it regarding you father?" she queried, hesitantly. Had Phoenix told her about Rycan after all?

"Oh no," Atlanta said. "Not dad." She took a deep breath. "It's about Faith."

The two women looked ahead at the little girl in red, dancing in the rain joyously and running between the gravestones, happy now that they were away from her grandfather's burial place. And who could blame her? Children weren't meant to see their loved ones in despair at a young age, but they had been incapable of finding sitters since everyone they knew had been at the funeral.

"Is there a problem?"

Atlanta squeezed her arm.

"Depends how you see it."

There was a pause, inviting her daughter to continue.

"Well don't leave me in suspense, honey. Tell me."

She nodded. "You know the day I gave birth to her?"

Kiya smiled in remembrance. "How can I forget the hour you brought that little angel into the world?"

"Well that's the problem-"

Kiya frowned. Since when had Faith ever been a *problem?* She was a darling girl after all.

"When she was born… she had…wings."

Silence.

"They aren't always there to see. They come every now and again, but we've managed to stop her from revealing them in public."

"You mean to say my granddaughter is-"

Atlanta bit her lip and finished her mother's sentence for her. "-part Angel."

"Which would make *Julian-*"

"A Fallen Angel. Yes."

Just as Kiya was trying to process everything, her

daughter spoke again.

"And there's something else."

"Dear Lord!" she exclaimed, drawing Julian's attention momentarily. "Are you trying to put me in that grave with your father?"

Atlanta looked nervously around at her family.

"She's... the one."

Kiya came to a standstill.

"Excuse me?"

"She's the one they've been waiting for...*apparently*. The one who will end the reign of darkness."

Kiya shook her head as it sank in.

She refused to believe it, for it meant more fighting and bloodshed in their lives. It meant her little grandchild was going to be introduced to knives, swords and stakes, much like her old friend Roxy all those many years ago- too young for war. Too young by a *long* shot.

"Just after you and dad came to see me on the maternity ward," she explained, "Gabriel came to see me."

"Gabriel?" she intercepted.

"The Archangel-"

A gasp of surprise escaped Kiya's mouth, along with an, 'Oh my!'

"He told me about some prophecy. A prophecy that my little Faith is a part of." Atlanta started crying now. "But I kept it a secret from people and now that dad's gone, I'll never get to ask his advice."

Kiya placed a hand on Atlanta's cheek and calmly gazed into her eyes.

"We're a strong family, sweetheart. You'll be okay."

Faith interrupted them at this point, tugging at her mother's hand.

"Mummy!" she called, "Daddy keeps chasing me!"

Hurriedly, Atlanta wiped her eyes so that Faith wouldn't see she had been upset. "Well tell Daddy I'll come and chase *him* in a minute if he keeps it up," she smiled, though it didn't reach her eyes.

Faith ran away giggling, and both Kiya and Atlanta watched as Julian swept her up into his arms, pretending to nibble at her neck and face as she screamed playfully for her mother to come and save her.

As he lowered her to the ground, only to raise her up again with a triumphant bellow, a pair of white wings materialised from the little girls back, ripping her jacket in two.

Kiya's hand reached for her daughter's instantly at the

sight.

"My, *my*," she breathed in astonishment. "What an extraordinary sight."

And for the moment, nothing more was said.

Karla J.M. Brading

Karla J.M. Brading

About the Author

Photography: KittyKems Photography

Karla Brading has a First Class Honours in Creative and Professional Writing. She models as a hobby and enjoys visiting the library. She currently has 25 tattoos and could happily write for the rest of her life.

Karla J.M. Brading

Made in the USA
San Bernardino, CA
14 December 2019